I0546275

DOMINION

Doug Goodman

Copyright © 2014 by Doug Goodman
Copyright © 2014 by Severed Press
www.severedpress.com
All rights reserved. No part of this book may be
reproduced or transmitted in any form or by any
electronic or mechanical means, including
photocopying, recording or by any information and
retrieval system, without the written permission of
the publisher and author, except where permitted by
law.
This novel is a work of fiction. Names,
characters, places and incidents are the product of
the author's imagination, or are used fictitiously.
Any resemblance to actual events, locales or persons,
living or dead, is purely coincidental.
ISBN: 978-1-925225-14-3
All rights reserved.

This book is dedicated to my friends, to all the lost boys (and girls) who have been a part of my life, and to "Barrio Whisperwood." You know who you are.

And God blessed them, and God said unto them, Be fruitful, and multiply, and replenish the earth, and subdue it: and have dominion over the fish of the sea, and over the fowl of the air, and over every living thing that moveth upon the earth.
Genesis 1:28

Part One: The Death House

Chapter One – Trustworthy

Opaque clouds hung low in the sky, like a gray, rolling ceiling. The boys did not like being outside on days like this, days that were especially cloudy. You couldn't see the monsters in the air. The boys knew they should have stayed inside where it was safe. But in the past week, they had run out of supplies, and they had become desperate.

Each day provided a four-hour timespan within which they could move outside the house. If they stayed outside beyond those four hours, they risked being captured, and the pile of severed heads at the subdivision's entrance reminded them of the consequences for being caught.

Jaxon and Peter played the role of the foragers, though sometimes Kirk joined them. Aidan and Colt never went. After Black Friday, Colt wasn't allowed outside the house and as for Aidan – somebody had to play the role of Dungeon Master. Alyssa was the Monster Handbook, and she saw nothing except an ugly grackle and an errant squirrel a few houses over.

"Okay," Jaxon said quietly to Alyssa through the FRS radio. "Just keep your eye on them."

Today was an important day. Not in a state championship way, or an SAT way or even a Friday quiz way. The day was important for survival. Everybody had to play their position correctly, and they had to trust that the others would do their job well. Failure to comply could be lethal to every one of the family.

Jaxon and Peter's success depended on their ability to remain undetected. So Jaxon and Peter opened the pouches in their fanny packs, which were full of pine needles. They smothered their hands with the needles. The rubbing left Jaxon's hands prickly and sore, but at least it kept him hidden. When they finished with their hands, they repeated the ritual with their feet. Both teens wore sandals made of wood and cloth. On one of the first nights, they learned that they could be tracked by the rubber in their shoes, so they had to find a less obvious way to protect their feet. The pine masked their scent.

Peter and Jaxon scanned the streets for any sign of life. Even with Alyssa watching from above, they had learned to double-check the broken-out windows and missing front doors on the houses for signs of activity. Seeing nothing, they opened the fence gate, crept around the house, and squatted behind Peter's old Chevrolet Cavalier. The Cavalier had taken the family to so many places before – to concerts, school meets, hangouts, movies, and on dates. With the flat tires, it wouldn't take them anywhere any more. That was how they kept them from mass exodus. They slashed the tires.

Jaxon took the lead, and the pair maneuvered between cars, shrubs, and pine trees. Jaxon felt like a Sioux hunter searching for buffalo. His family's survival depended on him returning home with a kill. Armed with only a large soft-frame backpack and what skills he learned over the past ninety days, Jaxon's spine tingled with the thrill of the hunt. While some avoided hunting and others resented it, he reveled in the time spent outside the house. Life was quickly becoming too complicated in the attic, and he loved the impending sense of peril, though he would call it adventure.

From the outside lawn, 1410 Vicksburg appeared empty. The lawn grass had grown as high as Jaxon's thigh, making recon difficult.

"How are we, Alyssa?" he asked.

"You're still clear. Don't forget to look for tampons."

"You really didn't have to remind me."

Peter said, "It's the end of the world, and that's still gross."

The door lay to the side of the foyer, thrown off its hinges. The foul odor of rancid meat permeated the humid air in the house.

There was a time when those nauseating odors made Jaxon want to puke, but over the past three months, he had grown accustomed to it. Instead of reaching for a barf bag, he reached for his Camelbak suction tube. Rancid meat would mean…

"Ugh. Maggots." A stove pot was full of bloated white bodies crowned with wheeling teeth. As Jaxon and Peter grimaced, the maggots moved as one, plopping out of the stove pot like boiling water and wiggling across the stove towards Jaxon and Peter like a slow, vermiculate wave. Jaxon hadn't seen many maggots, or flies, or any other insects since early September. He, like the others, assumed that all the bugs in the state were migrating to warmer climates.

Peter and Jaxon opened the valves on their Camelbaks and sprayed the maggots. The stench of bleach was almost as overpowering as the smell of offal. The maggots writhed torturously and melted in the chemical burn.

"Let's kill them all," Peter said.

"No, we can't spare the bleach." Instead, they sprayed a perimeter moat around the maggots, who had sense enough not to crawl over the bleach.

With the maggots at bay, Jaxon and Peter opened the pantry. Except for old mouse droppings and a few opened cans, it was empty.

"Son of a biscuit!" Peter cursed, or at least tried. "Well, that didn't work out. What do you want to do now?"

Jaxon pointed to a door. "We can at least check the bathrooms. You've got to be getting tired of carrying around all that shit."

"Language!"

The master bathroom was on the second floor. What caught their eye, though, was the extra-large pizza-sized hole in the middle of the master bedroom door. Jaxon pushed the door open, and they walked into the bedroom. The mattress had been pushed up against the windows, which meant these people had lived long enough to see the rocs and were trying to hide from them. There were a few old gnawed bones, but every strip of flesh and meat had been devoured. The shotgun lay next to the bed. They had probably hoped the gun would keep the creatures away, but all that changed on Black Friday like a flip of the switch. Jaxon checked the shotgun's chamber. It was empty, but there was a box of shells on the dresser. Jaxon grabbed both.

Peter jingled the toilet handle perfunctorily. The toilet did not flush. Water went out after the first month, though nobody knew how the animals did it. More likely, without workers the plant went down. They weren't sure. Public works wasn't part of their high school curriculum.

A heaping pile of human feces lay under the toilet lid.

"It will have to do," Peter said. He opened his backpack, and pulled out the trash bag. They opened the bag and leaned back as the smell of offal permeated the room. Coughing, they dumped the excrement into the toilet.

Eyes burning, Jaxon checked the sinks and medicine cabinet. This place had obviously been hit before, but whoever had been here dropped their shit and ignored the gun. Maybe they didn't have time, or maybe one of the creatures came after them. Hell if he knew, but if the shotgun was still available, then maybe something else was left. He grabbed a few items, including a bottle of bleach, and shoved them into their backpacks. As they backed out of the restroom, they hosed down their path.

"Aw, man," Peter said. He reached out to Jaxon. Turned the knob on his radio back on.

"How the hell did that happen? I must have bumped up against something."

"Jaxon! Peter!" came Alyssa's sharp voice on the radio. She ordered them, "Be very still. One of them is outside."

Tree branches shook as the misshapen moved from branch to branch, hidden among the leaves. It crept closer and closer to the house without leaving the tree, and then it stood very still and did nothing. Waited.

"Can you get it, Aidan?"

"No, it's behind the leaves. I can't even see it." He moved the Winchester around, but he could not get line of sight on the creature.

"Okay. If we wait, maybe it'll go away."

"We can't know for sure," Aidan said. "It could just be waiting for the others to get back, and then it'll corner Jaxon and Peter."

"Well, then what do you think we should do?" Alyssa shot back.

"Pray for a miracle. It'll be dark soon."

Jaxon's voice came on the FRS. "We're going to go around it."

"Jaxon, don't be stupid," Alyssa said. "It can see you almost the entire block."

"Not if we are stealthy."

Alyssa glared at Aidan. Aidan shrugged his shoulders. "If it hears them move, they're as good as dead."

She pushed down the button on the radio and said, "Aidan says if you want to die, that's your prerogative. We can't force you to not do something stupid."

"Hey, Mr. Whittenberg's on his roof," Colt said to everyone in the attic. Aidan retracted the rifle, and Kirk pulled down the ridge vent so that they would not be seen. Alyssa radioed to Peter and Jaxon that, "The dungeon is closed and the dragons are loose." Then everyone upstairs watched Mr. Whittenberg, who was standing on his roof. They could only see a partial view, though, since they were watching through the small opening they built using the ridge vent.

"Hell, another assisted suicide," Aidan said.

Mr. Whittenberg stood on the arch of the roof on his two-story property. His clothes were soaked with blood and he wore only one shoe, and when he spoke, he sounded loopy, like he hadn't slept in a thousand years. He could barely stand.

They had seen others like this, especially after the first week. That's when the assisted suicides became heavy rotation so that even Colt got bored with them. Mr. Whittenberg was the first one they had seen in almost two weeks.

Colt said, "He helped fix my bike chain that time it got bent in the gears. Dad was at a conference. Remember?"

"Yeah," Kirk said, having never met the man. He had seen the man once when he was visiting the Fannins, but never spoke to him. "Didn't he have a couple of kids?"

"Toddlers," Aidan said. "A pair of twins and a newborn, I think."

Mr. Whittenberg was a young father, pudgy, barely in his thirties. He had been in the subdivision less than a year before the change.

"I'm ready to die!" Mr. Whittenberg yelled at the air.

"So jump off the roof," Aidan said to everyone in the room.

"Callate," Alyssa chastised him through her half-mouth, but everybody knew she didn't mean it. Not completely.

"I can't do this any longer," Mr. Whittenberg said. "I've lost my wife and my children, and I've run out of allopurinol. My foot feels like it's been shot a thousand times," he cried. "I can't do it. Do you hear me? I'm ready. Come and end me! End me!" The man screeched the last words, arms raised out, head up to the dark, dense clouds. Just as he hit his highest note, another screech emitted from the heavens. It came up behind him, shot down out of those low-hanging clouds and hit him like a train wreck. Shoved him to the arch, and then adroitly flipped him on his backside. The grisly talons squashed him like a mouse. Arms and legs flailing, the man screamed and cried like a child. The giant beak poked his gut sack, and then pulled out his insides, which it tossed in the air. The man continued to scream, though with considerably less energy. The creature repositioned itself on him and popped his head off.

Alyssa turned into Aidan's shoulder. She never got used to that part.

The head bounced like a deflated basketball down the chimney rock roofing and came to a stop in the overgrown crabgrass in front of the Whittenberg's home. The weeds at the far end of the front lawn rustled back and forth. A small creature ran through the grass to the disembodied head. Alyssa was sure it was the squirrel she had seen earlier. It came from the same general direction. The creature grabbed Mr. Whittenberg's head by the hair and ran back across the lawns, dragging it to the front of the cul-de-sac. The squirrel rolled Mr. Whittenberg's head on top of the pile of skulls and partially devoured heads, then ran up the side of a pine and dashed across a fence and vanished. When they looked up, the Roc was gone, too, leaving only the discarded remains of Mr. Whittenberg draping from the eaves.

"Okay," Jaxon heard Alyssa say over the FRS, "the dungeon is open for player characters again."

"Who was it?" Jaxon asked.

"Mr. Whittenberg."

Jaxon thought of the pile of heads at the front of the subdivision and shuddered. He tried not to think about the pile. It was hard, though. His mother and father's heads lay there.

"Ask her where the squirrel is," Peter said.

"Where's the squirrel?"

"Don't know," Alyssa replied over the FRS. "It disappeared into somebody's backyard, so be careful."

"Got that," Jaxon said.

While waiting on the roc to finish its grisly business, Jaxon and Peter had planned their escape route. Since they lived on a cul-de-sac, they had decided to jump fences from house to house until they circumnavigated their way back home. By never being in the front, the grackle would not see them. That left the squirrel to deal with, but at least they didn't have the grackle.

Having grown up in this subdivision, the boys knew every inch backwards and forwards, and in ways their parents could never understand, like how certain sidewalks were easier to bike on because the cement wasn't cracked, or where to find all the good hiding spaces. It was a knowledge gained from years of hide and seek, cops and robbers, and pedaling to convenience stores. So Peter and Jaxon knew the Sanderson house would give them the most trouble because it had no coverage.

Jaxon led, duck walking across the lawn and climbing up an old live oak. Its giant arms reached over the fence and into the next backyard. Jaxon and Peter hopped from oak to shed to ground. This property had a thick bush line, which hid them as they crossed to the next fence. For the next few houses, they had to jump the fence, which they did as effortlessly as expected of two state finalists – Peter in gymnastics and Jaxon in Taekwondo.

At the base of the cul-de-sac, where the houses all circled in on each other, Peter and Jaxon were tempted to hop onto the subdivision's brick-and-mortar windshield. Then they could cross three houses in a fraction of the time it had taken them to get to this end of the street. However, the grackle might see them, or worse things that lurked outside the subdivision. Finally, they reached the Sanderson's home.

They entered the Sanderson's yard through a small hole in the fence. The yard was a long plateau of tall grass with purple stalks. No trees, no sheds or clubhouses, not even a damn patio overhang. Just open grass. They could be seen years away and not know it.

"You ready?" Jaxon asked Peter.

Peter looked around. There had to be at least five or six thousand cubic feet of backyard. He nodded.

They got down on all fours and crawled through the grass like snakes on their bellies. Hand over hand, Jaxon pushed through the lawn. They did not drop any bleach behind them as they had done all afternoon because they were touching too much grass. No matter how much bleach they poured, their scent would still be somewhere.

Low to the ground, the grass grew thicker around the bases, which slowed their progress. Jaxon wished he had a machete. Or a weed eater. Or an air conditioner for that matter. And a Gatling gun. He shook his head and reminded himself to stay focused. Stop fantasizing.

Grass seeds clung like spider webs to his arms and face. The wind blew over them. The purple stalks swayed in the breeze. They stopped and waited for the wind to pass over. Peter prayed the wind did not carry their scent.

Suddenly, Jaxon's palm landed on something that was not grass. He jerked his hand back and pushed up. His head emerged slow and easy from the grass line. When he decided that nothing was waiting to rip him apart, he moved into a stooped position and slowly stood up.

"What is it?" Peter asked, but Jaxon shushed him. "I don't know," Jaxon said. "I'm going to check it out."

The corpses lay sunken in the grass. The wind had carried the stench of death away from Jaxon and Peter. Decomposing bodies had a sweet smell, almost like cotton candy. It was weird, and not what any of them had expected, but what had they expected? Everything was different now.

Despite being headless, Jaxon recognized the bodies of the two sisters. He used to have a thing for the older sister, who was going to JuCo. The younger one was in junior high. She was on the swim team, he thought, but wasn't sure.

"What is it?" Peter asked from below.

"Remember Jennifer and Jessica?"

"Oh."

"Yeah."

"So they're?"

"Yeah."

Peter rose up in the grass behind Jaxon. "Not much left of them."

"Nope."

"They lived across the street. Why do you think they were out here?"

Jaxon checked what was left of the girls' hands. Pulled out some stems. "There must have been a garden out here somewhere. They were hungry." Jaxon pointed to the bloody paw prints on the door. "Wargs got 'em."

"I'm ready to get back."

"Yeah. Me, too."

But as they lowered into the grass, two things happened almost simultaneously. As Aidan came over the radio, warning them that the grackle had taken flight, it flew over the house and into the backyard. The black beast swooped around, landed on a fence, and started calling out madly, its eyes wide and yellow, and its feathers on end.

"Can you get it?" Jaxon asked into the FRS. A quick negative response came back.

"There are some trees in the way," Aidan explained.

Alyssa jumped in, "Run, boys! Run!"

Just then, an enormous sound, chthonic and booming, resonated through the subdivision like an earthquake. Trumpets of hell, Aidan had dubbed them. More than hearing the sound, they felt it. It was as if the air was sucked out of the world. Though they had heard the sound many times over the summer, they did not know what made it, whether creature or machine, but it always heralded the coming of the wargs.

Three giant black bodies loped down the highway and along the far end of the subdivision's windshield.

"Look how they move," he said, in amazement.

"Dude, they're like horses," Kirk agreed. "Demon fucking horses."

"And they keep getting faster," Aidan said. He picked up the FRS and said, "Hurry up." Then, to the others, "Crap. New problem."

They all moved to his side of the roof. Down on the streets, other Lakewood foragers, unseen until they began scrambling, were making mad dashes for their homes, having heard the call of the wargs. But one ran towards their end of the street. Aidan aimed the Winchester at the approaching teen and focused the scope on him.

"It's Aaron," Kirk grumbled. "I'd hoped he was killed in the first attack."

"Be nice," Alyssa said. "We have to let him in."

"No way. We have more than enough to deal with than to add some asshole to the group."

"You can't exclude a person just cause you pushed each other around in the schoolyard a million years ago. He's a human being, Kirk."

"If you let him in, he's just going to fuck things up. Trust me on that. He's going to get everybody pissed at everybody else, and then the wargs are going to follow our shouting all the way to the front door."

"You are such an ass."

A gunshot cracked in the air. Alyssa and Kirk turned to Aidan. The barrel of the Winchester was smoking.

"He had no bleach. He would have led them straight to us, regardless of whether we turned him down or not."

"Aidan," Alyssa said, her voice emptying. She couldn't say anything more.

"What would we have done if we let him in? We've got no food. We're barely surviving the five of us," Aidan explained.

Alyssa turned away, and a silence fell over the attic. They had done many things in the past three months that they had never thought imaginable, but killing another person was completely new territory. Colt finally ended the silence by saying, "Look. The wargs are coming."

There were five of them now. Two more had joined the pack, coming up from the western side of the subdivision. Most of the streets were cleared. People were hiding in their attics, hoping they would not be tracked, holding their breath to keep from being heard. The ones who hadn't been able to get back to their homes were trying to get out of sight and pray they weren't detected.

A middle-aged man wearing green-and-tan camouflage clothes ducked behind some shrubs just as two wargs entered his street. The giant, stocky beasts – each one as large and thick as an SUV – slowed down to an amble. They sniffed the air. The beasts eyed each other in silent communication, and then separated to different sides of the street. One went up the near side, the other up the far side. They walked with purpose, sometimes leaning down and putting their nose to the ground to scare up a path. Other times, they would shake their noses in disgust at the overwhelming stench of bleach, which was at least a hundred times more powerful for them than it was for humans.

The man lay perfectly still among the shrubs. Over his camo, he wore a makeshift ghillie suit, which had become popular in the past month. Even Jaxon and Peter were working on their own ghillie suits. This guy's was all leaves, sticks, and grass. Crudely created, but very effective, and it gave him hope. Aidan had almost lost sight of the man in the shrubs.

The warg trotted along the houseline where the man was hiding. In one sudden and fluid moment, the beast jerked its head to the side, lunged into the bushes, and pulled out the guy in the ghillie suit. The man tried to escape, but the warg clasped him tightly in its jaws. It shook him like a rag doll – leaves and grass and sticks flew everywhere – then it spit him out on the ground. He lay there, moaning in pain, blood mixed with the vegetation stitched all over his body. He looked up at the warg. The creature stared at him with malicious intent and opened its jaws so wide the guy could see all three rows of bloody teeth. With despair, he realized that the blood on the warg's teeth was his.

The beast snarled, then bit him again, but this time, the warg bit down on his leg, and all the way up Vicksburg they could hear the man's bones crunch. He cried out sharply, and once the warg let go, he tried to pull himself away.

The warg let the man drag his body out onto the asphalt. This was the worst part of the wargs. While most animals had developed some version of thicker hides, sharper teeth, and smarter brains, wargs had malicious intent. They had evolved a malevolent playfulness and sense of humor. The monsters didn't just kill, they seemed to enjoy finding new ways to torture anyone they found before they killed them. Case in point, the man's shinbone had been snapped in two, so his leg dragged behind him. The warg watched him with its serrated smile.

The other warg, which had stopped and cocked its ear in the direction of the grackle, turned to bark to the first one. It was a series of barks, in different pitches, and much more complex than anything Aidan or the others had ever heard escape the lips of a lupine creature.

The man, who was still trying to escape, cried out for help to anyone who would listen. "Please, somebody! Just shoot the damn thing!" he pleaded between sobs. "It can be killed. My life can't end this way. It Can't!"

The warg walked over, put its massive paw on the man's shoulder, and shoved the man's torso to the ground.

"No, no, no," the man insisted. Begged. "I still have things I want to do with my life. I have dreams to fulfill."

The man gave one last cry as the warg wrapped its maws with all those teeth around his dreams. A quick jerk, and the body crumpled. Bled like an oil leak from a hose, spurting softly. The warg spit out the head and started back up the street.

Jaxon and Peter sprinted across the lawn, and the grackle took to the air, circling over them and shrieking its piercing, noisome call. Then they heard the squirrel.

It hopped, tail twitching, along the fence line like any other squirrel they had ever seen. Then it perched up on its hind legs and opened a cavernous jaw. Two sickle-like teeth flicked outward.

"Fucking squirrels," Jaxon said. This time, Peter didn't correct him. He was too concerned with the threat glaring at them with black, pupil-less eyes.

"What do we do?" Peter asked.

"I don't know."

"What about the shotgun?"

"They move too fast. I got it. Go for the house. If we can lock it out, we can think of our next move."

Peter barely heard him over the raucous railing of the grackle.

"Okay. On three. One – two – three!"

However, when they darted for the door, the toothy monster easily dashed between them and their escape. It pounced at Jaxon, who tried to kick it, but as he extended his leg, the squirrel leaped on his leg and jumped at his throat. Two giant teeth were about to rip out half his neck.

Brain and fur blew over Jaxon, slapping him wetly in the face. Blood splashed like a water balloon bursting against his shirt.

"Got him," Aidan said over the FRS, "But the wargs are following the grackle. Get your asses home, pronto!"

The thought that wargs could be gunning for them made Jaxon and Peter react all that much faster. They hurdled one fence and sprinted another. The grackle followed them, always calling out with that horrible, noisome sound. It hovered over as they moved around the yards, glowering at them with its yellow, dinosaurian glare.

"Fuck this," Jaxon said. He pulled out the shotgun and aimed it at the grackle. The grackle saw the gun and stopped calling. It tried to fly away, but didn't make four feet before buckshot blasted it out of existence.

Running is hard when trying to cover tracks with bleach water, but run they did. They hopped the fence to the Christoferson's house, a burned-up corpse of its former self. It still stunk of burned bodies, though the remains had been devoured long ago. Jaxon suspected the stench was soaked into whatever remaining wood was left of the house.

"Hurry!" Aidan yelled. "They've finished Shiloh and Palmito Ranch Streets and are turning towards us."

"Almost there," Jaxon growled, knowing that Aidan couldn't hear him without the FRS talk button pressed down.

"The dungeon will be closing soon, with or without you," Aidan warned them.

Three streets down, the largest warg paused in the middle of the street and moved its head from side to side. When that failed, it raised its nose to the air and inhaled deeply. Then it jumped up on the roof of a car, its claws scraping against the metal hood. The alarm went off briefly, then weakened and died. The roof caved under the weight of the animal as it sniffed the air again. It snapped its black fangs in the air, and the other wargs turned, following it towards Vicksburg.

Sweating profusely, Jaxon and Peter ran out into the street, having decided that there was no further reason trying to elude any animals. Between the grackle and the gunshots, every beast in a one-mile radius was converging on Vicksburg. Besides, his arms felt limp and useless from jumping every fence on the block, and his legs were scraped up from catching on cedar wood.

Peter popped off the bit from his Camelbak. The bleach water ran down his legs and onto the concrete, hopefully covering their scent, though he had no idea if it would work. At least being on the concrete would help them. Grass collected scent better than concrete, and it was harder to get rid of all the scent in grass. Behind him, Peter left a trail of white water on the dark concrete.

A sideways glance down the street showed no wargs as they reached the house. They jumped a small hedge and ran up the walkway to their front door, which like all the others had been pushed in by the wargs. On the inside, the disheveled house looked like any other ransacked home in the neighborhood: broken furniture; giant water stains; dirt and leaves blown in through the open doors and windows, pictures knocked down, holes in the walls, scraps of trash left by possums, cats, and armadillos, and the acrid smell of animal urine and offal.

The stairwell was covered in discarded aluminum cans. A second look, however, showed a pattern. Each step was halfway lined with cans in an alternating pattern. Peter and Jaxon climbed up on the nickel-plated banister effortlessly and walked up it to the second floor. Though his feet were burning from the bleach water, Peter could not resist a dismount. The second floor, like the first, was a minefield of trash and disarray.

Down the hallway, they walked to the opening beneath the attic. They had to take a long step over a large play set that belonged to an action figure toy line that he outgrew ages ago. Peter looked around at the children's bedrooms. He had never known the people who lived here, and from time to time, he wondered about them, like why was there a stethoscope mounted to the wall of one of the children's bedrooms? It made no sense to him. Was the father a doctor? They found no evidence to suggest he was. Maybe the child had an older sibling or a close uncle. Some things just made no sense. Despite that, sometimes the whole gang sat around some days just talking about these phantom people they had never known or seen. It helped to pass time on the long, hot days. Peter would never know who they were or what happened to them after Black Friday.

Under the attic, Jaxon said, "Gunter Glieben Glauten Globen," and chuckled to himself. It was his idea to make the phrase their shibboleth. Nobody in their right mind would think of it, he had proposed to the group, and he felt pretty certain no animal could pronounce the nonsense words, unless of course they came up with a demonic parrot, but that would be crazy.

The attic stairs lowered, and Jaxon and Peter climbed up into the confines of their home. As soon as they were up, Alyssa and Kirk pulled the attic door shut.

Peter and Jaxon dropped their backpacks and took off their sandals while Alyssa checked over them. "You're not bleeding – thank God." She took an old shirt and wiped off the needles and the dirt, and noticed the burn marks on Peter's ankles.

"I'll be okay."

"Not if we don't get the bleach off you. It's corrosive."

She poured fresh water on his ankle. The water's coolness felt refreshing against his gnawed flesh. Then she took to cleaning Jaxon's feet. Jaxon jerked his feet away when she touched him with her soft hands.

"What?" she barked.

"My feet are just sore."

"Keep quiet, y'all," Aidan said. It was barely more than a breath, but the tone told them more than his words ever could. There were still wargs out there. Aidan had lowered the ridge vents, but left a small line open so that he could watch the beasts moving.

The same black-fanged alpha that had stopped and turned some of the others toward Vicksburg now stalked the street, moving slowly past the houses. The two betas each took a side of the street, which they searched in a grid formation. They were like a platoon marching across a field on the search for enemy scouts.

When the alpha came across Aaron's freshly killed corpse, Aidan told his heart to stop beating so fast. They thought sometimes that the wargs could hear their beating hearts if they thumped against their chest too hard.

The alpha stooped down and sucked the air out of the gunshot wound and into its nostrils. Aidan imagined the tiny scent particles of gunpowder and metal casing entering the warg's nostrils. He saw the synapses firing and carrying the information to the warg's brain, and he wondered if he had doomed them all. That by trying to keep the wargs from detecting them, he had led them straight to their doorstep.

Aidan raised his hand, the signal to be ready to run. Jaxon pulled his sandals back on. Peter's feet hurt too much, though, to put his sandals back on. And he was afraid the wargs might hear his feet moving across the floorboards. In the weeks immediately after Black Friday, Peter had tried to hold his breath as long as possible, but that only made him breathe hard when he couldn't hold his breath any longer, so he learned to just breathe slow and steady. Colt, being the youngest, scooted next to him.

The wargs are coming for us, Aidan feared. The alpha air-scented and turned to the house. For a second, it seemed like the large beast looked him in the eye. Aidan wanted to pretend he was staring the beast down, giving it the stink eye. In reality he just prayed he didn't blink so that the warg saw him.

Quietly, all three wargs made for the house. Aidan got ready to drop his hand, which meant it was time to run like hell. They had gone over this many times. It was a well-coordinated yet very simple contingency plan that involved burning the house and escaping to the nearest car with gas, then tearing out of Dodge like they lived in NASCAR City. *Hustle like you got a bustle*, his father would say, though Aidan had no idea why wearing a bustle would make you run fast.

The wargs approached the curb and sniffed around it, no doubt picking up on the bleach. When the boys had first started using the bleach, they feared it might lead the wargs straight to them. But throwing bleach on a trail was like asking a person to find a fluorescent-painted path at night, then shining a bright light in their eyes. Sure the bleach helped break down some of the smell, but mainly it just painfully overpowered their senses so they could not track.

The wargs' heads weaved back and forth. Tried to see beyond the bleach smell. With each step, they inched closer to their home.

Everybody in the attic watched Aidan's fist. And as he was about to lower his clenched fingers – his mind made up that it was time to make a run for the border – at that moment the cacophonous undulation that sounded like a hundred thousand elephants dying blared across the subdivision. The wargs responded, turning away, but not before the alpha took one last look to the attic, then raised his hind leg and urinated on the curb.

Once the alert was over, the teens in the attic breathed a sigh of relief. Shoulders relaxed. Lungs exhaled. Then Jaxon pulled out his backpack. Peter brought his out, too. They opened them to share their spoils.

First, they tossed their shit-sacks to the side. The sacks were always re-used. At first, they went through sacks about twice a week, but ever since the food began dwindling a month ago, so did their use of the shit-sacks. Now they used up maybe a sack a week.

Jaxon pulled out a bucket of bleach, floss, razorblades, cotton swabs, toilet paper, and moisturizer and set them aside. "And for the little lady," he said as he handed Alyssa a box of maxi pads and a *Reader's Digest*.

Alyssa's face lit up with that half-smile that had caught so many boys' attention back when there was a thing called high school. "Ooh, I haven't read this one."

"Well, it was *Reader's Digest* or *Home and Garden*."

"Thank you."

Aidan pointed to Peter. "What about you? Did you find anything?"

Peter unzipped his backpack and added to the pile several empty liquor bottles, string, a hammer, carpet cleaner, and fungicide. Lastly, he pulled out a notebook and a pen and handed them to Aidan.

"For you, bro." He slid it across the rainbow-colored gym mat floor.

Aidan picked it up and nodded. Alyssa poked him with her elbow until he said, "Thanks."

The rest of the evening, everybody did chores. It wasn't as bad as it sounded because nobody had to do anything like clear the table or vacuum the floor – chores that just kept up appearances in their old homes and lives. In the new world, chores were needed for survival. Bullets had to be inventoried, the attic had to be de-scented, and the power line to the solar panels had to be checked.

Everyone had their own duty, though none of them was assigned. People took care of what needed to be done until the sun began to set. With the first red and gold rays of the evening breaking through the gray lid of sky, Aidan and Kirk retracted the ridge vent while Jaxon filled several balloons with moisturizer and fungicide. Jaxon held up the open bottle of moisturizer to Kirk, who wrinkled his nose at the smell.

"Ugh, that's awful. What is it?"

"Lavender," Jaxon cooed.

"Don't be gay, Spike."

They took turns firing the water balloon hurler. Jaxon took the first shot. He scrawled "Cleveland Steamer" on the side, loaded the balloon, and pulled back the cup while Aidan and Kirk held the other end of the sling.

Jaxon shouted, "On my command, unleash hell!" They released the cup. The red balloon sailed out over the backyard and the alley and under the ocean of gray. The balloon splattered against a yellow and green garden gnome, spooging him with a moisturizer facial. They cheered as the balloon hit its target, and then spent the next half hour firing at random targets throughout the neighborhood.

While the boys played catapult, Alyssa collected the liquor bottles Peter found and filled them with the gasoline they kept downstairs in one of the boy's rooms.

Over the last three months, they had made many upgrades to the attic, such as soundproofing it with gym mats and egg cartons and adding a pulley system to raise the rooftop around the ridge vent like a trap door, which gave them an eagle's nest view of the neighborhood, but none of their innovations were as ingenious or as necessary to sanity as adding a second-floor bedroom. Of course, it had to be soundproofed and scent-proofed, too. But at the same time, it provided a storage area, a privacy room, and was ten degrees cooler than the attic – all things very necessary for not killing each other.

Alyssa opened the closet door. The closet was a carefully organized quartermaster's store of backpacks, pharmaceuticals, gallon jugs of bleach, bullets, and various items they had each dubbed necessary for survival at one time or another. She replaced the gasoline, and then added the new bottles. She counted them – 22 in all, plus an old-time wooden crate that was full of eighteen coke bottles, all Molotov cocktails waiting to be lit. Next to the bottles was a small stack of CDs. Alyssa pulled out a soundtrack. She loved soundtracks because the right ones compiled the best songs, like the *Sleepless in Seattle* soundtrack or the *Pulp Fiction* soundtrack. Classics. This evening, she held the soundtrack to another classic, The Mambo Kings. She started humming *Bella Maria de Mi Alma* and thought of her family in the barrio and hoped they were able to escape. Most of the houses were not as large as the ones in this upper-middle class neighborhood, so the logical side of her knew to be skeptical, but that was too much for her to give up on yet. Time must have eluded her, because a grackle startled her by flying past the boarded-up window. *Must be twilight*, she thought. Soon it would be dark and the bats would be out. She closed the closet door and climbed up the rope ladder back to the attic. She shut the attic door on the bedroom.

While Alyssa was in the bedroom and the other boys were doing their chores, Peter and Colt went down to the first floor and opened the door to the basement. They turned on their headlamps and descended into the basement, whistling like the seven dwarfs. Downstairs was another door, and it, too, had a lock on it. They unlocked it and went inside.

Before they arrived, the basement had been stocked full of grocery items. One of the things they had figured out about this family was that they were Mormons, so the basement was loaded with practical items for surviving a disaster like canned food and bleach. But now that they had lived off the family stockroom for months, only small pockets of random goods remained, like 28 boxes of fashion softener or 13 bottles of nail polish or 48 lines of USB cables – none of them over 12 inches long. These items were not considered necessary to survival, so the boys left them as-is.

In the far corner were the washer and dryer. The agitator had been removed from the washer and thrown aside like a pulled tooth (it lay in the middle of the basement floor) to make it lighter. Peter shoved the washer aside, and they crawled behind it. A dirt tunnel opened up before them. It went three feet, then cornered left another fifty feet to a concrete barrier. The tunnel was buttressed by various scavenged items like a standing lamp, a metal bedframe crossbar, and a curling bar. The tunnel was barely wide enough for two skinny kids to fit through, which was just the right size for them. For two months, they had been working on the escape hatch. Theoretically, once inside the sewers, they had a clear path to the drainage ditches on the side of the subdivision. They took turns using the back end of the hammer to scrape at the concrete. It was hard, difficult work in heavy, unventilated air and with little pay-out, but getting out through the drainage ditches was the linchpin in the escape plan. They had to have a way to escape without being detected, and the drainage ditch would take them far from any animals. By the time twilight arrived, they had added to a long, shallow indentation in the concrete.

"How thick is the concrete, do you think?" Colt asked while Peter took to the hammer again.

"It's got to be at least three or four inches thick, I suspect."

"And how far have we gone?"

"An inch or two." To Colt's despondent gaze, he added, "We're getting closer. Maybe tomorrow we can make it."

"Do you think Aidan will ever stop being mad at you?"

"I don't know. Maybe."

"I don't think he trusts you."

"Can you blame him?"

Colt didn't answer for a while. Then he said, "He's so serious all the time now."

"Now? Ha! He's always been like that. You just don't remember. Besides, somebody has to be serious. Too many people having too much fun in the middle of the apocalypse – we might make the neighbors jealous if it weren't for him."

Later, when the grackles started reappearing, Aidan called them on the FRS. While the risk with wargs was being smelled or heard, with the grackles it was a question of being seen. Like most predatory corvids, they had a keen eyesight far beyond the abilities of any human. Peter and Colt left the tools where they were and climbed back out of the tunnel. They wiped the sweat from their foreheads, repositioned the washer so that nobody could tell a tunnel lay behind it, and then climbed back up into the attic – washing their path with bleach as they moved.

The roar grew into something huge and deafening. There were more grackles out than they could remember hearing before. The grackles were so loud, nobody in the attic could hear the bats through all the raucous.

They peeked out through the ridge vent at the giant water oak across the street. What at first they thought were leaves had become the bodies of grackles. A thousand evil-minded eyes glared back at them from the tree, eyes that left no doubt that they once came from the heads of dinosaurs. Gently, the boys closed the ridge vent.

"It's like *The Birds* out there," Kirk said.

"Do you think they're on to us?" Jaxon asked.

"No," Aidan said. "I think it's a precaution because of what happened earlier. They're just ramping up the watch, you know?"

"What about the wash?" Alyssa asked.

Aidan had to repeat what he said, only louder.

The awful grackle noise was so loud that they didn't worry about bats that night. No way could bats feel their way through the dark with all those grackles screaming outside.

That meant they could party. No fires though. Fire was very bad.

Kirk pulled his box-top guitar from a cluster of boxes and mattresses. Then he started pummeling the strings. He sang a few lines, but once he sang, "There's a lot of people saying we'd be better off dead," everybody broke in with the chorus. Once they finished rocking in the free world, they played from Mumford and Sons, the Red Hot Chili Peppers, and even Def Leppard. They poured some sugar on each other. They poured it on loud, screaming at times so that they could be heard over the din that permeated from outside. They ended the night with Paradise City. They couldn't finish the song, though. Eventually, their voices fell hoarse from all the screaming, and the grackles drowned them out. All they had left was the noisome cawing. They went to bed, lulled to sleep by the birds that watched over the neighborhood, looking for them. Always looking for them.

Chapter Two – Loyal

The armadillo emerged from the underbrush and skittered up to the two-lane road. It began walking back and forth on the edge of the asphalt. There was no shoulder on the narrow road. The armadillo smelled oil lingering in the air, and paint on the asphalt. Suddenly, a blaze of lights and sound rushed by, and the armadillo ducked back into the underbrush.

After a moment, it stuck its gray nose back out from behind the bushes and sniffed the air. It clawed over a fallen log and plopped down in the grass. Sniffed around some more, its nose arching as the armadillo stood on its hind legs. When it decided it no longer smelled anything dangerous or threatening, the armadillo charged for the road. It had made up its tiny mind. There would be no stopping it this time.

Then the car came, unseen and unheralded until it was too late.

"What the hell was that?" Aidan wondered out loud, as the old van heaved over an unknown object in the road. There was a massive crunch as the van's contents, people included, shuffled from side to side.

"I don't know," Alyssa said, looking over her shoulder and out the back windows. "It looks like you definitely hit something, though."

"Unlucky for it. It is Friday the Thirteenth, after all."

Then the smell hit them, and Alyssa was the first to choke. "Unlucky for us. I think it was a skunk." She flipped the air conditioning to internal intake.

When she finally stopped coughing, she reached into the back and pulled out some of Aidan's books. They were hardbounds covered with the faded artwork of barbarian warriors and ugly monsters full of fangs and eyes and rage. The spines were broken, the covers were falling apart, and the page stitching was coming undone. She handled them like they were the severed arms of giant bugs, with as little tactility as possible.

"So this is what the boys do when I'm away."

"Yep. Me, my brothers, and Jaxon and Kirk are cool, happening studs. You just didn't' realize how cool till now."

She pushed the bangs of her shoulder-length hair behind her ear and opened the book. Then she closed it.

"This is stupid."

"So don't come."

"But I want to be with you."

"And I agreed to be with them. I'm the dude running the whole thing."

She put her hand on his arm and cooed through one side of her face, "I'll bet we could find ways to have fun."

Aidan liked that face. When she was a little girl, Alyssa had been struck with Bell's palsy. It had paralyzed most of the muscles on the left side of her face, giving her the crooked smile, but he loved how it looked. It was imperfect and asymmetrical and beautiful.

"I promised them. You don't want to see a bunch of guys in letter jackets cry, do you?"

"When you put it that way, that is pretty sad. So it's Friday night, and you guys could be anywhere doing anything you want, and you prefer to role-play?"

Aidan shifted in his seat. Kept his eyes focused on the road.

"What is it?"

He started to say, and then said, "I shouldn't say. I don't want to ruin anything."

"C'mon. You can tell me."

"I'm only doing this cause they asked. Kind of a last hurrah. Me and my wonderful fraternal twin, Peter are off to college, leaving Mike and Colt alone with Mom and Dad. Jaxon's heading to England to study under some martial arts genius. Kirk dropped out a year ago. We're on our way to different places, you know? We're not the same people we were two, three years ago. Am I making any sense?"

"Yeah, but you know, you get to fly away to Austin, and I'm stuck here pulling a senior year, so don't try to sound all doom-and-gloom about it."

"Sorry. I'm not trying to be a downer." He slowed down as the subdivision emerged from the woods on the right side of the road. On the other side stood a large pasture full of prize longhorns. Except for an errant calf and cow grazing through the barbed wire, the bulk of the herd had moved away from the road. They were huddled together beneath some oak trees, as if preparing for a storm. "You ever see some of the same people doing the same things year-in-year-out? Milling? Nothing ever changes for them, no matter what. It's like the world could fall away, and on Friday night, they'd still be cruising past the Dairy Queen. I think for us, for you, me, my brothers and our friends, it's going to be different."

"Ha! We'll be kings of the world!"

"That's not what I mean."

"Oh, I know what you mean. Don't be so serious. We'll have fun, and if it gets too dull, we can go out or something."

He grinned, which made her feel better. Aidan was a nice guy and all, but he could turn really sullen in a second. And she had to ask him something that might change his mood for the rest of the evening. There was something on her mind. Something she had to ask, just to make sure. She hoped she didn't make him mad bringing the subject up. Aidan was not easily stirred, but when he was, he had a bad temper.

"Speaking of us, you've been avoiding talking about us for the past few months."

Aidan groaned.

"Look, I'm not trying to bring up a sore subject, but it's something we need to talk about, and we need to talk about soon."

Aidan said, "It's all I think about. I think that's why I hate talking about it. I know it's something we have to do, but not tonight. Let's get through tonight, and we can talk about it next week. Okay? I promise."

Alyssa leaned into her seat. "Okay. Next week then, but no longer, cause you leave for college in three weeks."

Kirk walked into the living room, past the leather couches and the giant television screen, and sat down at the baby grand in the adjacent sunroom. Kirk had a face like a rock star, almost impish it was so angular. He also had long hair that reached past his shoulders. He set his shirt and cigarettes down on the piano bench next to him and lifted the key guard. Put his foot on a petal and pressed a few keys, his head cocked to the side like an inquisitive dog while he tried to figure out the right note.

On the television, a newscaster talked about the demise of the Kyoto Protocol and its effects on the environment. Kirk ignored it as he searched for the right key.

"Hey, my stuff's over here!" Jaxon yelled from his bedroom.

"I'll be right over!" Kirk yelled back, then began playing a melody on the piano. His head still cocked to the side, he did not look at his fingers as the notes began to assemble into a song. Music came easily to him. It was the only thing that came easily to him. These notes were crescendo, if he remembered correctly. He wasn't real good on the terminology, but it sounded like a rocket ship was launching from the piano.

Jaxon ducked his head out, a weird expression on his face. "I've heard this one before, haven't I? Is it All-American Rejects?"

Kirk rolled his eyes. "Think cooler. It's metal, but you've never heard it like this. Usually it's played on a guitar."

Jaxon had played this game many times before. Guess the really cool song I'm playing, but all you're going to get is the background music from one instrument. Jaxon never got it right.

"Cool. Come help me decide."

Jaxon walked into his room. Covering one wall was a television set, a stereo system, several game consoles, and a laptop with wireless. Covering the other were shelves of trophies –

mostly martial arts, baseball, and soccer. Mounted blades, knives, and posters of swimsuit models adorned his walls. He opened his closet door, which had customized shelving. Towards the top was a shelf with small see-through containers, like a jewelry box. Each box contained a set of jeweled dice. Sparkling onyx stone, metallic gray, bone-colored, and classic colored with wax lettering. It had been so long since the last time he chose a set.

"Just take the reds," Kirk said as he came up from behind.

"I was thinking the green."

"So whatever happened to you and Brandy?"

"Does it matter? My parents are sending me to England. We're done."

"Fuck them. They have no right, Jaxon. You should be the one to dictate what you do."

"They're my parents, and they're giving me a chance to study Taekwondo somewhere besides a hick town. They aren't exactly forcing me. Put out that cigarette. My parents hate it when you smoke in here."

Kirk looked around for something to put it out with and finally decided to toss it in the toilet.

"Waste of a good cigarette..."

Peter inhaled deeply. The hot dry summer air felt like fire in his lungs. He looked out at the burning evening sky and the ranch home they lived in. It was not old, but it wasn't as young as when they first moved in almost a decade ago. Their father talked about repainting the trim, and some of the bricks were chalked up from the natural wear and tear of a house full of boys. It may not have been the best house in the upscale neighborhood, but it was their home, and he was happy to have lived there.

He took two steps forward, and then began flip-flopping front handstands across the front lawn. He made it almost all the way to the drive before he started curling towards the street and lost his balance.

He hit the ground hard, to the laughter of Mike and Colt. He lay spread-eagled and sprawled out on the lawn as if he was imitating Da Vinci's painting of the Vitruvian Man, then sat up, acting dizzy and saying sluggishly, "And the lights went out, all over the world."

Colt and Mike laughed hard, bottles of Coke in their hands. Colt looked over at the carport at the vacant spaces and the missing Cadillac. His laugh faded. He felt frightened, not that he would tell any of his brothers. It was the first time their parents had ever left them alone in the house, and he was anxious of their absence, even though he had told his parents he was fine with them going and his brothers taking care of him. He didn't have an option, not according to his brothers.

Peter noticed Colt staring at the empty carport. Said, "Don't worry about them. They'll be fine."

"I know."

Mike's cellphone rang. He looked at the text message and smiled. "Pizza's on its way."

They could hear Jaxon and Kirk coming from a block away. The BMW coupe's stereo was blasting away to some frenetic rock group. Jaxon pulled in to the driveway, Kirk pumping his arms out of the window, a trail of cigarette smoke dragging behind the car like the steam from a tiny engine.

Kirk jumped out of the Bimmer before Jaxon could stop the car. Running up towards the three brothers, he did a front-flip in front of them, but it had been a while since he had tried flips, so he stumbled backwards and fell in the grass. This caused another round of laughter from the brothers.

As Kirk fell, a rabbit raced out of the bushes. Rabbits were common in their neighborhood on the outskirts of town. Still, it shocked them to see it dart in front of them, then stumble as if shot. A few dogs howled, and the rabbit started to twitch. The boys gathered around.

"What's going on?" Jaxon asked as he got out of the car, his backpack in his hand.

"Some rabbit's freaking out on our front lawn," Mike said.

They leaned down closer.

"Ew. That's wicked," Kirk said.

"What's it doing?" Colt asked.

"Convulsing," Peter said.

"Why?"

"I don't know."

Mike suggested chemicals. At seventeen, he was old enough to enter into such discussions that Colt felt ready for, but at thirteen, he was considered "too young" and inexperienced. Mike said, "Didn't Dad put down fertilizer and fungus killer on the grass last week?"

"Maybe," Peter said, then added, "Welcome to CSI: Vicksburg Avenue."

Kirk grabbed a branch and gently poked the rabbit. It was a small one, but it screeched loudly as soon as he poked it. It was a wild scream with all the volume of helium screeching out of a large balloon. It sounded as if they had suddenly brought it back from damnation. Its eyes rolled, and its tongue hung out loose and uncontrolled.

"Gross," Mike said.

The rabbit continued to wail. The sound was torture. It was unbearable. While everyone stared, mortified at the screaming rabbit dragging itself shaking across the lawn, Jaxon went to the garage. He came back with a shovel. He put the shovel in front of the rabbit to block its path. Then he ended it with a wet whack to the head.

"What the hell is this?" The sound was authoritative. It was Aidan. Nobody had noticed the van pulling up into the carport.

Peter answered. "Jaxon killed a rabbit."

"What? Why?"

"It was acting weird, man," Jaxon said.

Kirk said, "Come take a look. Its paws are still twitching."

Aidan frowned. "Throw it out, and clean up the shovel. I don't need Mom and Dad coming home and asking me why the garage reeks of blood."

Everybody came in through the garage door, which was always open and unlocked. There was a time when their parents used to lock the door, but since the older boys had started Junior High, their house had become like a hostel that kids ebbed in and out of, so they no longer locked the door. On various days, the house was full of either gymnastics teams, football teams, or even amateur rock bands. Certain teens, like Kirk and Jaxon, were near-constants. Kirk came from a single-parent home where his mom routinely worked double shifts and Jaxon came from a home of doctors who were always on call, so the twosome wee always open and willing to spend weekends at the Fannins' home. Kirk and Jaxon always had a bunk at the hostel and a seat at the restaurant. (Although Mrs. Fannin would complain that it was a sit-down restaurant, not a buffet, and there were no waiters.)

Because they were always in the house, Kirk and Jaxon already knew, where the Cokes were kept and where the cookies were stored when not in the ceramic cookie jar. The teens poured into the kitchen, gathered up what refreshments they needed, and headed into the living room. They found seats on couches, chairs, and the hearth, and then began talking about previous campaigns like old war veterans. Once the pizza arrived (three extra-large meat lover's, (thick crust, of course), two orders of cheesy sticks, six liters of Cokes, and cinnamon sticks), the giant-gelatinous-cubes-of-doom stories ended, and the boys took their food and went to the den.

Mike stopped Colt. "Not yet. You got to feed Cthulhu."

"But it's not my turn. It's Aidan's."

"And he's setting up the game, so if you want to play, you have to feed Cthulhu. Don't forget to give him his vitamin."

"But that's not fair."

"Life's not fair, and Mom and Dad aren't here to say differently, so go do it or we send you to bed. Your choice, *Colton*."

As Mike left, he yelled out, "Don't call me Colton!"

Alone, Colt made for the kitchen where the cellphones were charging. He picked up his cellphone, which was for emergencies only. *We'll be checking the phone bill*, his dad had promised him, and if Colt was calling for anything but an emergency, he would be grounded from Wii for a month. Phone in hand, Colt debated whether this was enough of an emergency. While he was not in danger, his brothers were bullying him, and he knew Mom and Dad wanted him to tell them when he was being bullied. But they would also be mad if he was calling for something other than an emergency. This was a difficult time for them. Aunt Renee was in surgery. If he called while she was in surgery, who knows how long he would be grounded. He took his hand from off the call button and closed the flip-phone.

Already the sun had set and it was dark outside when Colt opened the back door and picked up Cthulhu's food bowl, a shiny metal pan. He looked around, but didn't see Cthulhu anywhere, so he called out the dog's name. Cthulhu didn't come, so Colt went back inside without closing the door. From the laundry room, he took the old plastic gimme cup and shoveled two cups of dog food into the bowl. Then he opened a can of chicken-flavored dog food and spooned half of it into the bowl. Colt added the vitamin and stirred the food. Left the vitamin bottle and the can on the counter. Then he took it back outside and called Cthulhu twice. When the dog didn't come, he whistled. It was a pitiful whistle, but Cthulhu always came.

Colt went back inside and turned the outside light on and off. The bulb sparked, then went out. Colt growled. It was really dark outside. The camper blocked the streetlight, so the closest light came from porches several houses down. Colt pulled out the flashlight from the cabinet drawer and clumsily entered the darkness, flashlight in one hand and dinner bowl in the other.

Colt looked under the camper and out behind the shed. He double-checked the gates, but they were all closed. Just as the tears started to well up in his eyes and he was ready to run to his brothers, he saw the large body curled up by the side of the house. It was hard to make out the dog in the beam of light. Cthulhu faced away from him. His side rose and fell sporadically. He looked sunken in the ground.

"Cthulhu?" Colt called out. He felt embarrassed that his voice sounded so weak. He wished it would sound stronger, more like his brothers. He put the food bowl down and crept up to Cthulhu, the light shaking in his hands. Colt sat down beside his pet and placed his hand on the dog's side.

Suddenly, Cthulhu snapped. His teeth popped wetly and his head arched, all teeth and bite. Colt shrieked and jumped away. Cthulhu didn't chase the boy, though. He just lay there on the ground snarling and snapping. Something about the way his head jerked around scared Colt. Made him think something was wrong with the mechanics of the dog's body. Colt ran away, knocking over the food bowl, and slamming the sliding door shut behind him. He locked the door and stared out into the darkness. He couldn't quite see out there, so he shone his light in the darkness. A beam of light set a golden halo around the area where Colt had last seen Cthulhu, but the dog was no longer there.

"What's up?" Mike asked. Colt screamed, and Mike laughed.

"Shut up!" Colt yelled.

"What's the matter – why so tense?"

"It's Cthulhu. Something's not right. I think he tried to bite me."

"You *think* he tried to bite you? Let's see where you think he thought about trying to bite you."

Colt held out his hand.

"Well," Mike said in mock doctor's voice, "It looks like his thought was worse than his bite."

Colt jerked his hand away. "I know what I saw. Something's not right."

"Of course not. He's an old dog. C'mon, the game's set up. All we have to do is build some characters."

As the two boys walked back towards the bedrooms, a dark shape came up to the back door. The door began to rattle, quietly at first, then aggressively.

The hard part about role-playing is getting started. Once the game begins, the adventure commences. But until then, there was nothing for Aidan to do except watch everybody create characters, and everybody had a different theory about how to create a character. Some used generators to spit out characters, others made spin-offs of old characters, but most created super-sized versions of themselves. For Jaxon, that meant a mysterious ninja. Kirk, bard; Peter, thief-acrobat with an eccentric personality.

Aidan double-checked his references, and then braided some of Alyssa's hair. Her hair felt so soft in his hands. He thought about the possibilities of the upcoming year, what the dorm rooms would look like, who he would meet, and whether or not he would get to absorb any of the "cool" of Austin.

Somewhere out in the distance, he heard a scream. At least, he thought it was a scream. It sounded too inhuman to be a scream. Aidan looked around the room, but apparently, the sound was faint enough that nobody else heard it. Everybody was too absorbed in creating their characters. He shrugged it off as people partying way too hard for this quiet little suburb and returned to braiding Alyssa's hair.

Suddenly, the window rattled as if something hit it. The noise startled Alyssa, but the boys kept rolling dice and studying books as if nothing had happened. Aidan walked over to the back window that had rattled and hit the drywall beside it. "Cut it out, Cthulhu!" he shouted. "Go on."

"That dog always wants in," Peter said. "Dad says we could train him to track air conditioning."

"I don't like him," Alyssa said. "He has that weird look in his eyes."

"That's what makes him cool," Kirk interjected. "He looks crazy, so nobody'd fuck with him."

The shadow moved around the house, passing from window to window and pushing up against them, too. While the boys finished off their meat-lover's pizza, the shape jumped the fence and started around the front side of the house. First, it tested the windows along the front bedrooms, but they hadn't been opened in years. Then the front door began to shake on its hinges. The doorknob fumbled, then turned slightly, but the door was locked. The shadow moved on.

The symphony of pages flipping, pencils writing, and Cokes being guzzled was broken by a high-pitched ringing, like the kind landlines used to make in the sixties and seventies.

"Sorry," Jaxon said as he plucked out his phone to see who it was.

"What the hell kind of ring is that?" Mike asked.

"Dude, it's classic," Peter said.

"It's annoying. Like PewDiePie annoying."

"Mom and Stu," Jaxon said. "Want to bet they're calling me cause they smelled smoke in the house?" he said while glaring at Kirk. Kirk shrugged, as if there was nothing he could do about it.

"They can bitch about it in the morning," Jaxon said. He silenced the ringer and ignored the call.

The shadow quickly passed by the kitchen windows without stopping. The garage door, which was never locked, swung open.

Aidan's cell started buzzing. He picked it up to answer, when he heard another scream. This time it was much closer, and much less human. It was guttural and low, more a moan than a scream. From the look in Alyssa's eyes, he assumed she heard it, too. He glanced out the closest window, but there was nothing unusual in the backyard.

"What's up?" Mike asked.

"You didn't hear that?"

"I heard it. It sounded weird," Alyssa said. Aidan guessed that "weird" could easily substitute for "scary." Then he saw something both strange and frightening.

He saw a man run through the alley, past their fence, and continue on. This was the sort of thing that was usually more odd than anything else. Perhaps the guy was high on something, or maybe he was a jogger taking a short cut. But this guy wasn't jogging. He was running. Sprinting. Then the strange man turned to look behind him and saw something that made his eyes go wide and his face turn white. It was a brief, blink-and-you'll-miss-it look.

"Did you see that?" Aidan asked Alyssa.

Her eyes tightened as she tried to see out the back window. With the lights out, it wasn't easy to see.

"See what?" she asked.

"That guy with the crazed look running down the alley."

Peter and Mike's cellphones went off almost simultaneously, but they didn't answer them. They just let them ring while everybody gathered at the window to look for the crazy guy.

"Shut off the lights so we can see better," Aidan told Mike. The inside lights went out, and everybody stood at the open window, faces to the glass and hands above their eyes to cut out any residual light.

"It'll take a second for everybody's eyes to adjust," Jaxon said. Finally, everybody's phones stopped ringing. A few seconds later, they all started ringing again, but nobody paid them any attention.

"How did you see a guy in the alley?" Mike asked. "I can barely see halfway out of our backyard."

Aidan's stomach grew cold and his face darkened. He realized this was the part in the movie when everybody stopped and stared in shock at something inexplicable while the maniac with the chainsaw came up behind him. It was a paranoid delusion, but the night was turning weird, fast. The screams, the cellphones, the crazy-looking man – separate, they were coincidences, but combined, they were something else. But what?

Aidan stepped away from the glass and backed out of the den. Nobody asked him where he was going because they were all looking for the runner. Suddenly, a distant sound of wrenching metal resonated through the room, like a traffic accident out on the highway, but that was far away from them.

Aidan looked down the hallway towards the living room and the kitchen. Seeing only darkness and shadow, he retreated to his parents' bedroom. First, he crossed the room to his father's closet and pulled out the locked chest. He flipped through the combination with the numbers his father had taught him, yanked off the lock, and grabbed the family rifle, a powerful, high-caliber Winchester 70 that legend had it, his grandfather had used to hunt black bear in East Texas. It was a beautiful, well-kept weapon with a walnut stock that was worn from use. A few years ago, his father bought a new Leupold scope and had it custom-fitted to the rifle. He talked of hunting with it, but the only heads on their walls were passed down from their grandfather.

Aidan checked the chamber to ensure that it wasn't loaded – it was not. He hopped over the bed to the other side of the room and his parents' dresser. In the bottom drawer, he found the box with the bullets in it. The large 30-06 bullets felt cold in his hand. Suddenly, somebody screamed inside the house. Bullets spilled from Aidan's hands as he ran for the den.

The growl started low and rose up in the air, like a chainsaw ripping into action. Everybody in the room turned around. Cthulhu stood in the doorway glowering at them with that wild look in his eyes, the look that had always set people off, the reason visitors would say he was part wolf or coyote.

Alyssa tried to scream, but nothing came out. Colt was first. His still-childlike voice pierced the air, then everybody else joined the chorus of fear.

Cthulhu stood in the doorway on boney legs too long to be his. His horribly disfigured legs were each at least four feet longer than they should have been. There was no way this horror was capable of standing, yet here it was.

"Cthulhu, go home!" Peter yelled. Cthulhu ignored the command.

He barked at them, then leapt into the middle of them, like a wolf after sheep. And like sheep, they scattered away from Cthulhu, jumping to either side. Cthulhu targeted the easiest prey first. He clamped his tight jaws around Colt's arm, then jerked him back to the middle of the room. Colt made a soft sound of despair as the wind was knocked out of him. Stunned, he lay helpless while Cthulhu shook him like a rag doll.

They heard a wet pop, and Colt screamed with white-hot intensity. His brothers stood paralyzed as the death scene unfolded. They did not know what they could do. There was nothing about this in the Boy Scouts Handbook. (At least one of them wondered aloud how they were supposed to Be Prepared for mutant dog maulings.) As if looking at the room from far away, they were each consciously aware to some degree that they were in shock, yet they could not break its spell. Then a much larger pop resonated through the room, something like an ear-splintering blast, and Cthulhu flew sideways into the wall, a red Rorschach test where his head used to be.

Aidan lowered the smoking rifle long enough to release the casing and fully load five bullets into the bolt action chamber.

Peter and Mike jumped to Colt's side. His face and arm was covered in Cthulhu's blood.

Peter held up Colt's arm, and the youngest cried out.

"It must be broken," Peter said.

"Mike," Aidan said with urgency, "get the bandages and peroxide from the medicine cabinet in the pantry." Mike ran to the kitchen. By the time he returned, Colt was wiggling his fingers.

"That means it's not broken, right?" Mike asked.

"That's what I've always heard," Peter said.

"Then why does it hurt to move my arm?"

"Cause Cthulhu made you his chew toy," Peter said, and Alyssa giggled. She was always the first to be amused by Peter's wit. After she started laughing, everybody else joined in. It was more of a reflex than anything else. One of those "laugh or you'll go crazy" moments. By the time they stopped, Kirk and Jaxon had returned.

"What's so funny?" Jaxon asked.

"Chew toy," Alyssa said, "Peter called Colt 'Cthulhu's Chew Toy.'"

Jaxon and Kirk rolled their eyes and handed Mike a wet washcloth as well as the bandages and peroxide.

Mike wiped off the arm as Colt moaned. "This is for your own good, so quit bitching."

He poured the bottle of peroxide out on his arm, splashing away the rest of the blood. Colt's arm was already turning the color of the evening sky. Fizz seethed on the big puncture marks in his upper arm.

"He's going to need stitches," Aidan said. "We need to get him to a hospital."

Peter pulled out the keys in his pocket. "Let's go."

Mike and Jaxon helped Colt up. "I can walk," he told them.

Immediately, phones started going off. Jaxon checked a text message from his parents. "They say everything is fine, but Toby went into seizures. What is going on?"

Kirk lowered his phone from his ear and said, "My dad was attacked by our cat."

Aidan looked to his brothers. They were shrugging. "I can't reach them," Mike said as he put his phone away.

As everybody headed to the cars, Alyssa pulled on Aidan's arm. He leaned down to her, and she whispered something in his ear. He looked into her face and saw what was buried underneath.

"Okay," he announced. "New plan! You guys get Colt to the hospital. I'm taking Alyssa to her parents' house since she can't reach them. Once I'm done there, I'll call you. You take the van; I'll get in the Bimmer."

"I don't think so," Jaxon said.

"We've got some crazy guy running down the alley and every pet in the city going insane. I'm not driving a crap car halfway across the city with that kind of 'all hell' breaking loose. You've only got two blocks to your parents house, right? You take everybody there, but be careful. I'll take your car cause it has the re-inflating tires, the suspension, and the acceleration should anything happen." Aidan lowered his voice as he spoke, hoping Alyssa didn't hear. He didn't want her to be any more concerned about her parents because of something he said.

Jaxon looked from Alyssa to Aidan, then sighed. "Fine, but bring her back with a full tank of gas," Jaxon said, handing over the keys.

"Of course."

The boys climbed into the van. Aidan stopped Peter. "This is the part where Dad usually tells me I'm in charge, but I won't be there, you know?"

Peter gave him a "get to the point" look.

"Make sure everybody gets home safe, Peter."

"Gotcha, Captain Obvious."

Two minutes later, the Bimmer turned right and the van turned left, heading towards opposite ends of the subdivision.

As the van entered Lakewood Boulevard, a car came blazing up past them, lights flashing and horn blaring. The van slammed to a stop and the car swerved into the other lane, then disappeared down another road. Several plumes of smoke rose up in the sky. Jaxon, who was driving because like hell was he not driving the van if a Fannin was driving his Bimmer, turned away from the direction of the subdivision exit.

"The exit is the other way," Peter said. "Where you going?"

"There's no reason to go all the way to the hospital. We don't know what's out there or what's going on except that the whole world's freaking out. My doctor parents are just a few blocks away. They can stitch up Colt's arm."

The brothers looked at each other and nodded.

Something furry and thick ran across the road. It hit the Bimmer and kept on running, like a linebacker bursting through the offensive line on his way to the quarterback. The Bimmer swerved, and Aidan turned into the swerve. The car popped up on the curve. Alyssa screamed and grabbed the dashboard until the car was roadside again.

"You sure about this?" Alyssa asked. "Am I just being really irrational right now?"

"We'll see how far this road takes us," was Aidan's only response as he pressed the accelerator and the Bimmer throttled down the Boulevard. As it turned out, the road didn't take them very far at all. Aidan hit the brakes as soon as the subdivision's entrance came into view. Like so many other subdivisions, the entrance roadway to Lakewood was buttressed by two stonewalls, much taller than the rest of the subdivision's outer walls. From the outside looking in, each wall curved inward, with "Lakewood" ensconced in a central stone. Away from the entrance and in the middle of the boulevard's median stood a giant playground, its long jungle gym arms stretching like tendrils across the median. It was the largest playground in town, and stood almost three stories high at the top of the spiral slide. Besides the size of the playground, it was also probably best known for the tall climbing arches built to look like the metal skeletons of animals. A happy yellow dog with hanging cheeks playfully pawed at a scared cat with an arched monkey bars back.

Spread across the front of the boulevard stood dozens of longhorns. Bloody lines crisscrossed their chests and legs where they had broken through the fencing. Some of the creatures still had barbwire wrapped around their bodies and horns, which now had little spikes growing along ridges. The beasts moved without emotion or drive, as if some cowboy or field hand had herded them to the boulevard entrance, then left them there. They did not move away from the entrance either. Some picked at the grass. Others ripped out the cultivated pansies and azaleas from the entrance. If it had been any other day, nothing would have seemed so dangerous, but tonight was different.

"Maybe there's another way out," Alyssa suggested.

"This is the quickest route back to the Sixth Ward."

"Quickest doesn't necessarily mean safest."

"The other entrances are probably blocked, too, if you are going to believe that these cows are blocking our way."

Alyssa started to say that this was impossible, that there was no way that the cattle, like the dog, had gone through some kind of a change. But she remembered when she was little and her brother was very sick. In addition to the sickness, he was having visions. Her mother brought in a curandera who prayed over him and gave him a special tea that made him feel better. For better or worse, Alyssa came from a world where mal de ojo and susto was very much alive. She was definitely not the girl freaking out over the impossible.

"Turn around."

"You sure?"

She hated not knowing the fate of her family, but she was just as certain not to die trying to find out. Alyssa closed her eyes and prayed. Then she said, "Yes, I'm sure. Those cattle won't let you out. The same thing that got to Cthulhu got to them."

"You want me to run from cows? Cows? Look at them. They'll scatter as soon as I approach."

"If they're just cows, then why are you holding the gun?"

Aidan felt the weight of the rifle in his hands. He had picked it up as soon as they stopped. He hated to concede her point because it meant the world was a much darker place, but he had no choice but to agree with her. There were too many coincidences occurring at the same time. "Okay, so let's say the world is seriously messed up. What now?"

"Get the boys and find a place to hide. At least until we can make sense of all this and contact our parents."

Jaxon applied the brakes, slowing down to turn off the boulevard and onto Shiloh. He could not wait to get home. As much time as he had spent at the Fannins, no place felt as safe as home. He wanted to see his parents and know they were safe and everything was going to be alright. They were doctors. They would fix Colt's arm just as easily as they had fixed all Jaxon's broken bones growing up.

Suddenly, the road turned perpendicular to the world. Mailboxes jutted from the side, and the horizon unfolded vertically. Glass splintered and rained down on the world. CDs rose up in the air, then struck the side of the van. The boys screamed, but not like on a joy park ride. These were uncontrolled summonings from the roots of their spines.

Jaxon looked out at the sideways street, vaguely aware of two shapes sprinting towards the van. He looked to his left. Giant dents were caved inward along the driver's side of the van. He pushed against the door, but the door wouldn't budge.

"C'mon," he yelled to the brothers and Kirk. "We gotta get out of here!"

"What happened?" Kirk asked, his words groggy, lazy.

"We've been hit by something, but we gotta get out of here fast. Something's coming at us."

They looked down the street at two creatures. Could almost hear them panting as the panther-like creatures ran at them. Jaxon and Kirk unbuckled and crawled towards the back of the van. Mike, Peter, and Colt were already back there. They kicked out the doors as something large shoved up against the side of the van again.

They scrambled out and ran for the nearest house. Peter looked back and saw the dog-like monster butting against the van. The monster was built like a cross between a St. Bernard and a battering ram. The creature frothed at its mouth. A curl of blood oozed from an opening in its head as it struck the van's axle repeatedly. The sound of the skull smashing against the metal was wet and sickening.

They checked the front door, but it was locked, so they ran to the fence. Jaxon was the first to reach the fence. He turned around, folded his hands together, and lifted Kirk's foot as it pressed against his hands. Kirk flew over the fence, then Mike. Colt was too weak, so together, Peter and Mike lifted Colt up, and Kirk stood on a fence rail and helped him down.

"C'mon, c'mon, c'mon," Jaxon urged them. The two creatures, which definitely looked feline, like panthers, raced around the car and turned towards them. He booted Peter over, and then jumped himself.

As Jaxon landed on the soft grass in the backyard, the two panthers flew over the fence. The creatures turned in mid-flight to face their prey, but as they landed, a giant wolf-like creature snapped its jaws around the cat closest to its doghouse. The creature had been chained by its owners and could not escape yet, but it could unleash its anger on anything that got close enough for it to wrap its jaws around its neck. The other feline attacked the wolf, and the wolf mauled it, too.

They boys did not press their luck. They leaped into the next backyard. This yard was empty except for the moon glowing on the grass. Behind them, they heard the death throes of the panthers, then the backyard went silent.

"Okay," Jaxon whispered. "The plan is we can still make it to my mom and dad's. They are two houses down and across the street. What we'll do is make a run for it. I didn't see anything else out there, and the St. Bernard is busy head-butting your van…"

A low growl made Jaxon's voice falter and die. Behind them, he saw the giant wolf-like creature with its head leaning over the fence, its mouth contorted into a ruinous smile. The chain dangled broken from around its massive neck. In a single bound, the dog crossed the fence, but the chain caught between the fence rails. While the dog ripped the chain out of the fence, the boys scattered like herd animals when a predator leaps into their midst.

More screaming, and the boys came back together for the next fence line. This time, they leaped it without any assistance. Only Colt would need help. Peter stopped on the far side of the fence, Mike on the near side. Colt felt Mike pushing him up, then felt Mike fall away from him. There was another scream, and Peter ordered Colt to keep running, keep running.

They didn't make it to Jaxon's home. They got out into the street and saw more people flushed from their homes. They were screaming like victims in an old monster movie. One of those black and white movies where everyone is running pell-mell and without direction. From behind, wolf-like monsters dragged them down.

The sounds in Peter's ears came at him as if from far away, like his cellphone sometimes did. Before he could look around, Jaxon had shoved him twice. He followed the voice, followed it back to the corner house. The van was still turned over in the middle of the road, but the St. Bernard was gone. Only blood from the dog remained, pooling at the side of the van like leaked transmission fuel.

Then they were inside a house Peter was not familiar with. He wondered how long he had lived in this neighborhood, and yet he had never been in this house. He had only been in a few of the houses. He wondered how many people were home in their houses and dealing with similar calamities.

Jaxon disappeared, then reappeared with a gallon jug of gas, which he dumped on the walkway. Kirk lit a cigarette and flicked it, and the whole world went up in fire. Peter heard Kirk growl, "This'll keep them from following us," as he flicked the cigarette. Peter did not know he was crying until he heard the sounds gushing from his throat, but they were echoed by Colt, whose face was twisted into an ugly frown. Jaxon and Kirk led them upstairs, and closed the stairwell door and locked it. With all the lights off, they entered a corner bedroom, crawled along the bed, and looked outside to watch the carnage and hope that it didn't consume them, too.

Aidan held the phone to his ear, but none of his brothers was answering.

"Are they not answering, or is there no service?" Alyssa asked.

"I'm getting bars and a ring, so there's still service. Nobody's picking up."

He understood Alyssa's underlying concern. She was always quick to pick up on things, much faster than he did. If Lakewood was under this much devastation, what about the rest of the city or the state? How big was this? These were questions he would have to answer, but not until later when everybody was safe. Right now, he just wanted to find his friends and family.

Another car ramrodded down the boulevard. It took out a brick-enclosed mailbox, and then a small tree on the opposite side of the street as it bounced down the road like a pinball ricocheting from target to target. Aidan veered far to the left to avoid being pulverized by the out-of-control juggernaut, but the car came towards them. The two cars rubbed sides. Aidan looked across and into the car. He saw a lot of blood and fear in the passengers, and for a second, it looked like the driver had no hands. Everybody in the car was screaming as it continued for another block or two before finally coming to a conclusion into one of the subdivision's brick walls. Only the passenger's side doors opened. As people ran out, creatures appeared from the shadows to hunt them.

"We've got to get off the roads, Alyssa. They're too dangerous."

She nodded her agreement, and Aidan popped the curb and drove the Bimmer onto the wide boulevard's median. The freshly mowed median was full of pine trees and wood-and-steel-bar workout stations, like a balancing bar, a sit-ups bar, and a platform for working calves.

The Bimmer skidded on the pine needles and came to a stop behind the wooden platform. Aidan turned off the headlights as he heard another car in the distance swerving out of control.

Aidan tried his brothers and Jaxon again, and cussed when nobody answered. He texted them.

"I'm sure they're okay, Aidan," Alyssa said.

Aidan said nothing. Didn't have to. She knew his thoughts were as much on his family as hers were on her parents and siblings. She watched his eyes dart from people to the creatures, to cars and back again.

"They're attacking without purpose," he said. "Whatever crosses their path, they rip at it, even if it's another one of them."

"So?"

"So we just need to stay out of sight and out of mind."

"And how do you propose we do that?"

"I'm thinking."

Aidan opened the car door and leaned down to touch the dirt. The pine needles had kept the ground moist, relatively speaking for a hot night in the middle of July.

He took the moist dirt and rubbed it on his face.

"Are you serious?" Alyssa wanted to laugh.

"Out of sight, Alyssa."

He took her hand and slapped some mud on it.

She rolled her eyes. "Gee, thanks. You shouldn't have."

"Don't get sentimental on me." He rubbed more of the dirt on his shaved head, then his legs and forearms. Alyssa did the same. When they were as covered as possible, Aidan grabbed the Winchester, and they both crawled on the ground to the nearest tree. Aidan leaned into the riflescope and scanned the boulevard. The scope's night vision showed the subdivision crawling with these strange new creatures. And out of the shadows, one of the wolf-like creatures, one with long, crooked legs like Cthulhu, raced towards them.

"Be very quiet," Aidan barely breathed into Alyssa's ear. "There's one coming towards us."

He lay with the gun pointed in the general direction that the creature came from. He could not see the thing until it was almost in front of them. The boulevard had no lights, allowing the creatures to move between the shadows. All across Lakewood, lights were going out. Power was shutting off.

The creature did not so much as snort in their direction. It continued loping towards the crashed car, eagerness and hunger in its eyes.

Aidan and Alyssa army-crawled across the boulevard, and then waited for two cars to pass before they dashed for the other side. A small compact car came at them from the other direction, but it was too far away to be a threat.

They leaned against a brick wall and caught their breath.

"What now? I'm not going door-to-door. Besides, they're probably at the hospital by now."

"I don't think they made it out," Aidan said between huffs. "I think Jaxon took them to his house. His parents are doctors."

"And if they didn't?"

"I don't know. His parents are still doctors, right?"

As they passed in the shadows and among the shrubs from house to house and block to block, they saw many horrible and terrible deeds. All the animals in the neighborhood were reacting violently, as if taken over by some rabid disease. The ones who had escaped ran half-crazed through the streets, seeking out blood and death. The pets not fortunate enough to escape waited for unknowing owners to return home for the night. A bulldog with a toad-like grin of razor-sharp teeth barked from behind the glass door of one house. As it barked, its whole body hopped against the screen, as if the dog could no longer contain any of the kinetic energy building up inside. Perched on the inside windowsill of another house a large black cat with a twitching tail and lambent eyes watched them as they passed. One time at the zoo, Aidan and Alyssa had seen a tiger sitting in its cage glaring at them the same way. It was an expression that spoke to them from the days when man ran from animals. They knew who was predator and prey, and only a single-pane glass window separated life and lunch.

Aidan stopped Alyssa as they rounded another corner off the Boulevard. The van lay on its side, the back doors open and all its contents disemboweled on the asphalt.

"Oh," was all Alyssa could say. She clutched onto Aidan's shoulders.

"There's blood on the car," Aidan said. "It looks like something was slammed against the axle repeatedly."

Then a flash of something caught his eye. Across the street was a two-story house. On the walkway, a small fire lay dying, and in the corner upstairs bedroom, a light flashed at him. After a second or two, it flashed at him again, hitting him directly in the face and making him squint.

"They're in the house," Aidan told Alyssa. "Let's go."

He took her by the hand, and they ran across the street, stopping behind the van to get another look at the street and make sure they weren't being followed. When he was sure, Aidan led Alyssa up the walkway, over the fire, and into the house. Kirk opened the door as Aidan reached for the doorknob, then locked it behind them once they were inside.

Alyssa leaned into Aidan's frame and began to cry. He held her tight, then looked to Kirk. "Everybody okay?"

Kirk's jaw hung useless and powerless. Aidan read everything out of it. "Where are my brothers?"

"Upstairs. Corner room."

Aidan let go of Alyssa and ran up the stairway. He threw open the door to the upstairs and bulled into the corner bedroom. His eyes darted from Jaxon to Peter to Colt, who was still nursing his arm.

"Where's Mike?" Aidan asked. Tearful eyes met him, and he asked again, "Where's Mike?"

Aidan fell to his knees. Colt and Peter kneeled down with him, arms all around him.

Peter said, "I'm sorry, Aidan. I'm sorry." He couldn't stop saying it, just repeated it over and over.

Very quietly, Aidan said, "You were supposed to look after him, Peter. You were in charge."

Aidan glared at his brother like he was going to lay him out, but he didn't punch him. He wiped his red-rimmed eyes and got up. He sniffed his nose a few times while everybody watched him to see what he would do. He pulled out the phone and called his parents again. Nothing. He dialed again.

"Pick up, pick up," he pleaded with the dial tone. Nobody answered. He looked at the blank space where Mike should be sitting, at the arm limply hanging at Colt's side, and wondered if his parents were ever coming back. With all the chaos swirling around them, only one thing was certain: they were all alone.

Chapter Three: Helpful

The deep inhalation woke Aidan. He rubbed his eyes and looked around the room, chastising himself for snoring again. The curved humps of egg cartons stared back at him like a thousand gray and green eyeballs stapled to the walls. He could feel dawn pressing against the boards on the window, soaking the room in new warmth. Alyssa lay next to him. What little light passed through the boards cast an iridescent amber sheen to her almost waist-long black hair. He started to smile, but the grin was cut off before it could fill the corners of his cheeks.

The sound of another deep inhalation suffused the room. Aidan froze. Fear jolted him awake faster than any caffeinated beverage ever did. He reminded himself to steady his heartbeat, to keep it from pounding against his chest.

There was more sniffing in the bedroom adjacent this one. Probably another warg, Aidan assumed, though rats had been known to work with them. Briefly, he remembered the horrible night the rats invaded their house. It was one of the longest nights they had spent in the house, collecting and killing and disposing of all those rats.

Alyssa's warm fingers gripped his bare arm, and he knew she was aware, too. He said a prayer of thanks that he had fallen in love with the kind of girl who didn't overreact, the kind you didn't need to remind to keep quiet. Her soft hair fell on his shoulder as her head rose up. He could feel her deep eyes gazing over his shoulder.

The attic door slammed open, and a body fell down.

"Aah!" Colt yelled.

Alyssa shrieked. Aidan took a rubber ball and chunked it at Colt, who couldn't duck out of the way in time. Giggling, he flipped back up into the attic.

Aidan smiled while Alyssa laughed. She had an embarrassing laugh when something really got her going.

"Very classy," Aidan suggested.

"Oh, stop it," she said and mock-slapped him. He took her face in his hands and held it close to him, admiring the beauty of her asymmetry, then he kissed her. Alyssa hoped it wouldn't end. Then a ball came flying down from the attic.

"Breakfast," Kirk moaned.

"Help us...we're hungry..." Peter gasped, his hands clawing at the air in pain. "If we don't get something to eat, we'll die."

"Or turn into zombies," Kirk suggested.

"Dancing Thriller zombies?"

"Dancing with the Stars Thriller zombies! "

"Shutup!" Aidan shouted jovially, then rolled on his back while Alyssa put on some shorts and a high school tee, then climbed over Aidan and up into the attic.

"Who wants pancakes?" she asked, and the boys cheered.

Alyssa looked at the dead grackle lying in the tub. "Gross," she muttered. It was slightly wet to the touch and felt limp in her fingers. Its head flopped to the side, and she winced.

"Who found it?" she called to the back of the attic.

"Jaxon," Colt cried out. The attic was filled with the muffled thud! Thud! Thud! of his feet as he ran across the mats. "He found it outside by the house. He said he thought it got confused with all those grackles flying around last night and flew right into the wall and killed itself."

Alyssa started yanking out feathers. She remembered being horrified as a child when her mother had plucked one of their chickens, the ripping of feather leaving pale naked flesh. Now cleaning a bird was second nature. She stuffed the feathers in a sack, then handed the sack to Colt. The boy took the sack of feathers to the other boys, and they began looking for a place in the wall to stuff them.

Alyssa set the naked bird aside. Into a small bowl she poured a can of black beans - water and all.

When she was finished making the mashed beans, she returned to the grackle. She cut off its wicked glare, then sliced it open and pulled out the bird's insides. All this she set aside. Later, it would be thrown in the shit sack or added to a balloon.

After she finished cooking the bird, she placed the food on paper plates on the floor. The boys devoured the meat and beans quickly, with a song of "thank you" and "tastes just like chicken."

Aidan leaned back and watched Alyssa watching the big teenagers as if they were the children she used to babysit in her neighborhood. Kirk, Jaxon, Peter, and even Colt were all much older than the toddlers and kids she used to babysit. Those kids she fed snacks and kept out of danger. These kids, it was the same thing, but different. Then Aidan leaned forward and announced, "Today is the day we leave."

All the boys, except Peter, put down their meal. Peter kept eating until Kirk flicked his ear.

"If we head north, there will be less bugs to deal with and just the animals. All the bugs seem to be moving south or going dormant."

"But we have a good house here," Jaxon said. "It's practically a fortress. There are trap doors, hidden passages. Hell, we got booby traps."

"No, man. It's like Night of the Living Dead. The creatures haven't come to kill us yet. We've been lucky, but we can't be lucky forever. Eventually the wargs are going to come for us – they'll smell us, or hear us, or a damn grackle or squirrel will tell them, and just like in the movie, we'll be cornered. This is a death house. I said as much when we first came here, remember? That's why we've been preparing for two and a half months to leave. We have weapons and we have a way out of here that will be hard to track."

"But we're not finished yet. We haven't even broken into the sewer," Kirk added.

"But we're close. What – an inch or two, Peter?"

"Something like that."

"See? We can't wait any longer. They have come close to getting us before, but last night, we had every damn grackle in the county parked outside our front door. We had wargs scenting for us. I say we take a hammer and find out what's on the other side of that concrete."

"Be honest," Jaxon spat. "You just want to go find your parents."

"That's not true."

"Don't lie, Aidan."

"I'm not."

"Bullshit."

"Bullshit, you. Maybe I want to find my parents, so what? There are other reasons to leave. You're just mad cause…" But he couldn't finish, cause nobody wanted to say that Jaxon's parents were the only confirmed dead.

"Mad cause what? What, Aidan?" Jaxon yelled.

"Boys," Alyssa urged.

"Alright, tell you what - we'll put it to a vote."

"Ha!" Jaxon chortled. "That's not fair. You know you already got Colt and Peter on your side cause they're your brothers. They want to go find Mommy and Daddy, too."

Aidan lunged for Jaxon, who jumped deftly out of the way. Everybody else got between them.

"Don't push me," Aidan warned.

"What about the vote?" Peter asked.

"There's nothing as democratic as a vote," Alyssa added. Everyone was eager for Aidan and Jaxon to back off each other.

Jaxon looked to Kirk for support, but Kirk just shrugged. "Any form of decision-making sucks."

"Okay, we have a pretty good idea who wants to go, so all for staying in this house, raise your hand."

Aidan counted the hands. Three. Surprise splashed across his face. Why did Alyssa want to stay?

"I thought you wanted to go."

"We don't know what's out there. Besides, we've done really well scavenging here. And like you said, the bugs are going south or hibernating. Maybe the other creatures will, too. That could buy us time to be ready for spring. Everything could go back to normal."

Kirk added, "There's too much risk in leaving. We don't even know where we would go. Just north."

Aidan slammed the wall.

"We will be safe here," Alyssa said. "It took a lot of hard work to build up our house of bricks. Let's not run from it just cause a couple of big, bad wolves have tried to blow it down."

"Why are you so afraid of the unknown? For all we know, in some parts of the world, people are fighting back. There could be strongholds or green zones. My parents could be out there somewhere. Your parents could be out there."

Silence filled the attic. The sun was rising, and though the heat was not as unbearable as it was in August, Aidan was beginning to sweat already. The attic fan kicked on, and everybody turned and watched it.

Colt was not old enough to ride his bike on the major roads outside the subdivision, but he was drinking a whole glass of whiskey. He hated the taste, so Kirk mixed some Coke in it. Colt said he still felt like puking. They gave a few minutes for the whiskey to set in, then Alyssa put a pillow over Colt's face while Peter and Kirk pinned him down. Aidan grabbed Colt's arm and reset the bone. Colt screamed, high-pitched and undignified, like a child and not a 13-year old kid. To Alyssa, the sound was soul shredding, but she did not let up on the pillow pressure. A lot of noise had just been made in a world that was attuned to seeking out human noisemakers and killing them. They looked down the attic door to Jaxon, who was looking out a window with the binoculars. He gave everyone in the attic a thumbs up – if there were any monsters outside, none of them were investigating the muffled screams. Alyssa pulled the pillow off. Aidan wrapped Colt's arm the way he learned in Boy Scouts. Colt rolled away, crying.

"I'm sorry," Aidan said.

"I'm sorry," Peter said.

Aidan rubbed the sweat off of Colt and went back to the computer, which they had moved upstairs. Before the Internet died on the third day, Aidan spent the day downloading texts about animals, doctoring, wilderness survival – any information he could think of that would help their situation.

From the Internet, they learned that whatever was happening was happening worldwide. The day after Black Friday, CNN reported uprisings of giant-sized hawks in England, six-legged bears in China, and murderous lions in South Africa. Crocodiles assaulted Australia, mountain lions the size of saber-toothed cats throttled Mexico, and tigers and elephants hunted maliciously in India. And of course dogs and cats, or at least monstrous beings that once were dogs and cats. They were everywhere.

Everybody had a theory. The religious-minded claimed Armageddon. The science-conscientious reminded everyone of megafauna during the Ice Ages. They talked of rapid mutations as a response to the environment, but they could not explain what the animals were reacting to. Nobody had an explanation that could stick.

Later that night, CNN went off the air for good.

The lists of dead and alive were provided through social media. This is also where people found friends and family.

"ALIVE/WELL in Reno." Like.

"We r safe n Seattle." Like.

"They took my bro and sis. I'm trapped in a closet. I can hear the dogs outside, but they can't get in. I think something must have fallen over the door. Not sure how much longer I can keep posting, but I will stay on as long as I can."

That was Wendy, and she went to JuCo. She lived two streets down, and from what they heard and saw, her house was covered with wargs and panthers.

"We should tell her she is surrounded," Peter said.

"Why? What good will it do?" Aidan countered.

"We must get her," Alyssa said. "She is going to die if we don't help her!"

"There is no way any of us are going outside, much less to a house surrounded by wargs," Aidan countered. "That would be suicide."

Aidan went back to the computer. There were more posts from people they knew.

"Mom and Dad love you. Stay safe."

"Te amo, Mama y Papa."

But their parents never posted. Like so many others, it was as if a giant hole in the ground swallowed their parents up and everything they belonged to or ever did. There was no trace of them anywhere, except their last posts on the Internet. From Black Friday:

"Watch over each other. Be back later. PS – Don't forget to feed Cthulhu."

Peter read over Aidan's shoulder. "They're out there, man."

The next day, Wendy posted about being scared that this was her end. She was hungry and tired, but mostly thirsty. She had no water, and the heat was incredible. She could hear the wolves scratching, scratching. "If I dont post agn, luv you mom and dad. Peace to every1." Her friends and family told her not to give up hope and keep posting. Somebody would come soon. They were trying to get through to the police department and the fire department, but nobody ever came. Not the police, the fire department, or the army. Wendy didn't post again.

For whatever reason, the panthers left after the second day and were not seen again in their subdivision. The wargs stayed, though, like wardens of Lakewood Prison Facility. On the third day, the wargs started going house-to-house.

"We got to do something," Kirk said.

Aidan found fifty gallons of bleach in white and blue jugs in the basement. They bleached the entire first floor and most of the second, then shut the attic door and prayed that the wargs would not track them.

They got lucky. The wargs went up the flight of stairs, but the stench was too powerful. They went to the next house.

The third day, they lost connection to the Internet. They would have believed that the wargs or rocs had snapped a power line, but the lights were still working, yet their cellphones died, too. They were ostracized from the Internet community. Later that night, the power followed the Internet and cellphones into oblivion. First, the streetlights blipped into darkness. The halogen glow stopped streaming through the vent fan. Then the fan, the only respite from the overwhelming heat, slowed down and stopped. Almost immediately, warmth began to creep into the attic like some hot-tentacled monster.

By mid-morning, the thermometer outside said 95°, and life in the attic had become unbearable. Breathing became exhausting. The hot-tentacled monster had transformed into some smothering, carpeted creature that suffocated life and made movement difficult. There was nothing to do in the attic but sit and sweat. By the time Aidan broke into welts in the evening, a decision had been made. Unvoiced because talking only made you hotter, the decision had been made. In less than 24 hours, the most important step in their survival had become reactivating the fan. Screw food and water. They were going to die without some ventilation.

"I've got it," Aidan said. "Two houses down, they have solar panels."

Later, they would look back and realize how foolish and lucky they were. Nothing could be done without strict planning, like depositing a shit-bag or searching a house for supplies. But in the early days they were still like children who, when they see something they want, they take. If you want something, get it. There was nothing beyond the immediate. Want to watch a show that's not on television? Pull it up On Demand. Want to find out about something? Wikipedia. Want a solar panel in the middle of the night? Grab some pliers and cable and go.

Only Colt stayed home.

As new as they were to this world, they had enough common sense to stay off the road and move in the shadows. They climbed under cars and over hedges, but always out of sight of the main road. They never saw a warg while they went to the 1-story brick house with solar panels on top.

"Alyssa, stay and watch while we figure this out," Aidan said.

"Why do I have to stay here? I can do anything you can do."

"Can you climb a house?" Aidan asked.

"Do you want to climb a house?" Kirk added.

"Fine."

Routing the cable from the converter box took almost two hours; none of the boys were electrical engineers, or even handymen. But by ten pm, they tossed the cable down. They ran the line back to the house (thanks to the extreme couponing family, they had more than enough cable) and connected it to the vent fan. In fact, the photovoltaics were large enough that by 3 am they had also connected the air conditioning unit. By 5 am, they were no longer sweating.

By 7 am, the wargs were following the lines back to the house.

They listened to the wargs crawling through the first and second floor, knocking over furniture, tearing up walls, and sniffing along the floorboards. Then the wargs entered the hallway below the attic, and everyone stopped moving. They had no way to muffle any sound. They watched the attic door and stretched their hearing as much as they could.

There was silence.

Then some movement.

Sniffing.

Suddenly, the sniffing stopped.

All eyes were on the attic door. The long black cord snaked from the cable splitter to the attic door.

The coax budged with the smallest movement. Like a little mouse raising its head off the ground. Then the splitter slid, ever so slightly, towards the attic door. Further, further it slid. Everyone watched as the splitter dragged across the boards. It made a small noise of metal being dragged across wood. Behind it, the lines were beginning to go taut. One line went to the vent fan; the other, the air conditioner.

They were caught in a Catch 22. Move and the wargs would hear them. Don't move and the wargs would rip out their air conditioning and vents.

Aidan, who was close enough to the attic door that he had to move his foot so the splitter would not get caught on it, gripped and re-gripped the rifle. Alyssa and Peter held Colt. Kirk and Jaxon watched and waited.

Aidan rolled over to the attic opening, stomped it open, and put bullets in the wargs. The first one died on the spot, but the second one took two shots to the head before it went down. Aidan quickly scanned for any other wargs, then fell back against the floorboards, breathing heavily.

They were fortunate none of the other wargs came back that day, but they knew they would return the next day, so they moved the carcasses two doors down (they were not yet ready to eat warg) and covered their tracks with bleach. They also rerouted the cable so that it came up the side of the house and through the attic, rather than through the house. Then they cleaned the cable to get rid of their scent.

When they finished at 11 pm, they came back to the attic to find the vent and A/C not working.

"The power just went out, like it did yesterday," Colt said.

Aidan had everyone check the lines, but Kirk was the first one to say it.

"Our lines are fine. We're not the only ones wanting power."

Jaxon concurred. "Somebody cut our cable."

"No way," Alyssa said. "Why would they? We can share the power."

"A few solar cells are barely enough to power our A/C and vent fan during the day. Nobody is going to want to share this," Kirk countered.

"Let's go check it out," Aidan said.

Sure enough, Kirk was right. A new cable dangled over the brick house, and theirs was cut and lying in the bushes.

"What do we do?" Peter said.

"I think you know what we're going to do," Aidan said, and climbed up on the house, rifle slung over his back.

Jaxon raised the cable to him, and Aidan started to cut the cable.

"I wouldn't do that if I was you," a voice came from above. Aidan looked up and saw a man, his wife, and their baby. The man and wife both had guns pointed at him. The baby was breastfeeding. "That's our power now, son. You need to go find your own."

The funny thing was that all Aidan could think was *who are these people?* He didn't recognize them. They were not that much older. Aidan thought they might be in their early twenties. Maybe they were from out of the neighborhood, like most of his friends.

Hell, Aidan wasn't living in his house. They were living in the attic of people they never met. For all he knew, the young couple with the baby were at a party on Black Friday and they found refuge in the nearest house.

Aidan dropped the pliers and said, "I don't want any trouble."

"If I see you here again, I will shoot to kill. That's my power and my power alone."

"Okay." Aidan backed away slowly.

"Leave the rifle."

Aidan acted as if he didn't hear him and kept backing up.

A bullet bounced within five feet of him. He leaped aside.

"I won't waste bullets. Drop the rifle, or I drop you."

"It's a family heirloom."

"Unless you want to die for your heirloom, I think it's time for this rifle to leave your family's history."

"Maybe I can offer a trade. I killed one of those dog-wolf things. I call them wargs. You can have the meat. I'm sure you're hungry."

"Need bullets more'n meat. Drop it."

Aidan pulled out the Winchester.

"Slowly!" the man shouted.

Aidan was just a foot away from falling off the ledge, but before he could make his move, giant talons ripped out of the air and lifted the man, wife, and baby up in the air. Like something right out of Tolkien, the eagles lifted the people up in the air, but this time, they dropped them. Man, woman, and babe fell screaming and then were silenced by the front lawn.

Aidan jumped down off the roof. Above him, the roc landed on its victims, pulled off a leg, and gobbled it down. It looked at Aidan with those cold, avian eyes, then returned to its meal.

This was the first time they had to fight off survivors for access to the solar panel, but it would not be the last of what they would come to call the "solar wars of Lakewood."

Chapter Four – Friendly

"We need warg piss," Aidan said. "Nothing distracts a warg like a female warg in heat. Even the females have to stop and sniff it."

"I'm calling bullshit," Kirk said. "I want proof."

"I read about it, and I saw it on a Mythbusters about guard dogs."

"Mythbusters? I'm convinced," Peter said.

"Are you crazy?" Alyssa said to Aidan. "Do you know how much danger you are talking about getting into?"

"We are going through bleach like there is some endless spring in the basement, but there isn't. We only have twenty gallons left. What are we going to do when we run out? Go to the convenience store and pick some up? We were lucky to stash ourselves in the extreme coupon family's house. But it won't last us two months. We need another way to keep the wargs away, especially if we're going to stay here like y'all wanted."

"I hate to say it," Jaxon said, "but he's right. The only problem is how can we tell if a bitch is in heat?"

"Then there's the part about getting bitch warg vaginal fluid," Kirk said. "I don't expect a warg to split her legs for anyone, not even a handsome fucker like you."

"We get it off their urine," Aidan said. "And I know which one is in heat."

"Good. Should be easy from here on out," Kirk said.

Jaxon and Kirk ran out into the boulevard under full daylight.

"This is a bad idea," Jaxon said. "No cover and nowhere to run. If a grackle sees us, we're dead."

"No way, man. It's the ultimate in anarchy. We are handing over our chances of survival to Lady Chaos. I love it."

They stopped at a slanted wooden beam. It was an exercise station for pushups. Jaxon removed a maxi pad from out of the backpack and strapped it to the post. Kirk duct taped the maxi to the post. Then they did the same to a few nearby oaks, placing maxis at various heights on the trees.

"Is it just me, or does it seem like every time we go out, we're doing something with feminine hygiene products?" Jaxon asked.

"I think it's just you, man."

Jaxon and Kirk put maxi pads on the tallest of the step-blocks and on the chin-up bars, which were stations spread out over another hundred yards. The longer they were out there, the more they watched the trees for squirrels and the skies for rocs and grackles. Too bad, they weren't watching the ground.

When Kirk was five, his father gave him a sparkler, and he dropped the sparkler on his foot. The little firework flashed on his feet, burning them. That was how he felt now, like little fireworks were going off all over his feet. By the time he brushed his feet, the pain electrified. It felt like dozens of sparklers had been dropped on his feet and his ankles, and the fireworks were turning from sparklers to Black Cats and M-80s.

"Crap in a casket!" Kirk yelled and jumped away. He looked down and saw dozens of black-headed ants climbing up his legs. He pushed them off, but they wouldn't budge. They bit him again. As they bit, they twisted his skin. His skin was starting to bleed in dots. Kirk screamed and rolled on the ground. "Get them off! Get them off!" he cried out.

Jaxon felt the fireworks going off on his feet, too. There must have been a hundred fire ants coming at them. They were almost on top of him. Ignoring the excruciating pain in his legs, Jaxon grabbed Kirk and dragged him away from the oncoming ants. They crossed the boulevard and fell behind some juniper shrubs.

There, the boys pulled out pocketknives and attacked the ants. They had to kill each one individually and ended up cutting themselves more than the ants.

Pain woke Jaxon. Judging on the amount of sweat on his forehead, he assumed he had been out for an hour. He looked down at his swollen, throbbing legs. Dozens of large, red splotches bubbled on his legs, each one crowned with a painful white head. He thought of the Solarcaine relief back in the attic and started to get up. Kirk stopped him and held his index finger to Jaxon's mouth.

On the other side of the shrub sat a large, quivering rabbit with long ears and bloodshot eyes. A little bit of brain exuded from a crack between the creature's ears. The hairless beast looked almost wax-like and bulbous in the afternoon light. It limped on wretched, gnarled feet to the juniper and bit on some grass.

Then it stopped and growled. Jaxon pulled his knife as the gruesome beast leaped into the juniper tree, screaming like a murdered woman. Jaxon rolled on top of the rabbit, which bit at him and bit at him. It was missing half its face, like it was some sort of demon zombie rabbit. Jaxon held it down with one hand while he stabbed it with the other. The rabbit kicked him, and red ribbons of flesh and shirt ripped off. Jaxon kept stabbing the rabbit, and then Kirk started stabbing it, too, but it wouldn't stop fighting. They couldn't let it escape, though. If it escaped, the damned thing would bring the wargs down upon them. It had to die. It had to die.

Jaxon slipped his hand from its shoulder to its neck and squeezed as hard as he could. He felt its neck snap in his fingers.

Twenty minutes later, they slumped into the attic with forty pounds of zombie rabbit meat.

Jaxon again refused to let Alyssa touch him when she came to him with the salve.

"What is wrong with you?" She tossed the salve at him. "Do it yourself."

"Thanks, bro," Kirk said. "I would have liked it if she rubbed some of that sweet stuff on my legs, but no – you'd rather have Colt or Peter do it."

"Just shut up," Jaxon said.

Jaxon and Kirk slept through rabbit stew supper, through the grackles that sat in the giant water oak across the street, and through the drowning sound of bats flying around at night.

When Jaxon woke, the attic was quiet except for the sound of air conditioning. Colt playing with a Rubik's cube, and Kirk was talking softly to Alyssa, who was only paying him half-attention while she read through the Reader's Digest. Kirk saw him, and Alyssa followed his gaze.

"I'm going back to the tub," Kirk said. He passed by Jaxon and opened the attic door. Jaxon saw that Kirk's legs were covered in welts as big as keloid scars.

Alyssa scooted next to Jaxon. Jaxon looked at his legs, which were covered in salve. "I guess I should thank you."

"No, Peter did that. You should thank *him*. You could thank me, but you wouldn't let me help you. You don't want me to touch you, like I'm poison or something. You don't talk to me, either. It's like you're ignoring me."

"No, I'm not trying to ignore you. Trust me."

"Then you hate me, but why? Because I'm not one of the guys and I break up your little boy group? Or because you just don't like me? There is something inherently wrong about who I am that you don't like. Which is it? A or B?"

"How about C, none of the above?"

"So you do have a problem with me. At least we're getting somewhere."

"No, I didn't mean it like that."

"Then what did you mean?"

"Will you stop that?"

"Stop what?"

"Asking questions." He looked over at Colt, who had moved his attention from the Rubik's cube to the two of them arguing.

"Why don't you go downstairs to the basement and help Kirk with the tub, sweetie?"

"Okay, I guess." Colt took the cube with him.

Once they were alone, Alyssa turned her sharp eyes onto Jaxon. "Spit it out. What's the problem?"

"Where's Aidan?"

"He's with Peter. They are checking on the pads to see if it worked."

Jaxon rolled his eyes.

"What was that?"

"That was the problem."

"What? Spit it out."

"Look, I don't want to talk about it."

"If we don't talk about it, then I'm going to go on thinking you hate me."

"What you have is a good thing," Jaxon said.

She threw up her hands at him. "What's *that* supposed to mean?" She threw her hands up again.

"There is no way I know of saying what I want to say without it affecting everybody in the house."

Jaxon looked around at the crawl spaces that had become their home. All the egg crates, the mats, the wires, and the vent they added.

"Before all this, Kirk had his music, Peter had his gymnastics, I had Wendy, and Aidan had you. I never heard back from Wendy, and that's fine. I was going to break up with her anyways. But now there's just…" and he let his hands drop into hers, and she knew. Alyssa stared at his hands. She never in a million years would have guessed. She put his hands back in his lap and didn't say anything. She climbed down out of the attic.

An hour later, Kirk, Alyssa, and Colt were back in the attic with Jaxon, and everybody was uncomfortable. When Peter said the password, all the tension was sucked out of the room. The attic door dropped, and Aidan came up with a plastic bag that contained something small and round.

"People," he announced triumphantly, "We have bitch warg urine!"

"Oh, baby, you bring home the best things," Alyssa jested as she hugged him.

It was then that the trumpets from hell blasted through Lakewood.

They pulled up the attic door and shoved rubber piping into the wooden seams. Except for a small opening in the ridge vents, there was no way of scent getting out. Aidan watched the streets through his riflescope.

"Shit! Shit! SHIT!" he growled. He raised his hand.

"What?" Alyssa.

"They're coming straight back here. Black Fang is with them."

Eyes widened, Alyssa began mouthing the words to the Lord's Prayer, and everyone else tried to slow their heartbeats. To anything that could hear well enough, it must have sounded like a drum line in that attic.

Black Fang and the two other wargs approached Aaron's dead body. Black Fang licked it, then went over to the fire extinguisher and sniffed it, too. He barked at the other two wargs, and they approached the Vicksburg house. They growled and snapped and fought against the pervasive smell of bleach, but they moved across the lawn.

Alyssa watched Aidan's hand lower once, then twice, and she closed her eyes. The sound of shoes running back and forth on the attic told her more than anything else.

Within 30 seconds, Peter and Colt were already down the attic and running down the stairs, no longer mindful of their scent. As they rounded the front door, the ugly visage of a warg growled from the other side of the beveled glass door. But before it could lunge into the house, flames shot up on the porch.

The warg looked up and saw where Aidan and Jaxon were throwing lit Molotovs on the cement entryway. Tendrils of fire curled outward and climbed up the house walls as the wargs barked angrily.

While they tossed Molotovs, Kirk and Alyssa grabbed the backpacks. There was one for every member of the household. Each hellpack had two to three liters of water, a tarp, canned foods (and can opener), whistle, a small container of bleach, FRS radio, flashlight, extra batteries and clothing, and a first aid kit of Band-Aids, gauze, aspirin, and antibiotic cream. In addition, every pack was tailored to its owner, such as the small portable hard drive for Aidan, paperbacks for Alyssa, a harmonica for Kirk, and iPads for Peter and Jaxon and Colt.

Peter and Colt shoved aside the washer and raced to the concrete. Hammer in hand, Peter ran at the wall and hit it as hard as he could. The wooden handle split.

"NO!" he shouted.

Fortunately, there was just enough wooden handle left to grip, though it was split open and cut into his palm when he smacked the hammer against the concrete.

He hit again and again and again. Concrete dust billowed around them in the tunnel. They had no idea when the rest of the gang would get there or whether or not wargs would be right behind them. All they knew was that everything was counting on them busting through the concrete. No matter what.

Aidan and Jaxon flung more cocktails onto the ground. One nearly missed lighting up a warg. Black Fang stood back and watched the boys while the two wargs began to circle.

"Quick – we've got to barricade the other side as well!" Aidan shouted.

Jaxon lofted a few towards the back door, but they hit the bottom of the roof instead.

"Problem!" Jaxon shouted back at Aidan.

Then Black Fang jumped at them. His paws caught the first-floor gutter, but his weight ripped it off and he fell back down on his back.

"We need to use the bitch urine!" Kirk shouted.

"No way! It would be a waste at this point!" Aidan shouted back. "We need to escape. It's time to run for the basement."

"What if Peter and Colt aren't finished?"

"Then we won't have to run very far."

A crash of glass broke out. The wargs were inside!

"Chang of plans," Aidan said, and he raised the vent.

"Are you crazy? Why are you doing that?" Jaxon said.

"Cause we got to find another way out. We can't go to Peter and Colt. They will have to make it on their own."

"You can't abandon them!" Alyssa yelled. "They're your brothers."

"The rendezvous point is still the Dodge Viper outside the subdivision. Besides, they are safer than us. No way can a warg crawl into that hole they made without crushing itself."

With the ridge vent fully raised, Aidan climbed out onto the roof. For a second, he scanned the skies looking for low clouds. The ceiling was high today. He gave Alyssa a hand up while Kirk and Jaxon climbed out onto the roof. Except for Kirk, they were each carrying an additional backpack. Alyssa and Jaxon carried Colt and Peter's packs while Aidan carried the bag of urine.

Black Fang lunged again, and this time, he hit the side of the wall with enough force to almost knock them off balance and off the two-story roof. The only thing down there was broken bones and a really pissed off warg.

"Now where?" Alyssa asked. Flames were coming up from the front porch and the backyard.

Suddenly, Aidan felt the eyes on him. Just like Mr. Whittenberg two days ago, today they were the ones being watched by the hiders, the people who hid in crawlspaces and attics and basements of the neighborhood. Only this time, they weren't going to be assisted suicides. They were going to be hunted down and murdered.

Aidan dropped to the roof tile and slid down towards the tip-off. At the bottom, he kicked off, dived, and rolled onto the first-floor house. Jaxon followed him next. Once he was safely aside, Kirk told Alyssa it was her time.

"I'm no athlete. I can't make that jump."

"Aidan will help you across. Look – he's waiting for you."

"That's good and all, but I still can't make that jump."

"Then we'll do it together."

On the count of three, they slid down the rooftop, both of them screaming. Alyssa just knew she wasn't going to be able to stop in time. She saw her body going over the edge of the slanted roof and crumpling on the ground.

"Now!" Kirk yelled, and they both kicked off together.

As their feet left the building, Alyssa looked to Aidan. She saw great fear in his eyes, but there was more to it than just the jump.

From underneath her, a giant maw full of gnarled black fangs reached up to bite her foot off. Narrowly, Kirk and Alyssa avoided the warg as they crashed into the side of the house. Jaxon and Aidan pulled them up as the warg jumped again, this time catching on the side of the house and pulling himself up.

They all jumped into some bushes and trees on the far side of the house and sprinted across the street. They moved fast, their speed fueled by adrenaline.

"Where the hell are we going?" Alyssa yelled.

"I don't know, but follow me!" Aidan yelled. It was as good a suggestion as any. Alyssa looked behind her. Black Fang had disappeared. Maybe he returned to the house.

Colt traded turns with Peter for the broken hammer. Coughing in the dust, Peter examined his bloody hand. There were three large cuts that would probably require stitches – assuming they could ever get to a doctor. The pain was electricity jolting through his hand and searing up his forearm.

"Think that'll need stitches if we can ever find a doctor?" Peter asked.

"Don't be a pussy," Colt shot back.

"I'm serious!"

"I think that's a running gag with us."

Behind him, wargs growling stopped any chance to humor the moment for Peter. He ran back to the tunnel's turn and straight into the eyes of one of the beasts. The creature jabbed its head at the tunnel, but the tunnel was barely large enough to fit Peter – there was no way the warg could get anything more than its head inside. The warg knew it, too. It ducked out of view. Peter smiled. Maybe this would work out after all. In the blank area where a warg's ugly face used to be, Peter could see smoke. The house was on fire. Then he saw something remarkable and truly terrifying. Something he never thought he would see. The warg reappeared, but this time it raised and lowered its paw. It did this two times, three times, then stopped and looked into the hole. Was this really happening?

"We got trouble!" Peter yelled down to Colt as he ran back to the concrete.

"What is it?" Colt stopped hammering. They just weren't making the progress they needed.

"They're smoking us out."

Aidan, Alyssa, Jaxon, and Kirk rounded Vicksburg and headed towards the Lakewood entrance. Aidan thought of the last time he saw the entrance to Lakewood. There was a herd of demon longhorns playing the role of centurion guard there. He hoped they weren't still there.

Up ahead, Aidan saw what he was after. Giant metal animals with climbing ribs, and behind them, big metal beams jutted out of the ground. A narrow, grated staircase led five feet up to the first tier. Insect-like climbing arches, fireman's poles, and smaller slides formed the legs of the play structure. Rock-climbing walls were the spider's sides. Almost 30 feet in the air, the corkscrew slide was like giant spider's teeth. This was where they had some high ground. If they could make it here, they could make a stand.

Then Black Fang leaped over the red-brick walls and jumped across the boulevard. The monster came out on the far side of the playground.

They raced the warg to the spider play set. The warg toppled the happy-faced yellow dog with the hanging jowls and jumped at the spider play set. From the opposite side, Aidan lit a Molotov. Aidan used the first level of the playground set as a leaping ground and lunged at Black Fang. In mid-air, he slammed the Molotov on the monster's face.

Black Fang collided with the rock wall, screaming. The creature fell down and shook his flaming head while the others climbed up the playground. Aidan rolled on the mulch, then ascended the climbing wall back to the narrow barred corridor that was the spider's spine. Jaxon pulled his shotgun, but before he could shoot, something mindboggling happened. Suddenly, a group of six or eight high school kids – he assumed they were all jocks and cheerleaders based on their letterman jackets and outfits – burst out from underneath the playground. Yelling, they scattered. Black Fang, most of the flames vanished from its now hairless head, was enraged and confused. It took advantage of the fleeing teens like a wolf landing in the middle of a chicken shack. Jaws snapped and head lunged. Black Fang slammed one of the jocks into one of the playground set's metal beams so hard that his massive paw caved in the kid's chest. He turned and ripped the head off a cheerleader, then plunged into the escaping kids, throwing bodies from side to side.

Jaxon aimed the shotgun and fired. With only birdshot, the blast did no harm to the warg, but it was enough to keep the alpha from finishing its massacre.

"Thanks!" Aidan yelled. "You just reminded the damned thing why it was here in the first place!"

Aidan pulled out the Winchester while Kirk, Jaxon, and Alyssa crowded the very top of the corkscrew slide.

Black Fang walked over to the equipment, ignoring the carnage in front of him. He lifted one paw up on the grate, and then his toe seemed to pop out of socket and wrap around the grate. The boys and Alyssa stared in shock at the new evolution in the wargs. Black Fang pulled himself up on the set, his enormous form ridiculously perched on the narrow equipment.

The warg growled low and long. Snapped his giant serrated teeth. His disfigured face sneered at the impudent humans. At this close range, the more dog-like features of the beast surfaced. The wedge-shaped muzzle, the stout neck, and the slight black and tan markings told Aidan that, on the other side of reality, Black Fang had been somebody's German Shepherd.

Aidan leveled the barrel. There was no reason to take aim. The creature was too close to miss.

He fired. The creature didn't yelp. The bullet glanced off his shoulder.

Black Fang crouched for the pounce. Aidan leaned into the cool walnut stock while Jaxon aimed his shotgun. Then an explosion ripped the playground into a hundred pieces.

The black smoke was reducing visibility in the tunnel, even with the headlamps on the highest setting. Colt was coughing. Peter's lungs felt like they were on fire. He slammed the hammer down on the concrete and cussed.

"Just more nicks."

"We gotta keep trying," Colt said. "It's our only way out."

Peter looked around. Unless they dug up into the lawn, this was their only way out. He considered pushing through the dirt and emerging that way. They would probably come out somewhere next to the sidewalk. Assuming the wargs didn't pick up on it, maybe they could escape…

"No chance," Peter said. "We just don't have the strength to go zombie here. Besides, the roof would probably cave in on us, which, if it didn't bury us alive, would make enough commotion to attract the wargs."

Colt coughed again. "My lungs ache."

"Mine, too. Let's not give up yet, though. There are people in worse places than us. I mean, just think about it. There are some people living in starving countries or living in other countries where they are running from their overlords. Oh, wait…" He smiled, and Colt did, too.

He hammered again. This time, the concrete broke. Rotten, stale air billowed into the tunnel.

"Yep, we made it!" He coughed. "Not sure this is an improvement in air quality, though."

Trying not to use his bleeding hand, Peter pushed through the concrete. With all the stress fractures, it had broken into pieces. Peter crawled first into the sewer. Colt followed.

"Now we only have about a hundred yards to crawl through lemonade and mud," Peter said.

"You mean…"

"*Lemonade* and *Mud*!" Peter reiterated.

Peter and Colt crawled through a hundred yards of the kind of unimaginable foulness that nobody wants to talk about. For almost twenty yards, Peter held his breath, but the smell was so fetid it really didn't help. After a hundred yards, they slithered out of a blue tube like two turds from the subdivision's rectum. They landed in the ditch. They were free.

Lying on his side, Black Fang pawed at the air like a spinning tire on an overturned car.

"I know you. You're Riley Overstreet, cheerleader. And Charlie Tate, linebacker," Jaxon said.

Riley and Charlie looked at the dead bodies, the devastated play gym, the fallen warg, then back to them.

"Who are you?" Riley asked.

"We went to high school together. We were in the same English class."

Riley looked at Jaxon as if from years away. Some slight recognition crept into her blue eyes.

"You were dating Wendy, right?"

"Listen, guys, I'm not against the icebreaker, but we still got wargs back there. We gotta run," Aidan said.

"Wait. First, just tell me what happened," Kirk said. "We were all waiting to turn into warg cheeseburger, then there was this explosion."

"Oh, that," Riley said, still a little shell-shocked. "I threw a grenade."

"Oh. Well, thanks for that. Let's go. There's a Viper with our name on it."

They started running for the subdivision's entrance. Jaxon looked back, and neither Riley nor Charlie was moving.

"You coming?" Jaxon said.

When they didn't respond, he went back to Riley, took her by the hand, and led her away. Charlie followed from afar. His legs didn't seem to be capable of running at linebacker speeds yet.

Aidan said a silent thank you that there were no psychotic longhorns out in the open. There were cars everywhere, though, and a few bodies that died months ago, their remains scattered by animals. A huge chunk of barbwire fencing was missing from the pasture across the street. The Viper lay as it died, with twin curls of burnt rubber arching away from it. They didn't know what had happened to the owner, but from the vent ridge on Vicksburg, they had seen that it still had its keys in the ignition.

From across the road, Aidan saw Peter and Colt running. They looked like black smudges.

"You made it!" he cheered, and then, "You stink."

"Quien se pelló?" Alyssa said while waving her hand over her head.

Aidan held the seat back.

"Shotgun!" Kirk called out.

While Kirk went to the passenger-side door, Alyssa, Jaxon, Riley, and Charlie climbed in the back. There was barely enough room to fit Peter in the back, too. Colt had to sit up front under the dashboard.

"Oh, man, that is awful," Charlie moaned.

"Sweet ride, though," Kirk said. "If you're gonna drive around the apocalypse, you might as well do it in style."

"Easy for you to say. You're not crammed in the back like a damn clown car," Alyssa said. "I'm not sure I can breathe."

Aidan turned the ignition. The Viper popped forward and stopped.

"What the hell!" Alyssa yelled.

"Hang on," Aidan said, as he tried again, with the same effect.

"Don't you know how to drive a clutch?" Alyssa said.

"No. I said I didn't know. I said I would try, but I didn't know."

"Good God," Alyssa said. "If you don't know how to drive a stick shift, somebody else drive."

But nobody moved.

"Does nobody know how to drive a stick?" Alyssa asked everyone.

Again, no answer.

"Hell, no! I am not going to die in some high-end sports car cramped up with a bunch of stupid white people and two that stink like a landfill just because you want to drive through the apocalypse in style. Get me out of here! Now!"

Everybody jumped out of the car. Just then, the two remaining wargs ran out into the road. Everybody looked to Aidan.

"Quick, try every car, and we'll take the one that's working, even if it's a bike," he said.

They fanned out into the road, but every sedan and SUV they tried either had no keys or the battery was dead. The wargs were closing in fast. And impossibly, now Black Fang was back with them.

Aidan looked at the dead body ripped to pieces in front of the mini-van. He scrunched his nose and looked away as he reached into the pocket of the unattached leg. He pulled out the keys and pressed the unlock button on the car's remote. The car lights blinked, and the buttons on the doors unlocked.

"I think I've got a live one here!" He yelled as he jumped into the van. He turned the ignition, and the engine hummed mercifully to life.

"Come on!"

"A mini-van?" Kirk chided. "Really?"

"No time to make fun of my ride, Kirk. We gotta go."

All eight poured into the van. Kirk didn't call shotgun this time, so Alyssa rode up front. Only Colt had to sit on the floor. Kirk looked back at the Viper and moaned. "You'd think the one good thing about surviving the apocalypse is you'd be able to choose whatever car you wanted to drive, and you'd be able to drive it."

The wargs didn't catch up for a long time.

Part Two: The Long Bridge

Chapter Five – Courteous

The first night on the road was by far the scariest. In contradiction, the first day had been their best. Their world was no longer closed in by the subdivision's walls. They were free to explore the new and terrifying world. For Peter, Aidan, and Colt who had lost their brother, a silent pact had been made, to find their parents.

The seven drove a state road northward out of town. They were shocked by how much distance they could make. Within an hour, they were outside of the metro area. By their first bathroom break (a funny picture of seven people forming a circle around the mini-van, too scared of the outside world to be any farther away from each other than the distance needed to not urinate on the next person's shoes), they had entered the long-limbed pine forests.

"It looks like somebody drove a bulldozer through here," Jaxon said. All the cars lined the sides of the road like the wake in mechanical waters. Aidan wondered what kind of boat drove through a scrap metal lake.

"What are you thinking about?" Alyssa asked him.

Aidan pointed to the crossroads signs. "I'm wondering which way to go."

"Well, where do you want to go?"

"Vegas, baby!" Peter shouted.

"Chicago!"

"Atlanta!"

"Hell, no! Have you seen The Walking Dead? No way we're going to Atlanta!"

"Hollywood!"

"I want to go as far north as I can," Aidan told Alyssa. "So far north that nothing lives there except lichen and moss."

"I could go with that right now," she said.

Nobody else disagreed, so Aidan took the northbound lane. They drove for hours deeper into the forest.

As night fell, they stopped in the middle of the state road. The engine stopped, and Aidan reached for the lights.

"No. Not yet. I need just a minute," Alyssa said.

After a few seconds, the lights went out on their own. Suddenly, the trees on both sides of the road felt a lot closer than they had when the sun was up. The line of pines was like giant walls pressing against them. Their tops were like the teeth of a giant saw blade striking at the sky. A sense of dread crept into the backs of all their minds. For the past two months, they had lived safely in an attic surrounded by barriers to keep them protected from animals. But sleeping in the minivan, they were almost completely defenseless. No high ground, no soundproofing, no scent proofing.

"We're like the kids from Jurassic Park, holing up in an SUV and hoping it will keep us safe from the T-Rex," Kirk said.

"Think on the bright side," Peter said, "At least we haven't seen any dinosaurs yet."

"I wouldn't put it beyond them," Alyssa added.

"Who's them?" Riley asked as she handed Charlie a Clif Bar. Charlie didn't eat it.

"Them are the people responsible for this clusterfuck of a world we live in now," Aidan interjected while he chewed on his own bar.

"You don't have to cuss," Peter said. Aidan ignored him.

"Okay, but you don't know who did it, right?" Riley said.

"Sure I do. It was Mr. Johnson, my chemistry teacher. I think he did something with one of his chemistry experiments."

"No, it was Republicans," Kirk said.

"UIL," Peter suggested.

"Justin Bieber," Alyssa said while rolling her eyes.

"You?" Riley said to Colt.

"Lex Luthor."

"And what about you, Jaxon? Who do you blame for this mess?"

"I don't see a point in blaming anyone. I just want to survive it and protect the family."

They were all nodding together at this. Talking helped. Somehow, it created a barrier against the mysteries of the night and the woods. Then a long howl broke their comfort, and despite the heat, they all shuddered.

They tried to sleep with the windows closed, which would reduce the amount of scent being sent out into the world, but the heat was oppressive. They had to open the windows, which made them that much more vulnerable to detection. Aidan elected to take the first watch. He was too hot to sleep, anyways.

As he sat in the minivan, he felt little rivers of hives exploding along his sweat-soaked back, arms, and legs. So he left the van and climbed on top of an overturned RV, which gave him a little wind and allowed him to see farther. A moment later, Alyssa climbed up with him.

"I didn't like being away from you," she told him. A minute later, Peter brought Colt up there, too. Riley, Jaxon, and the rest followed behind.

None of them slept that night. There was a time when they used to listen to crickets chirping and owls hooting and it was a good thing that reminded them of the simple things in life. Now they wondered if the crickets were somehow communicating to wargs or rocs about the location of the teens. A long time ago, lightning bugs were a welcome sight. Now they all sat and wondered if the bugs were up to something, like the maggots in the houses. They watched the roadside for any sign of an animal. From time to time, they would hear twigs snapping or footsteps in the trees, but they never saw anything, and nothing came on the road.

Sometime around dawn, they fell asleep.

Aidan woke later in the morning. He was hot and thirsty, the sun was in his eyes, and something was tugging at his leg. He looked down and saw an oversized blackbird picking at his boots. He swung the rifle like a club and knocked the bird off the RV. The others were waking to the same predicament. They shooed the blackbirds away, but the greedy little rats flew to the roadside and watched. Aidan said a little prayer of thanks that even in the apocalypse, blackbirds were nothing more than annoyances.

"Every day it's something new," Kirk growled.

"Where's Charlie?" Riley cried out. They looked around. Everybody was accounted for except the linebacker. Charlie was nowhere. Aidan looked over the side, expecting to see Charlie being devoured by blackbirds, but he was not there and there were no signs of an attack.

They spread out across the four-lane state road and began to search. Jaxon with the shotgun took one side of the road, and Aidan the other. Ten minutes later, Aidan found a path leading away from the road and a fresh footprint.

"Oh, God. What was he thinking?" Riley said when everyone came over.

Slowly, carefully, they entered the path. Aidan saw him first and tried to tell the group to keep Riley away, but it was too late. Riley saw Charlie strung up on jumper cables and gagged.

The next few nights Riley would sleep close to Jaxon.

Within hours, the wake disappeared and the scrap-metal waters flooded the state road.

The first sign of the massacre was a station wagon squashed in the middle of the road like a smashed cockroach, its guts hanging out of the side like Mr. Whittenberg's bowels and its carapace paper-thin against the floor. If there were people in that station wagon, nobody would ever know. The station wagon was pointed in the opposite direction they were traveling.

"That's not a good sign," Peter said.

"What is that up ahead?" Kirk added. Nobody had brought the binoculars from the house, so they pressed on, but the mini-van was driving less than 10 miles per hour now, weaving back and forth through a maze of smashed cars and scavenged bodies.

The wall looked like giant child's car toys stacked all over each other. At the center of it lay a tanker truck with the tank collapsed in the middle. At least a dozen junkyard cars shadowed the truck.

Aidan stopped the mini-van, and everyone got out.

"I don't know if it's comforting that I can no longer smell the fumes from the tanker," Aidan said.

"No, it isn't," Jaxon told him. He helped Riley out of the car.

Aidan slung the rifle over his shoulder and wandered into the carnage.

"What are you doing?" Alyssa whispered to him.

"I'm going to check it out and see if there is a way around this. Why are you whispering?"

"I don't know. Be careful." She kissed him again, and he climbed onto the first car. It was a sedan, but he couldn't tell what kind. Metal plates had been bolted to its sides before it was smashed.

Peter and the other boys came up behind him, and they quickly passed him up. Peter quickly ascended to the top of the tanker and began walking along its top with cat-like ease. Not for the first time, Aidan wished he had the balance of his brother. Aidan came last, walking slowly along the tanker.

"Dude, you gotta see this," Kirk told Aidan from atop the rubble pile.

"That's new," Peter added.

When Aidan finally caught up to them, he was shocked, too. From the roof of the big rig, they could see a ladder truck had been leading the caravan when it came to its eventual end. A bulldozer's blade had been mounted to the front of the ladder truck. The ladder truck had been doing a good job of creating the wake of cars they had passed through all of yesterday, but now it was smashed between a wall of cars and the front of the big rig the boys stood on.

"Why didn't we think of that?" Colt asked.

"First thing we do next town we come to, we're getting a ladder truck," Peter said.

"Fuck that. Let's get an army truck or a tank," Jaxon countered.

Aidan looked at the wall of cars that the ladder truck was imbedded in. The wall was at least three or four cars thick, and it went off into the trees and then stopped.

"Didn't help them much," Aidan said.

"Well, whoever did this, they wanted to keep cars out. You can walk around it," Kirk said.

"Do you think it was the monsters?" Aidan asked him.

"I don't know."

On the other side of the wall, the road was clear of cars for about a mile, and then the stream of cars on the road started up again. Aidan imagined the road had looked like this soon after Black Friday.

"All these cars lined up for evacuation. Then they killed everyone. Like cattle waiting for the slaughter."

The corpses inside the caravan had been dead for no more than a week or two by everyone's guess. Since Black Friday they had become amazingly adept at determining how long a body had been dead. Most of the bodies in the caravan had been so horribly disfigured by scavengers, it was impossible to tell how they had originally died.

"So what do you think happened here?" Alyssa asked when they returned from the wall.

"Best I can piece it together this wall was built to keep people out. What I don't know is if it was built to keep people on this side or on the other side. But this caravan, must have got to here, then something slaughtered them. I don't think that was people."

"So what I'm hearing is we shouldn't stay here."

"Go back or press on?" Peter asked.

Aidan looked at everyone. The other six were looking at him.

"Press on. I saw an opening on the side that I think we can get the van through."

"North, still?" Kirk growled.

"Yep," Aidan said.

As the others began planning how exactly to get the mini-van to the other side of the wall, Jaxon went to examine a Jeep Wrangler with railroad spikes welded to its roll cage. Riley followed.

The car lay on its side like a dead cow with its guts eaten out and only the roll cage and ribs remaining. The body inside had been ripped into so many pieces that only shredded clothes remained.

Jaxon stepped over the roll cage and entered the Wrangler's cab. He pushed aside the remains.

"What you doing, Jax?"

Jaxon looked up. He had soft eyes and a wide forehead. His thick lips hooked mischievously. Jaxon held up the curved blade of a parang for her to see.

"Wicked."

"You got no idea. I can do a lot of damage with this baby."

When Riley and he returned to the others, Jaxon handed Kirk the shotgun.

"I shouldn't hold something this deadly," Kirk said. "If I get in the wrong mood…" He gave the weapon to Peter.

"Gee, for me? You shouldn't have. But why give up the shotgun?"

Jaxon said, "That shotgun was almost useless against the wargs. But get me close enough to one of those sons of bitches with this," and he showed them the parang, "and it is going to be a crazy-ass night."

It took them most of the afternoon to move the mini-van to the other side of the wall. Aidan was right. There was an opening, hidden to most, but getting there meant that the mini-van had to drive off the road to get to it, and the mini-van – as useful as it was on the road – was not an off-road vehicle. It got stuck once, and then they had to search for something to prop under the wheel. Finally, Alyssa found a sun-bleached keyboard pushed against the back window of someone's car. They were able to jimmy the keyboard under the tire and free the van in a plume of QWERTY. Then they had to make the hole a little wider, which meant they all had to push a couple of cars off the wall. This was very tiring activity, and had to be pushed carefully. It was like a Jenga of cars, each heavy enough squash whoever was underneath them if they fell. The cars bounced and jostled until they came to a rest in the ditch. The van was able to push through the remaining cars to get to the other side of the wall, but on the other side of the wall was a sea of abandoned vehicles. They didn't get very far because they had to get out and push the cars out of the van's way.

Most days, they traveled less than a mile or two in the van. Moving cars off the state road took most of their time. Colt suggested they find a monster truck. Besides moving cars, they also took the chance to scavenge stores and houses as they passed, but they stayed away from all subdivisions, no matter how welcoming and inviting they looked.

"We need a map," Alyssa declared one day.

"For what?" Aidan asked. "We go north. We don't need a map to tell us which way north is."

"I got one better for you," Kirk said. "First, we gotta find a map, and I'm telling you. There ain't no fucking maps. People don't make them anymore, and the ones they did make, people snatched them up and lost them before they died. Maps are as extinct as cappuccino lattés. Everything went electronic. Fucking GPS. And now they don't even work."

"Still, we need a map," Alyssa said.

They did not really sleep at night until one night Kirk announced a solid, "Fuck it." He climbed down off the big rig trailer that they were sleeping on, laid his sleeping bag out on the pavement, and curled up to sleep. Within half an hour, everyone but Aidan was sleeping on the ground.

"Tired of this shit," Kirk said to the first person who went down with him. "We can't do anything about it, and nothing's happened, so why fight it? Gotta sleep."

Nothing attacked them that night or the next. They were always on their guard, though. Months of playing hide and seek with monsters in Lakewood had left them all leery of trusting their surroundings. At any moment, they expected an army of men or wargs would charge them from the woods.

The front pushed through in the morning while they were eating Pop-Tarts and stale cereal. It lowered the temperature enough that they all got out of their bathing suits for the first time since they left the subdivision and put on jeans and rain gear. Thanks to some keen scavenging from Alyssa, even Riley had new clothes.

Once the rain started, they climbed into an overturned trailer and waited out the rain.

"It's not that bad," Aidan yelled over the drumming of the rain.

"Fine, you go push the cars and I will stay here out of the rain," Alyssa suggested.

"No, that isn't what I'm thinking," Aidan replied. He picked up his gun. "I want to see about some meat."

"Are you crazy?" Alyssa asked. "There are monsters out there. And it's raining!"

"And I'm getting tired of granola bars and soup. I want some meat. The rain will keep me from being detected. I won't go far."

"Be careful, or I will come after you," Alyssa warned while she kissed him.

"I'm comin' with," Kirk said.

"Sounds good. Let's go."

Fifteen minutes later, they were running for their lives.

Aidan and Kirk walked down the side of the road looking for a break in the barbwire fencing. While Kirk checked out some damaged fencing, Aidan turned and strode to a nearby Cadillac that had been t-boned during an accident. It was dark navy blue and the side was crumpled like a skull of a rat bashed in. He tried to read the plates, but they were damaged, too. He checked the front and back seats, then saw where the impact car had crashed through the barbed wire where Kirk stood. Aidan entered the mess that was East Texas scrub pine woods and found an animal path. Kirk followed him as Aidan wandered down the path and came into a clearing. While they wandered, the rain regressed into a sprinkle, then into a spit.

"Aidan," Kirk said. "Aidan!"

"What?"

"What are we hunting for? Really?"

"I told you, meat."

"No."

"Why would I lie about that?"

"Cause as soon as we left everyone, you went straight to that Cadillac that looks just like the kind your parents had, and now you're running up and down game paths looking for them, aren't you?"

"I just thought there might be a chance. I couldn't make out the license plate. It could've been them."

"You've got to give it up, man."

"Would you?"

"I already have. I lost my mom, too. Haven't heard a word from her since Black Friday. But you have to trust the chaos, Aidan."

"What do you mean, *trust the chaos*?"

"Chaos rules everything, as was proven on Black Friday. And chaos means our parents are lost forever. Millions of people were killed, and those that haven't been killed are probably holed up somewhere waiting for death. What are the odds that you will actually find your mom and dad?"

"I don't know."

"Exactly. That's chaos. You can't fight it. Look, if it is meant to be, you will find them, but you are going to drive yourself crazy if you search every blue Cadillac between here and the rest of your life. You got to give up looking for them."

"They could still be out there."

"What if they are? What can you realistically do about it? You can spend the rest of your days going John Walsh, but that won't guarantee that you find them. You have to give into chaos. I want you to say something, right here. Just between you, me, and your God, I want you to say, 'I give up looking for you, Mom and Dad.'"

Aidan scanned Kirk for some understanding of his predicament, but he found none.

"We are in the same boat, Aidan, but if you are not focused on our survival, then you are a risk. Say it. Say, 'I give up looking for you, Mom and Dad.'"

"I...I...See a deer."

A single white tail mule deer entered the meadow through some scrub not fifty yards away. They had been lucky, and the doe did not hear Kirk and Aidan arguing. Its back was turned as it sniffed at some leaves.

From behind him, Aidan heard another wave of rain approaching. *Good,* he thought. *This will keep the deer from hearing me.* He raised the barrel of the Winchester and sighted the crosshairs on the back of the animal's neck.

"Oh, shit," Kirk said. "Run." He charged towards the deer.

"You're ruining my shot!" Aidan yelled at Kirk. "It's just rain!"

Then Aidan started to get that 'I should be hiding in an attic somewhere instead of out in the open where any monster could kill me' feeling. He glanced behind him in time to see that the sound he thought was a wave or rain was actually a cluster of hornets, each the size of a Chihuahua.

Aidan ran, too.

At the trailer, the rain dribbled on the black asphalt, smearing the edges of the road. Without much to do, Peter and the rest of the boys had begun re-enacting video games. Riley went over to Alyssa. Riley was smiling.

"You're a lot cheerier," Alyssa said.

"I like it here."

"They like you," Alyssa said.

"What about you?" Riley asked. "Do you like me?"

"You are good for Jaxon. That sounds a lot worse out loud than it did in my head." Then she added, "But I like having you here to break up the testosterone."

"Yeah, what is that they are re-enacting? Some video game about elves and princesses and swords?"

Alyssa rolled her eyes. "You have no idea. Wait till they break out the role-playing games. That is something I haven't missed."

"I miss eyeliner and Facebook."

"Facebook, yes, but what I really want is some Jane Austin. I'd settle for Jude Deveraux. I could use some escapism."

"We've come a long way from Elizabeth, haven't we?"

"The more I see of the world, the less inclined I am to think well of it."

Riley guffawed, then held her hands to her lips. For a moment, the boys looked over at them, and then they returned to their game. Riley nodded to the boys and said, "*It behooves us all to take very careful thought before pronouncing an adverse judgment on any of our fellow men.*"

"Look at us, Riley. We are as bad as they are," Alyssa said. Then she gave her half-smile and said, "*It is a universal truth that a boy in possession of a role playing game will* not *be want for a wife.*"

Before she could laugh, something in the woods caught Alyssa's eye. She tried to see through the curtains of rain that had started in force again, but she couldn't make it out.

"I think someone's out there," she said.

Riley stiffened and turned. "Do you think it's Aidan?"

"No. He wouldn't come back without Kirk."

Riley cupped her hands over her eyes and searched the side of the road. "I don't see anything."

"You don't? Over there. It's like a shadow in the rain."

Without another word, Alyssa pulled the hood up over her raincoat and walked out into the rain. The boys suddenly stopped playing.

"What's going on?" Jaxon asked Riley. Peter and Colt were right behind.

"She said she thought she saw something in the rain."

"Stay here," Jaxon said to Riley, and they all went out.

Riley tried to see what was going on, but all she could make out were that her friends' shadows were gathering at the edge of the road. Then all four returned, but there was someone else with them. An old man. He had a big black jacket, pants, and boots, and he walked kind of funny, like maybe he had sprained both his ankles, or something.

The man was cold to the touch, so Alyssa took him away from the opening of the trailer. The man said not a word. Just sat down on one of the boxes of cola. Peter offered him a drink, but the man shook his head.

"Are you okay?" Alyssa asked him. "You look like you've been out there a long time."

The old man wheezed as he breathed. He looked forward with the thousand yards stare that they had seen in so many people over the past two and a half months.

"What's your name?" Peter asked. "I'm Peter. We come from south of here down in Houston. Lakewood." When the man did not respond, he raised his voice. "Where are you from?"

The man said nothing.

The first hornet buzzed by Aidan's ear as he caught up to Kirk. They were both dead sprinting through the mud and trees with no direction in mind. Aidan felt the hornet's wings beating so close he could feel the filaments. He twisted his head away, and the bloated body of the hornet zoomed past him. He leaped over a rotted log and turned as they came into a nest of thorny vines. A hornet jabbed at Aidan and missed. They ran some more. Another hornet knocked Aidan in the back and he stumbled. He put his left hand down and felt a sharp pain in his hand. He also lost the rifle. He didn't stop, though, as he tried to keep his balance and run deeper into the forest.

Up ahead was a small abandoned house. The doors were closed and the windows shuttered. Vines and leaves covered the sunken roof. He wasn't sure how much protection it would provide, but if it gave them a chance to catch their breath and think, it was a gift from heaven.

But as they ran to it, a creek bed with steep sides appeared between them and the house. Aidan and Kirk jumped, but this time, Aidan slipped and fell backwards into the mud and water. Two hornets lanced their stingers at him. He was too quick, though, and the first hornet stabbed a stump. The second one cut his pants open and tore a ribbon of red into his leg. Aidan cried out as he tried to climb out of the creek bed.

A hornet flew to the side and knocked into a tree. Wood exploded above them, covering them in rotted-out wood. A thick, rotten stick landed in front of Kirk. He picked it up as a black and yellow hornet rushed towards him. Kirk swung hard and connected with the hornet, which he sent crunching wetly against a pine. Then Kirk dropped the stick and hoisted Aidan up, while several more bloated bodies, full of enough venom to kill thirty men, slashed at them. They ran into the house and slammed the door shut. There was no way to close the door, so Kirk braced his foot against the bottom of the door while he held to the knob.

"Holy, hell!" Kirk said through deep breaths. "Those things are monstrous!" Then, he said, "Your hand!"

Aidan leaned back against a 1970s-era stove and gasped for air while he looked at his hand. Adrenaline was pumping so hard through his body that he hadn't realized what happened when he stumbled and fell on his hand. His little finger on his right hand was pointing in the wrong direction. Before he could think about how much pain he was in or how wrong the finger looked, he popped it back in the correct direction. A shower of pain rained up from his arm, and he screamed.

Momentarily safe and secure, the energy rushed out of Aidan like the air in a popped balloon. Aidan sat down on the floor and moaned.

"Did you see that?" Kirk asked. "I totally Pujoled that hornet!"

Using his legs only, Aidan pushed himself up off the floor and looked out the shutters. The buzzing had stopped. Except for the ones at the front door, the hornets were crawling on the walls. Their legs made little ticking sounds as they walked along the paneling.

"They are searching for a way in," Aidan said.

They both scanned the room. The place was a dump and was probably used by squatters, so there were small holes in the siding, but otherwise it looked intact.

"Well, I wouldn't like my odds against a warg in this place, but I think the holes are too small for the hornets."

"I can't hold this door forever."

"I think there are only four of them."

"I thought I saw six. When we've caught our breath, we should run for it."

"Where? I can't run forever."

"Good point. It will be nightfall soon. Don't wasps go to sleep at night? Maybe we can wait them out."

"Maybe. But what if these guys don't go back to the nest at night. Since when has any animal acted the way it was supposed to in the past two to three months?"

"That brings us back to running."

A sound of wood popping echoed in the one-room house.

"We need a decision quick, Aidan."

Aidan looked back to the stove.

"I've got an idea."

Peter handed the old man an open can of beans. "Sorry, but we don't have a campfire, or I'd warm it up for you."

The old man turned his watery eyes away, and then towards Peter. The old man dropped the can and muttered something.

"Okay, did he just say hymen?" Peter asked.

"No, not that," Jaxon said.

The old man muttered again, but this time a little louder. His voice came out in ragged, forced syllables.

"Dry her?" Peter asked. "Dry who? Alyssa and Riley are toweled off."

"Dryder?" Colt offered as he approached the old man, who turned his vacant gaze on the boy.

"Dryder," Jaxon confirmed. The old man croaked the sounds, "Dry-der," encouraged by the five.

Peter reached down to pick up the can of baked beans. They were unusually red, like somebody had mixed tomato sauce in the beans. Then he realized he was staring at blood. His blood.

"I think it's working," Kirk said as the fire blossomed in the chimney. They were lucky to find some old cans of gasoline to help ignite the blaze. Aidan had used his fire starter on a stack of gas-soaked magazines and broken futon legs. Now, Aidan brought more trash from around the room – fast food bags, cardboard boxes, and porn magazines – and he tossed them in the old red brick chimney. He put most of the weight on his right hand. His left throbbed like crazy.

"I just hope the chimney doesn't catch fire," Aidan said.

"Are you kidding? That would be awesome," Kirk said. "The ensuing chaos and the flames taking over the house would probably save us. I could finally let go of this doorknob and we could make a run for it. Did you just throw away porn?"

"Well, it was to save our lives."

"Good point. Did you just throw away the porn?"

From behind them, they heard the buzzing of insect wings. Kirk and Aidan turned around and saw one of the hornets had forced itself through a narrow opening in the wall and now stood on the inside of the house. Its large insectoid eyes glared at them while the creature crawled click-clack-click-clack down the wall. Its bloated thorax seemed to throb with venom.

Kirk saw a bat in the trash. Slowly, he stretched his arm to it, but it was too far away.

The giant hornet flitted its wings and took a few more steps into the house. It seemed to be trying to come to a decision about what to do with the boys and the fire.

Aidan coughed, then realized that the smoke was filling the room. Either the flue was not open or it was broken, but fortuitously at least some of the smoke was staying inside.

The hornet took to the air and circled the room while Aidan and Kirk flung their arms. Aidan grabbed a burning futon log and Kirk grabbed the bat. They both started swinging wildly at the giant hornet, hoping that something would hit. At the same time, the door of the old ramshackle house swung open.

Kirk screamed at the giant hornet, which swiped at him. It missed its target, then aimed for Aidan. Aidan fell backwards as the hornet landed on him. He felt its long black stinger knifing his abdomen as he threw it to the side.

The smoke was filling the room, and it didn't seem to calm or scare away the hornet. It only made the damned thing madder. Soon, flames danced on the ceiling. From the other side of the room, he heard Kirk yell. Out of the corner of his eye, he saw hornets swarming into the room, their giant black and yellow bodies filling the air.

Touching the bulbous creature's body sent a ripple effect of shivers up Aidan's spine. There was just something unnatural about the sensation of the creature's hard exoskeleton, which was covered in prickly fibers.

In the excitement of the moment, Aidan forgot about his hand. He pushed up with his left, immediately felt the pain railing up and down his arm. He fell back down next to the hornet, which bit at his face. He felt slashes of pain, and then kicked it away. He stood up with his right hand this time and ran through a wall of bloated black and yellow bodies.

Aidan came out the other side of that wall and realized he had somehow escaped the abandoned house. As he looked up, he saw a strong wind pushing the flames to the trees.

"Forest Fire!" Kirk yelled as he came running out of the old house. They both ran from the fires, which were now raging out of control around them.

Aidan felt the heat rushing towards him. He jumped over the creek, and this time, he cleared the gap and landed on the other side of the steep edge. Rather than stop to appreciate his feat, Aidan followed Kirk on a direct line out of the forest. By luck, he saw the family Winchester and picked it up.

Something hit the trailer roof and made a big bang, and Peter was pretty sure it was him. He landed on some boxes, and the wind got knocked out of him. He stood up and pulled out his parang.

The thing – because nobody could really tell what it was – stood in the middle of the trailer. Its broken carapace showed two sides of the old man's face and body. Underneath the old man's body sprouted bat-like wings and giant knobby legs. Bright yellow eyes looked out from his waist, and his legs now ended in the front-most feet of the monstrosity, which was neither mammalian, avian, or insectoid, and all three at once.

"Dryder!" The thing screeched as it thrust a leg at Peter. Peter, whose lip was busted wide open and blood was gushing out, lowered his body in a way that only a gymnast could and flipped out of the creature's kill zone.

Colt and Alyssa stood on the far side of the monster. Alyssa was trying to reach her backpack where she kept a pocketknife, but the creature was between her and the knife. So she placed herself between Colt and the monster and prepared to die fighting for him.

"If it comes for us, run," she told Colt.

"But…"

"Ya! No buts!"

Instead of Alyssa, the monster lashed out at Riley. It did not strike her. It grabbed her with its spike-haired claws and rolled her in its legs. It hugged her next to its thorax-body. "Dryder!" it screeched again.

"You can't have her!" Jaxon roared and bull rushed the monster. He blocked the creature's first strike, and then hacked through a leg with his parang. The appendage bounced and wiggled on the ground as it spewed blood. The monster wailed as it released Riley. Jaxon pulled her towards him as he ran outside of the trailer.

Almost by instinct, everyone knew what they had to do. They did not need to communicate with words. By the time everyone was outside, Peter had already lifted himself up on top of the trailer and heaved the door down. Alyssa, Colt, and Jaxon raised the bottom door while Riley locked it.

They all backed away from the trailer.

"You're bleeding, Peter!" Colt exclaimed. Peter had felt weak ever since the Dryder hit him, but the adrenaline had pulled him along. Now he looked down and saw a wet black stain across his chest.

"That looks unhealthy," he said with a smile as he slumped down.

Alyssa pulled him up. "C'mon. We need to get you somewhere safe and look at that."

"Does anybody smell smoke?" Colt asked.

They turned to see the flames rising up through the rain like some vision of hell, and out of the inferno, Kirk and Aidan came running.

"Go! Go!" they shouted without stopping. The seven jumped into the van and turned it around. They would not come this way again. They had to find another way north.

Chapter Six: Kind

It took them two weeks to find a better way north. First, the seven traveled south back the way they came. But they did not want to go so far south that they returned to Lakewood, so once they re-entered the metro area and the land of buildings and subdivisions, they turned west on a different state road, which took them into a Mordor of industrial zones, refineries, and factories that leaked so many noxious gases that the seven decided to spend a day scavenging for gas masks. Alyssa finally found some military-grade gas masks in the back of a gas station of all places. She found them in the gas station's back office, which was covered with pornographic pictures. Riley took one look at all the photos of naked women and left the room. Alyssa rolled her eyes and began searching through the storeowner's cabinets and drawers, which is how she found the gas masks in an opened safe. There was also a place for keeping pistols and bullets, but those were all gone. The storeowner also kept a stack of cash that he left behind. Alyssa left it, too.

Back outside, Alyssa found everyone circled around the station's gas well, wearing bandanas over their mouths. Peter was pulling up a narrow bucket attached to some string. Aidan had a white scar across his belly where the hornet got him, and he still favored his left hand. Peter had a similar scar from the Dryder and Riley had a couple, but otherwise, the group looked in pretty good shape compared to the past couple of weeks when Aidan was pissing blood and both brothers were in-and-out of consciousness.

"There's gotta be a better way to do this," Kirk said.

"When you can turn on the pumps, you let me know," Peter said.

Alyssa pulled down her black bandana and said, "Hey, guys. Look what I found." She held the gas masks up as if she was holding all that cash.

"Oh, cool!" Colt said.

"How did you find that?" Jax asked.

"I guess the guy who owned the shop was always worried about gas fumes from the refineries," Alyssa suggested.

They stopped driving the van and elected to push it. They pushed it because running the engine with all the traffic to slow it down was a waste of gas.

Each day began with more cars to be shoved off the road. They worked under the sun, but were usually comfortable. Only once or twice did they have to walk down the road wearing nothing but swimsuits and gas masks. Another cold front kept the temperature moderate, but the humidity remained constant and permeating, like the aunt at family reunions who nobody wants to talk to but everybody must deal with. The roads were not as bad as the overpasses, which were frequent and difficult to push the van up.

Peter looked at the latest overpass and sighed. "Can't we just teleport the van to the other side?"

He slid his gas mask like a ball cap on his head and fumbled around in his backpack, then looked around. "I'm all out. Anybody got some waffles?"

There were shakes of the head from everyone.

Alyssa searched the back of the van. "We've got Raman and...more Raman. You want beef or chicken?"

"Never mind," Peter groused.

"I think I might have a couple of Clif Bars remaining in my backpack," Riley said.

"Good," Aidan said as he jerked her backpack from her. He pulled out the Clif Bars and started handing them out to everyone.

"Hey, you didn't have to do that," Jax said. "She was going to share."

"We are running out of food, and she isn't one of us."

"I'm sorry," Riley apologized.

"No, you don't have to apologize," Jax said. "I'm tired of this bullshit, Aidan. She's been with us – what? A month now? Stop treating her like some second-class citizen!"

"He's got a point, Aidan," Alyssa said. "You shouldn't be so mean to her."

"I'm not trying to be mean. I'm trying to save you," he said to Alyssa. To Peter and the others he said, "And you, and you, and you, and you. But not her. She eats last, she eats least. That's the way it goes."

"Go to hell," Jax said.

"Fuck off," Aidan growled as he shouldered the rifle and headed towards the cars. "Anybody doesn't agree with me, give her your breakfast."

"What's up?" Alyssa asked Aidan as he finished pushing a Prius off the overpass. They were alone except for the dead. The Prius careened down the hill, barrel rolling until it collided into another train of cars.

"I don't have anything against her. She's been good for Jaxon, I mean Jax, and I think you've enjoyed having another girl in the boy's club."

"But she's not one of us."

"Exactly. Look at it this way. If you had to choose between her and me, who would you choose?"

"That's not a fair question."

"A couple of months ago it wasn't a fair question. It was like the whole *if I lost all my arms and legs and was horribly disfigured, would you still love me,* question. But babe, any one of use cold lose an arm to a warg or a dryder or whatever other kind of F'ed-up monster is out there now. So these questions that sound so callous and horrible are fair, and the truth is, every day she's with us, she's eating food that was rationed for six people, not seven."

"Have you looked at her? Riley's nothing but skin and bones. She just picks at her food."

"But if it came down to you or her, I would put a bullet through her head to save you."

"Would you put a bullet through Kirk or Jax's head? What about one of your brothers?"

"I'm trying to keep it from ever getting like that."

"But the way you're doing it is all wrong. It's not very Christian of you."

"Christian? You want to talk family values, and I'm trying to keep us alive."

She caressed his arm. "But we are alive, and we do have values. And you may not believe in God anymore, but…"

"I believe in God. I just have no value in Him."

Aidan smashed in the window of a Mercedes with a hammer and unlocked the door. He turned the wheel and began pushing it off the overpass. Alyssa walked away.

She gasped sharply as she saw a dead body standing on the other side of the road. Alyssa was used to seeing dead bodies lying in cars and on the floors of stores and houses, often pulled apart and mangled, but never had she seen one standing. This corpse was pretty dried out from being on the overpass throughout the summer. It was not very disfigured. Something about it looked kind of odd. Was it doing the jerk?

Colt and Peter came out from behind the nearest car, carrying another dead body.

"What are you up to?"

"Oh, this? Well, we had this idea," Peter said.

"You had this idea," Kirk said, dragging another body over.

"Okay, I had this idea. I remember reading about I think it was Pompeii, and how some of the people who were uncovered there were found in weird positions, and now archaeologists are spending their entire lives trying to figure out how they died that way and what were they doing that was so important they were going to risk dying for it. So I got this idea. One day, people will look back on all this and try to piece together what we were doing and why. I wanted to throw them a curveball. I decided we could pose some bodies in dance positions along the road, and that way, the archaeologists could spend their entire careers trying to figure out why people were dancing while others were being attacked by monsters."

"You have got to be kidding me."

"Tomorrow, we are going to make a flash mob," Kirk said.

"How is it going to be a flash mob if—never mind. Why do I bother asking?"

Behind them, in the distance, Alyssa saw something that made her pause. The boys were too busy positioning dead bodies to notice Alyssa staring out in the distance. So they didn't see the joy spread across her face like lights flickering back on after a long blackout.

"Look! Look!" she shouted. Everyone within earshot turned and stared where she was pointing.

"What is it?" Peter asked.

Colt cupped his hand over his eyebrows. Then he jerked back. "The bridge! Look at it!"

"What bridge?" Kirk asked as he came over.

"The bridge over the ship channel," Alyssa said. She pointed at it. "It's full of buildings!"

Aidan came over, too. "Buildings on a bridge?"

"Don't believe me, hater, but it's true!"

"We really need a pair of binoculars," Peter reminded them.

From where they stood, they could barely make out giant blocked shapes on the bridge. "I'm not sure what it is," Aidan said, "but it's definitely not cars or trucks."

Then a bright light flashed at them.

"Somebody's over there!" Alyssa cheered.

"Let's not get too jumpy. Remember the last time we met people, they were stealing our solar panels."

"They weren't *our* solar panels," Alyssa said.

"Same difference. You know what I mean."

Back at the van, Riley lifted her head from Jax's waist. "Did you hear that?" she asked.

"No. Don't care."

"I think they saw something."

"Sure. Fine. Whatever. Just finish."

She smiled mischievously. He frowned at her, and she finished him as the others returned.

"Oh," Alyssa said, seeing Riley and Jax. She turned her head. Jax buckled his pants.

"Sorry!" Alyssa said.

"It was nothing," Riley said. She got a water bottle and drank deeply as the remaining four walked up behind Alyssa.

Kirk could feel the tension in the air. "Did I miss something?"

"Nope," Jax said. "What'd y'all find? A working television?"

"Better," Peter said. "Civilization."

"Civilization. I thought it died last summer."

"But what kind of civilization?" It was Aidan. "We need to take it slow. Approach them, but on our terms, and with a get-away option."

After much discussion that went long into the night, the get-away option became a BMW. BMWs were common, and they had high top speeds and excellent acceleration. Their tires also didn't run flat, so that made them good running-from-the-law cars. One time, they had all sat around a television set watching a man in a BMW who was able to run from the police for hours on end until he finally slammed into a car coming up an on-ramp he was trying to go down.

The problem was gasoline. The irony was not lost on anyone that they were running out of gas while moving through all the refineries. They hadn't seen a gas station since the one with the gas masks, so they had to siphon the gas from car fuel tanks. Only problem was, they needed a hose and a gas tank. Finally, they decided to rip hoses from stranded cars. The gas tanks were easier to come up with. A couple of cars had some old gas cans, even if they were empty because the owners spilled them in their efforts to run from whatever hideous monster was attacking them.

Peter and Kirk took one lane, Aidan and Colt the other.

Aidan sucked on the hose until gasoline poured out. He quickly jammed the hose into the red gas tank and sat back. He watched Colt holding the tank with his one crooked arm, the arm that Cthulhu mangled.

"How does it feel?"

Colt looked up and saw Aidan staring at his crooked arm. He started to pull the sleeves down.

"I'm sorry," Aidan said. "I didn't mean anything by it."

"It's okay. I mean, no worse off than your finger, or your belly, right?"

"I guess so. I'd never set a bone before. I wish I could have done better for you, Colt."

Colt shrugged. "Is this going to be one of those brotherly moments where we say things about each other and cry?"

Aidan laughed. "Hell, no. This is going to be one of those moments where I grab your cap and run."

It was a Texas Longhorns cap, and Aidan waved it in the air as he ran past the cars. He was not much of a runner, especially not compared to his little brother, who would probably have ended up on a junior high track team because he was so fast. But he was laughing. He tried to stiff-arm Colt, but his kid brother pushed his arm out of the way and tackled him. The kid hit hard for a 13-year old. Maybe he could have been a cornerback instead of a track star. They fell in a ball of laughter.

Kirk wanted to drive the Bimmer they found, but he couldn't handle a stick-shift, so he led with the van on the final push to the ship channel bridge. They found they were closer to the bridge than they thought, and as they got closer, the cars thinned out. Riley, who could drive a stick shift (which was much to everyone's surprise until they remembered her telling them once that her dad gave her an old Pontiac Firebird for her Sweet 16), drove the BMW.

"I thought you couldn't drive a stick," Kirk said. "I remember Alyssa asking explicitly back at Lakewood when we were in the Viper if anyone could drive a stick, and nobody said anything."

"I was a little out of it that day, I guess, having just seen my friends blown up and eaten by wargs."

"You still bitching about that Viper?" Jax said.

"It was a Viper, man!"

Colt stayed with Riley in case anything went seriously wrong. Aidan decided that he, Peter, and Jax, who were armed, would walk in front of the Bimmer and mini-van. Alyssa, to nobody's surprise, refused to be anywhere but at Aidan's side.

Since the ship channel bridge was actually part of the interstate, they had to climb up the on-ramp to get to the bridge. They found that the wide bridge was blockaded, but unlike the great wall of automobiles they found weeks ago in the pine-wooded forests, here large cargo shipping crates were carefully placed along the edge of the bridge's low point. Two prominent crates were painted up like the Texas flag. Between the two, a large metal gate had been placed. Two towers were erected behind the crates, one on each side of the north and southbound lanes. About ten people holding various rifles, pistols, and crossbows were aiming their weapons at them.

Each side waited for the other to do something.

"We're gonna have to run," Aidan said under his breath.

"Just chill, Aidan," Jax said. "They will be okay about it."

Still, the people in the towers didn't say anything. They didn't drop their weapons, either.

"Somebody should say something," Peter said. "Aidan, say something."

"You say something and get shot."

Alyssa took a step forward and pulled off her gas mask. Everybody reacted. The people in the towers started shouting, and the boys raised their weapons.

Something caught her eye, though.

"Val, is that you?" she yelled over the shouting.

One of the people put their weapons down. "Alyssa? Hey! I didn't recognize you!"

While Val had the gate opened, the boys stood paralyzed. Alyssa ran up to the gate. As soon as Val appeared, she gave him a giant, full-bodied hug.

"Who is Val?" Peter asked.

"Her ex," Aidan said.

"Oh."

"They went out on a date or two, but nothing happened."

"Clearly," Peter said.

"Nothing happened. They just haven't seen each other since the beginning of the apocalypse."

"I'd crush on her too, if it meant I got to hug her like that."

Aidan didn't reply. Of all the people to survive Black Friday, why Val? Couldn't he have been carried off by some roc and fed to its little roc babies? Val was a charming, pretty man with fair features. Val was like a really tall Zac Efron or Ryan Reynolds to Aidan's Shrek. He was so tall that in hugging Alyssa, he had to lift her off her feet to hug her properly. She giggled while he twirled her.

Val looked over to the others. "You can take your masks off. We've tested the air and it's okay to breathe."

"Thank God!" Peter said to Val as he ripped his mask off and tossed it. "That thing was murder. You have no idea what it's like to sleep in a gas mask."

Aidan was the last to pull his mask off. He collected the others and put them in the Bimmer.

"C'mon in!" Val said. "You can bring the cars if you want, but drive slow. We don't have much street room."

Aidan guessed there were 200 people living on the giant arched bridge. It was almost completely walled in by the large cargo crates, which were often layered one on top of the other with nothing more than a ladder to get people up and down.

"We used cranes to move the crates from the shipping docks. You can't imagine what we find in them. It's like one day we find an entire crate full of Hello Kitty or Power Rangers, and the next day, we find one full of noodles or cokes. Speaking of which – I'm guessing you guys haven't eaten good meat in a couple of months. Who wants barbecue?"

Peter said, "I must have died cause it sounded like you said you had barbecue."

"C'mon. I'll take you to the kitchen."

As they made their way to the kitchen, Aidan noticed that Alyssa and Val were still arm-in-arm. As they walked through the makeshift town, people stopped and watched them. Aidan noticed that none of the people looked too happy to have his friends and family there.

The kitchen was a big red crate with golden arches on it. "Don't get your hopes up. It was full of kid's toys," Val told them,

"But I thought it would look good on our kitchen. It breaks the monotony of all these same-colored cargo crates."

The sweet smell of barbecue wafted to them from a hundred feet away, and they were all salivating by the time they reached the kitchen crate. The doors were open, and inside they saw metal picnic tables like the kind normally found in parks. At the far end of the crate was a small counter, and on the other side, stacks and stacks of MREs, all still in their cardboard shipping boxes.

"Edna, could I get some barbecue for my friends? They are new here."

"We only have the best for the newbies," Edna replied. Edna had the look of a woman who was older than she appeared, with deep laugh lines and tallow skin on her narrow frame. Her smile covered half her face. Aidan thought all she was missing was a hairnet and a burning cigarette to look like the cafeteria lunch lady. She cut open a box and gave Val eight MREs, but Val handed his back. As they sat down at the picnic tables, she brought out a gallon of water.

"Been filtered, darlins," she said. "Happy eating."

Val showed them how to add water to the barbecue, which cooked the meat. In five minutes, they were eating it without abandon. Barbecue sauce and crackers drizzled down their chins. They ate not completely unlike wild, half-starved dogs. They squirted tubes of jelly down their throats and gulped the Powerade-reject drink mix almost without stirring. For a full minute, there was complete silence except for the sounds of chewing, glurping, and smacking. Even Aidan had to admit to himself, though he would never say it out loud, the barbecue was the best food he could remember.

After the minute of silence, Val noticed Alyssa crying.

"What's the matter?"

"I'm sorry, but it's just – I haven't had beef since Black Friday. It just tastes so good!"

Val noticed how quickly they were all finishing their meals, so he brought them each two more of the barbecue MREs and began cooking them.

"It's been tough for everyone," Val said, "But somehow, we all find a way to survive. How did you guys do it?"

"Holed up in a two-story house in a subdivision," Alyssa said between mouthfuls. "What about you? I mean, clearly, you guys went a different route."

"Yeah," Val said. "I don't think we could have survived if we went in the direction you took. My dad was out on the oilrig on Black Friday. I was back home. You know my cousin has a monster truck, right?"

"So it's agreed – we chose the worst escape car in the history of the apocalypse, right?" Kirk asked.

"Did you get to drive out on a monster truck?" Colt asked.

"Pick your jaw up off the floor," Aidan told Colt. In reality, Colt was admiring the monster truck idea through mouthfuls of barbecue.

Val laughed at Colt. "Ha. More than that. We took a few of those things down on the way out. We knew the suburbs would be a deathtrap, and from everything I've heard, they're nothing more than prisons, which is partly why I am surprised you got out of there, Alyssa. No, like everyone else, we first thought of evacuation. We tried, but you can't get far in a monster truck unless you are willing to run over some cars, and I didn't want to injure anyone, even if it meant harming myself."

"That's very brave of you. I wish everyone had that sentimentality," Alyssa said.

"Thanks, but mainly we were just trying to escape. Before the power went out, I was able to get in touch with my dad. We met here at the bridge, and that's where we got the idea to stack crates and build the fortress."

"Who is this?" A big man with broad girth said as he entered the kitchen. He came upon them so suddenly that Jax and Aidan reached for their weapons out of surprise. The large man wore a black leather jacket and pants. A salt-and-pepper beard teased his face. When he spoke, his voice was like mortar and concrete. "More lost boys?"

"Dad, this is Alyssa. You remember Alyssa, right?"

"The one that got away. I'm glad to see you survived. Welcome. And these are your friends?"

"They went to high school with me. Kirk, Jax, Riley, and the brothers Peter, Colt, and Aidan, my boyfriend."

He looked sternly at Aidan while shaking his hand. "You I have to thank for my son's loss."

"No, it wasn't like that," Alyssa said.

"No te preocupas," he said, waving his hand and smiling. "Water under the bridge, right? Nothing could please me more than the news that more people survived. Your self-preservation shows you to be a credit to our species. We need more people like that, since the food chain has been turned upside-down on us. I am Señor Victor Olivarez, but you can call me Mr. Olivarez. You know my son, Val. Together we founded Bridgetown. At first, there were just a few of us, but now several hundred call Bridgetown home."

"Sir, if I may," Aidan said, "How did you fight back the wargs?"

"Wargs? You mean the giant dogs? We call them *perros de apocalipto*. Hounds of the Apocalypse. In combat, they are indomitable. You can't defeat them." He looked at them sternly. "You really don't know anything, do you?"

"We hid out in a house for two months, and we've spent almost a month wandering around East Texas since then," Aidan said.

"You must leave the math to someone else, boss. You're off on your dates. You say it's been three months since Black Friday, but it is not October. It is nearly Thanksgiving."

The lost boys looked at each other in shock.

"Wait," Peter said, "We missed Halloween?"

"Almost three weeks gone. Come, you all look wasted away and drained. Val will show you to your quarters and you will get some rest. We can talk again tomorrow."

With that, Mr. Olivarez departed. As Val led them away, Aidan glanced back at the kitchen. Edna's face-spanning grin had inverted into a giant toad-like frown. She turned away as the boys left.

Val showed them to their beds, which were in a large red crate at the low end of the bridge on the far side. Their lodging was the third crate up. Aidan couldn't help noticing that their quarters were close to the guard towers.

Val said, "I'm sorry, but you will have to climb ladders to get up to your beds."

"I would climb razors if it meant there was a bed at the end of them," Peter said.

Val ignored Peter. He stared at Alyssa for a bit, then told her good night. She tried to hide her smile from him as she said, "It's really good seeing you again."

The crate had been used to import smartphones, and stacks of the boxes rose to the ceilings. The beds were Tempurpedic. A thick curtain had been strung up to create two adjoining rooms in the crate. Riley and Alyssa slept on the far side of the crate. The boys slept on the side closer to the entry. For the first time in months, they each had their own bed and nobody slept on the floor. Aidan tried to fight the sleep, but between his full belly and the sound of water lapping against the ship channel bridge, he could not resist and soon fell fast asleep.

Kirk was almost the last person awake. Only Peter was still asleep. The smell of cooked eggs woke him. Kirk rubbed his eyes and brushed his hair out of his face. Colt built a house of cards using smartphones he'd removed from their packaging. Colt was wearing new GAP clothes that looked straight off the rack. Then Kirk saw something that made his senses almost go haywire. In addition to the new clothes and breakfast MREs set out for him, not two feet in front of him rested a carton of cigarettes. He reached for the carton, smelled the tobacco and imagined the smoke filling his lungs.

"You really need that, man?" Peter asked him from his bed. He yawned.

"Been three months."

"Exactly."

Kirk put the carton down. He got out of the bed and put on his shoes.

"Where you going?" Peter asked him.

"Well, if I ain't smoking, I might as well take a leak."

"Careful, bro," Jax said. "They got escorts."

Kirk climbed down the ladder. He had to pause halfway down because he was still too drowsy to climb. He hadn't slept that well in…well, as long as he could remember.

As he landed barefoot on the ground, he felt the coolness of the November asphalt rising through his feet. For the first time, it felt like November to him. What was it – sixty-some-odd degrees outside? It was a good chill, a wake-up chill.

An oversized woman holding an AK-47 and wearing a black windbreaker stood outside the cargo crate.

"I guess I know you're tough cause you're wearing a black jacket," he told her. She didn't respond.

"Up here." Kirk followed the sound to Aidan, who was standing a little farther up the bridge, leaning against the concrete dividers that lined the side of the street. He was watching something higher up on the bridge. Like the rest of the lost boys, Aidan now looked like a walking GAP commercial ad. He wore a bright blue-collared shirt and khakis in addition to the old rifle slung over his shoulder.

"I dig the new look, Aidan. You're the gun-toting Boy Scout yuppie I always wanted to be." Kirk walked up to him, found a space between two dividers, and pulled down his boxers.

"Hey, we got places for that!" the woman with the AK, who had never stopped watching them, yelled at Kirk. He flipped her off and kept urinating off the side of the bridge.

"Always the rock star."

"I just got a thing against authority," he yawned. In nothing but his boxers, Aidan realized how sinewy Kirk was. Before Black Friday, Kirk had been the skinny type, so skinny you would miss him if he turned sideways, but since the apocalypse, well, he was pretty ripped. Aidan wanted to ask him when that happened, but decided against it. They had all changed since Black Friday, some for the better.

"What are you doing out here by yourself anyway?" Kirk asked.

Aidan shrugged as he turned his attention back to the bridge. Kirk followed his line of sight and saw Alyssa and Val talking to each other. Val must have said something slightly insulting because Alyssa punched his arm. Playfully.

"You should go up there and say something," Kirk said.

"No, it's not my place. Alyssa was in the same classes as Val and all those GT kids. I was never that smart."

"Smart enough to keep us out of trouble for the past couple of months."

"Not smart enough to count days. I can't believe it's November."

"Beat yourself up all you want, but that girl loves you."

"Yeah, but am I right for her? Look how happy she is. With all the shit we're going through, she needs somebody who can make her laugh. She deserves it. I'm too morose for her."

"Listen to you talking like some emo. You saved her ass, and she saved yours. You can't break that kind of bond with a couple of one-liners. Go fight for her."

Aidan started to go, and then said, "There was something else. Maybe I'm being paranoid. I know I have a history of being paranoid, but I saw something in the channel below. Watch the currents. There's something there. I'm not sure what. Shadows in the currents."

Kirk looked over where he was just urinating. "If you're telling me I just pissed on some monster, you could have warned me."

Kirk waited for the laugh, but it never came. Aidan was already walking over to Alyssa and Val.

"Hey, Aidan," Alyssa said when she saw him walking over. "Val was about to give me a tour. He's been explaining all the improvements they've made. Plumbing, insulation, and they even have central air conditioning and heating in some of the crates."

"What's in the water?" Aidan said without acknowledging Alyssa.

"What are you talking about?" Val asked.

"Watch your tone, Aidan," Alyssa urged. "We are guests."

"Don't lie to me," Aidan said to Val. "I saw it with my own eyes. There's something beneath us. Some monster. What is it?"

Val looked to Alyssa for help.

"I have no idea what he's talking about," she said.

"You bring us here, show this perfect world of beds, air conditioning and cooked meat, but it isn't so perfect, is it? There's always a monster around. A dryder, a roc, a warg – what is it this time?"

Hearing the argument, some of the bridge people approached Val and Aidan.

"Is he bothering you, Val?" a particularly brutish-looking man with a face tattoo asked.

"No, I think he's just confused," Val said. Then to Aidan, he explained in his most placating voice, "There's nothing to worry about here, Aidan. Look, I won't lie to you. There probably are creatures in the channel, but there are creatures everywhere. The difference is, we are protected here. You don't have to worry, boss. We have it all under control." Val held Alyssa close to him.

"Get your hands off her!" Aidan shouted. He tried to split them up, but the man with the face tattoo grabbed him by elbow. Pain splintered and cracked up and down his arm.

"Okay, that's enough," the large man mandated. "You need to take a walk and cool off."

Later that day, Alyssa came and found Aidan with Kirk. Kirk excused himself to look for a guitar. "All these crates, one of them has to have a guitar in it."

Aidan noticed that in addition to new clothes, Alyssa was also wearing new earrings and jewelry. They were real diamonds.

"Val give you those?"

"Gee, hon, you look so pretty in the new dress and those wonderful earrings. What's wrong with you? Why are you being such an ass?"

"I'm not being an ass. I'm trying to take care of us. And you look very pretty."

"Too late, you lost your chance to flatter me. And no, you're not just trying to take care of us. You're being an ass, and it's annoying."

"This morning when I got up, I was watching the ship channel. I swear I saw something in the water below. And yesterday, when we went to the kitchen, I looked back at the kitchen lady, and she was giving us dirty looks like we stole her baby or something."

"Well, I'm sure the monsters own the water, so you probably saw something, and after your blow-up about rations the other day, we can't be surprised that somebody here is getting mad if they had to give away some of their food. That doesn't mean you have to flip out."

"No, something's not right here. Can't you see? I can't put my finger on it, but there's something about how we're always being watched. It's not just the guards, either. Everybody watches. It's like they're waiting for something."

"Okay, there's something I think you haven't picked up on. They have a rule about not carrying weapons here. You're walking around with a high-powered rifle, Aidan with a scope that looks military bad ass. I'd be watching you, too, if you showed up at my house looking like some Army sniper. You want them to like you, give them the guns."

Aidan put his hand on the Winchester. "They told you to tell us that, didn't they? Val told you."

Alyssa groaned. "They've been very cooperative so far. And we don't need the guns. Look around, baby. This place is safe. Wargs can't jump this high, and they've mounted spikes to keep the rocs out. Bridgetown's militia would blast them out of the sky before they landed."

"So they get to have a militia, but we have to give up our weapons?"

"It's not like that. They don't know you like I know you. I'm sure once they get to know you, you can have the gun back."

"This place is bad for us, Alyssa. We need to rest up, then we need to keep heading north."

Alyssa put her hands on her hips. He knew she was really pissed if she did that. She flung her arms up in the air. Finally, she said, "What the hell, Aidan? We finally find a good place. A safe place. And you want to 'pack 'em up and head 'em out?'"

"We will be safe when we are someplace the monsters aren't."

"Right, the cold tundra. I got to remind you, I'm a Texas girl. I'm Mexican-American. We don't like cold."

When he didn't say anything, Alyssa walked off.

"Fine! Go be with Val!"

As Kirk walked up and down both sides of the wide, eight-lane bridge, he checked behind curtains, beneath stacks of boxes, and inside crates, but he didn't see anything that looked like a guitar or even a banjo.

"You need to be careful," the chubby woman with the AK-47 said as Kirk opened a trunk. "That's individual property. We have rules here just like any society, and stealing is one of them."

"Are you really going to follow me around all day? Don't you have something better to do? Dreams to fulfill? Children to bake?"

"Sorry, cupcake, but tailing you is my dream come true."

"Really?"

"I'll be with you all day."

"Good luck."

And he was off, sprinting uphill as fast as his legs would carry him. Kirk was surprised at how well he climbed to the top of the bridge. There was a time when sprinting twenty yards would leave him out of breath. *Maybe it was the cigarettes,* he thought. *Maybe it was the past four months spent running for my life.* The uphill climb was still a bitch, though, so he stopped three-fourths of the way up and looked behind. The lady with the AK stood there at the lower end of the bridge giving him the evil eye. "Oh, c'mon!" he yelled. "You're not even trying!"

Not worried about his 300-pound shadow any longer, Kirk returned to his search for a guitar. He would take anything at this point. It didn't have to be a Gibson.

Kirk took in Bridgetown for a moment. Beyond the light posts and crates, it had a feel of the familiar. Kids rode bikes on the bridge, parents watched children from under little plastic or plywood awnings they had built for their crate-homes and friends sat around enjoying the cool breeze while they watched the clouds or read books. The town was communal and tranquil in an almost idyllic, Blue Bell commercial kind of way, which was weird since Bridgetown was also a post-apocalyptic shanty-town of giant industrial shipping crates stacked on top of each other like children's blocks, all of which was connected together by a couple hundred thousand pounds of concrete and asphalt hanging over the shipping channel.

What really struck him was the absence of animals. There were no kids playing with dogs, no cats reclining off ledges, no mice scampering between crates. The place was completely and totally devoid of animal life. He remembered when he was a kid that his parents were too poor to own a dog. He had a gray gerbil that he kept until he forgot to feed it and it died. It felt odd not having animals around, even gerbils, despite everything that had happened, whatever it was that had happened. He still wasn't sure of that. Genetic mutations? Radiation? Super virus? Who the hell knew? Who the hell cared?

From somewhere in the distance, a tune tickled his ear. At first, he thought he was imagining the sound. It had been months since he last heard guitar strings plucked. Nevertheless, as the sounds grew in his ear, it was as if the strings were plucked from his heart. Kirk casted like a hound dog in the middle of the road while he tried to figure out the source of the sound. Then he found her in a yellow crate with posters lining the inner walls. She was definitely older than he was, possibly twenty. A clove cigarette dangled between two peach-colored lips. Long straw hair hung over her leather guitar strap. A faded green tank top barely concealed her thin figure. Her nimble fingers danced along the frets of the guitar she was playing. The tune was Ledbetter.

As Kirk climbed up into the crate, she didn't look up or react, but kept on playing. A second guitar lay on its side, unused, right next to her. Kirk seated himself cross-legged next to her and attempted to join the song. Only after he struck the right chord did she look up at him. She smiled. She had blue eyes.

Aidan and Peter and Colt walked the bridge at mid-day. They were eating peanuts since the kitchen was limiting them to two spaghetti dinners but would allow them to eat all the peanuts they wanted. (Bridgetown had an entire crate loaded with peanuts.) Most people were outside walking the bridge, either going to get their lunch rations or returning home to eat them.

In the middle of the crowd, not far from where they were walking, two adults walked together. Their backs were to them.

They walked like people who were lost and abandoned, like zombies. One wore a suit jacket and blue jeans. The woman was shorter and had cropped hair. She, too, wore a cream-coated jacket the boys knew too well.

"Mom!" Peter yelled. "Dad!"

Aidan and Colt ran behind Peter, full of longing and relief. Their parents turned around and started to cry. "Dodger!" the woman exclaimed. "I always knew we would find you!"

Then five astonished, shocked faces looked at each other and saw only strangers. The parents' faces turned into grim jack o'lanterns, and they turned around and renewed their zombie walk.

Aidan shoved Peter hard enough to knock him down and walked away.

As Peter stood up, two boys helped him. One was Indian and the other was black. They wore polos and khakis like everyone else, but to Peter, these looked like the kind of guys who would wear those clothes naturally.

"Thanks. I'm Peter. This is my brother, Colt."

"Mayuran and Kobie," the Indian boy said, thumbing at himself and his friend. "We were lost boys, like you guys."

"Your friend has a nasty streak," Kobie said.

"Yeah, well, he's my brother," Peter said. "Can't live with him. Can't live without him. How did you guys make it here?"

"We flew," Kobie said. "Mayuran's had his pilot's license for years. So when everything else went down, me and my friends decided no way in hell were we sticking around on the ground. We would fly to the coast and outrun the monsters."

"Boy, were we wrong," Mayuran said. "And I wouldn't recommend flying. The rocs own the skies. And if they find you, they will have no problem taking you out. Trust me. I've seen them take out Hornets, Warthogs, C-130s. It's pretty impossible to avoid them. Maybe if you were in a Blackbird, but eventually you'd have to land, and then they'd really get you. I landed the Cessna down on the interstate about three weeks ago. We've been living here ever since."

"We looked as skinny as you when we first got here," Kobie said. "Don't worry. They will fatten you up real quick. Mr.

Olivarez probably hasn't shown you, but there's like four crates full of MREs, more than enough to sustain Bridgetown for years."

"Hey, you want to see something cool?" Mayuran asked. "We can show you the generators."

Peter and Colt looked at each other. They had just been assaulted with a lot of information to take in all at once. "Um, okay, I guess. But could you guys slow it down?"

"Sorry," Mayuran said. "We can overwhelm. This way."

Mayuran and Kobie took them past a few crates. A ladder lay on the far end of one, and it led up five stories. At the very top, the wind was even gustier.

"So is it just you two? What happened to the rest of your group? The rest of the 'lost boys,' as I think the term is being used?" Peter asked.

"Careful. It gets windy up here," Kobie yelled. "Last week, wind sucked two guys off the crates. They are trying to rig a safety system up here, but we haven't found anything, yet."

In front of them lay three giant generators, each half as big as a crate.

"Mr. Olivarez found them in a warehouse. They were supposed to be shipped to Denver to power the house of some rich guy who doesn't want to pay for energy anymore. We got them instead, and now two of them produce enough energy to power all of Bridgetown. So the other one is a backup. The only trick is making sure they stay fueled, so Mr. Olivarez has crews set up to go looking for fuel."

"That's weird. We had no problem finding fuel not half a mile from here."

"Oh, but you came from the south. We never go south. Nothing good comes from the south."

"What do you mean?"

Kobie and Mayuran looked at each other as if they were having some sort of mutant power-twins, wonder-nerd communication.

"Look," Mayuran said. "There is something we wanted to tell you, but we didn't want to tell you down there. It's about what happens when…"

"Hey!"

Everyone looked back. A man with tattoo sleeves and another AK-47 was waving to them. "Get off of here. You could get sucked out into the shipping channel!" He ushered them off.

Once they got down, Mayuran and Kobie ran off.

Kirk was explaining about his jam session with the girl named Alex to Aidan and Peter and Colt when the guards received a signal on their walkies. The guards looked at each other, then motioned. "C'mon, lost boys, time to head to the top of the hill." The guards collected Riley and Jax, who were still up in their quarters, and herded everyone uphill.

At the bridge's highpoint, they met Alyssa, Val, and Mr. Olivarez. They stood in front of some large gunmetal-grey school lockers. The lockers looked like they had been ripped out of a school and brought to Bridgetown. Next to the lockers sat more of the large shipping crates nicely stacked one on top of the other. OLIVAREZ was painted in black up and down its sides.

"So I guess the rich folk live at the top of the mountain," Aidan said.

"I hope you are enjoying your stay with us," Mr. Olivarez said, ignoring Aidan. "But in order to extend that visit, you're going to have to give up your weapons."

"No way in hell," Aidan growled. Even Jax put his hand on his parang.

"I know it has been rough for you, living on your own with nobody to rely upon, nobody to trust. And I know I am asking you to take a leap of faith. So I will tell you that they will be kept in these lockers, and you will have the combination, 0812, so you could always get to them if you needed. In return for giving up your weapons, I will give you a gift of unimaginable value."

"No deal," Aidan shot back. "We keep our weapons. If you don't like it, we can leave."

"But wait, you haven't seen the gift." Mr. Olivarez leaned against a wall and turned a knob. A groaning, hissing sound shoveled through hidden pipes, and then behind him, a showerhead erupted with water. A small shower stall had been improvised using PVC pipe and shower curtains. Mr. Olivarez produced from his pockets shampoo, conditioner, soap, and a washcloth.

Riley squealed. "Is the water warm?" she asked, hopping up and down.

"The steam rises quickly on cool mornings," Mr. Olivarez said. As if on cue, water vapor began floating up in the air.

"But I can't just give this away," he said. He turned the faucet off, and just like that, the lost boys were returned to their filthy, unclean apocalypse.

"I need your weapons in the lockers."

While the boys didn't seem to mind the promise of more days in grime, the girls were begging Aidan to release their weapons.

The lost boys stood around smelling very clean and talking about their options as the light began to slant and turn golden. Aidan's head was shaved down again and his nerves were tingling with exposure to the wind. Clean went a longer way than any of the boys wanted to admit, but Riley was almost glowing, she felt so good after the shower. She of course, spent the longest time in the shower. Between the shower and the new denim shirtdress, she looked less like a survivor and more like one of the popular kids she had been in school.

None of this changed how Aidan felt about staying in Bridgetown.

"And now they've taken our guns," he said.

"Give it a rest, Aidan. It was worth it," Riley chided. It was the most outspoken, defiant thing Riley had said since joining them. Aidan glowered at her.

Jax interceded, "Aidan, I didn't want to give up my parang, either, but even I got to admit, it's nice to be clean. And Bridgetown has everything we need. Food, clothes, pumping water, electricity – even Kirk has a new guitar and someone to jam with him. You have to admit, this is a sweet deal."

Before Aidan could retort, Colt came running down the bridge, his eyes wide with excitement.

"You are never gonna believe this!" he shouted. Peter was coming up behind him.

"What?" Jax asked.

"They have a movie theater with popcorn and Cokes and everything! C'mon!"

The theater was made of two crates standing end-to-end with the walls broken out between. The crates were welded shut and support beams added to hold up the roof. There were five rows of folding chairs – enough to fit almost half of Bridgetown's populace – between the crates. A projector hung like a mechanical crab from the ceiling and played images on the far wall. A concession stand was set up closest to the opening. Somebody had draped velvety curtains along the inside walls to make the crates look more like a theater. The room was full of the wonderful smells of fresh, buttery movie popcorn.

"I didn't know it was possible to miss something this much and not know it," Peter said. He took a tub of the popcorn and inhaled deeply and blissfully.

Most of the town was showing up for the movie. Mr. Olivarez and Val were already there with a few others who were making the popcorn and handing out drinks.

"It's our way of giving back," Val said.

"Don't you give back enough?" Alyssa asked.

"What are we watching?" Colt interjected. Like a typical child his age, nothing mattered but the promise of CGI graphics and lots of bullets.

"Anything you want," Mr. Olivarez said. "You are the new ones here. You get to pick." He opened a case full of discs.

"They have Transformers!" Colt shouted with complete giddiness. "You gotta play it!"

Mr. Olivarez smiled. To Aidan, he said, "There is nothing like children. After Black Friday, we lost so many." As Colt lifted a large cup of Dr Pepper mixed with Coke, Sprite, and Fanta Orange to his mouth, Mr. Olivarez nodded at his crooked arm. "I see your brother didn't escape unscathed."

What happiness was in Aidan's face soured, so Mr. Olivarez said, "Of course, things happen. We do the best we can. Please, sit down and relax. Enjoy the movie."

Suddenly, Colt let out a giant bellowing belch and smiled broadly. "Wow."

The movie was pure fun. The time passed so quickly, the lost boys didn't notice the sun setting or some of the people going back home. By the time Optimus made his final soliloquy, there were only about fifteen people remaining in the theater, most of them other lost boys like the seven.

As the lights came up, Mr. Olivarez stood and stretched. He looked around at the mostly empty theater and said, "The rest of you can go home now. You seven, though, hang back. I think we should talk now. You must have questions about what has happened in the world. How Bridgetown survives without the intrusion of the animals."

The projector was turned off. They pulled the folding chairs into a semi-circle around Mr. Olivarez and Val.

"I was working on a rig the day the animals attacked," Mr. Olivarez said. "Unlike most, we had some warning of what was to come, though we weren't sure exactly what it would be. The mutating animals first struck in the cities and the suburbs. Mostly it was pets. God, I will never look at one of those YouTube cat videos the same way.

"Guys were trying to get off the rig as fast as they could. They were fighting over the chopper. Either they wanted to get home to find their families, or they thought the rig was nothing more than a chicken coop waiting for the fox.

"I don't know why I didn't go. I had Val back home. But cellphones were still working, so I was able to keep tabs on him. I guess I hoped I could be his eyes and ears to what was going on elsewhere. Give him a full account. Then the Internet died. We haven't been able to get it going since. Best we can figure today, it was a combination of insects shorting out power plants and cell towers being toppled. That, and a couple of bombs went off in New York. I don't know how or whether they were nuclear or if it was done by us or them, but the result was the same. Lights out." He snapped his fingers for emphasis.

"Those were the worst days. I knew Val had made it to the bridge, but now I couldn't talk to him, couldn't reach him. A couple of days later, they attacked our rig. It wasn't with sharks or krakens, either. As seems to be the pattern, it started with the smallest things, like mollusks and starfish. We had noticed them accumulating on the foundations since Black Friday. But one night after the lights went out – maybe it was a week after Black Friday, but I'm not sure – they got on top of the platform. We took our knives to them, and that worked at first, but they were relentless. We worked in shifts. We took knives, screwdrivers, wrenches, whatever we could find to scrape the things off, and we worked at it all day and all night. A couple of shifts into it, we were all getting tired. Lots of headaches, too. That was when we figured out what you guys figured out.

"Which is what?" Aidan asked.

Mr. Olivarez looked at Aidan's blank face strangely. "You don't know?"

"Know what?"

"They're psychic."

Chapter Seven: Obedient

Aidan nearly choked. "Psychic?"

"Yeah. How else do you think birds and dogs and fish can fight together against mankind? When they have their big conversations, when they talk to each other a lot, it gives us headaches. That's how we know something's about to happen," Mr. Olivarez said. "You never got the headaches?" Their shocked faces told him everything.

"There are things we know and things we don't know. I can't tell you how it happened or what caused it. Evolutionary jumps, the wrath of God, or toxic waste – I don't know. But it is clear what they are after."

"What's that?"

"Dominion. When I was on the rig and people started disappearing, we became frightened. Nobody wanted to go out and scrape mollusks off the rig. We had no idea what was taking people or how. It was like we were in a monster movie, and we hadn't figured out the rules yet, so we didn't know how the monster fed or lived or whatever the hell it did to kill people. So when it was my turn to go on deck, I took my pocketknife with me. It was a gift from my grandfather when I joined scouting. I'd had it since I was ten. I now know how ridiculous this all sounds. What can a one-and-a-half-inch blade do against these beasts? But right then I needed anything to boost me up, and that cheap little knife gave me confidence, so I took it with me.

"The platform was getting worse. The mollusks were on all four sides by at least a foot in some areas. I got down on my knees and began to scrape the shells off. The shells were sharp, though, and I cut my hand. I started wiping the blood off, when something wet and slippery, yet strong like an eel, grabbed my arm. I looked up and saw something that even to this day is hard to describe, though I have described it often to lost boys like you all.

"It was dark like Gulf water, and reeked of sediment. It was leviathan. It was kraken. It was dragon. It was all these things and much worse. Gripping the platform, I saw seven more dirty tentacles, and every four tentacles was like the fingers to another tentacle. The largest tentacles were like whiskers coming from a mouth full of vulture-beaked teeth. I knew I was nothing to it. I was less than a morsel. I was a tiny, insignificant crumb.

"I sat squatting on the platform's edge looking at this god-like creature and thinking, *this is how I am going to die*. I thought of my son and of the missed opportunity with the helicopter, and I just wanted to see him one more time. That's when the creature revealed itself to me.

"Revealed itself to you?" Kirk asked. "What do you mean?"

"Through its grip on my hand, it showed me images of the world to come. Cities laid waste and turned into fiery infernos. The world's population enslaved. Stockyards full of people crammed together for slaughter. And much, much worse things. I was given a choice. I could either die there on the deck of that platform, or I could betray my species and live."

That paranoid monster that lived in the pit of Aidan's stomach was growling at him again. A darkness passed over Aidan as he started to rise. "What did you do?"

"What any parent would do: I agreed. By my seven murdered crewmates who I tossed into its open maw, I swore allegiance to our new gods. In return for my loyalty, the creature showed me Bridgetown. That same day, giant eagles carried me to this bridge. The god we call Malifax offered us peace in return for sacrifice. So just like I was given a choice, every new group to come to Bridgetown is given the choice. They can sacrifice one of their own and live here in peace free from the monsters, or they can move on and return to the world of slave drivers and human-hide hunters.

"But don't you see?" Alyssa said. "This thing, this Malifax, is just using you to collect people so that it can kill them at its own convenience."

"Your pride is getting in the way," Mr. Olivarez responded. "You want to believe that they are just trapping us because you think we are a significant threat to them, but you're wrong. They just want us out of the way."

"This goes beyond unspeakable," Aidan fumed. "You betrayed us all!" He spit in Mr. Olivarez's face.

Val jumped up, but Mr. Olivarez stopped him. He wiped the spit from his weathered face. "This happens every time. But in the end, you realize that the comforts of our world are too important. As a people, we need safety. And as a society, we need arts and entertainment and plumbing and air conditioning. We crave our electronic devices. We crave them because they are as much a part of us as our right arms. To reject them is to reject thousands of years of evolution. We can't do that. You have until sunrise to give me your answer."

"And if we refuse?"

"We have never forced anyone to make that choice, but just know that if you refuse, you must leave immediately. And you will not be let back, either."

As the lost boys walked defiantly out of the movie theater/cargo container, Val stopped Aidan.

"Just give up Riley. You don't want her or need her. Give her up, and everything will be okay for as long as you live."

Aidan walked out.

Nobody talked during the short walk back to their container. Knowing the decision the lost boys were given, the guards kept their distance. While the others climbed up in the container, Aidan crossed to the opposite side of the bridge. A giant crane with thick trestles blocked his view of the downtown. The crane had been damaged at the base and was lilting to the side. He bet he could make it if he jumped, but he didn't want to find out. He wasn't a

Peter or Jax. Instead, he climbed up on the bridge rail and walked up the bridge far enough to get a good view of Houston's downtown. It was a long ways off, but not so far he couldn't see all the skyscrapers. The downtown looked like a massacre of headless buildings and leaning bodies that had not only been slaughtered but also picked apart by vultures. For a few of the buildings, smoke jutted out like blood from a severed artery. Every once in a while, a flash of light would resonate, and he would hear the rumbling echo of pyrotechnics. He wondered if it was people fighting or being killed. In the skies overhead, he could barely make out the shadows of rocs.

By morning, nothing had changed. Everyone was up because no one had slept. Jax and Riley had whispered to each other all night long. Around mid-moon fall, Colt had started naming all the different movies in their movie collection. Every once in a while, he would stop, make a correction about the name of a movie actor or character, then return to his list. Alyssa had removed her earrings, her jewelry, and the nice dress. She was back in her shorts and boots and had her pack ready.

Peter and Aidan sat at the edge of the container, their feet dangling in the air.

"We met these kids," Peter said. "Nice, but talkative. I think they were trying to warn us about this. What are you thinking?"

"They want Riley."

"What was that?" Jax said from deep inside the container.

Aidan turned to him. "Val told me last night. They're after Riley."

"No way. Not going to happen. I will fight anyone – including you – if you lay a finger on her."

"Shut up, Jax," Riley said.

"Riley, they are going to feed you to some monster."

"I said shut up." She turned to Aidan. "Is that really what they said?"

Aidan nodded.

"Do you want me to go?"

"It's not that simple," Aidan said.

"No, I think it is."

Aidan looked away. Riley looked around the container, and then said, "Fuck y'all. I don't want to go. I want to live. I'm tired of living like a third wheel here and being treated like a second-class citizen. I'm not your slave, and I'm not your lover, either," she said to Jax. To the rest of the group, she said, "I was popular. I was a cheerleader and a member of student council. I was supposed to be prom queen! But I don't give a damn about that. It's not important. I don't want to die, and I sure as shit don't want to die so that you guys can sit here and wait for some demon monster to come eat you. I want to live. I want to live as far away from these monsters as I can."

They climbed down the ladder. They were shocked to find most of the guards asleep. Only the fat woman was awake, and she was massaging her head.

"Tough night?" Kirk asked her sarcastically.

She glared at them and grunted that they should head to the top of the bridge. There, next to the Olivarez home, they found some of the townspeople gathered. Mr. Olivarez and Val were there, too. They looked tired and weary, as if they had struggled to sleep, too.

"Malifax is near," Mr. Olivarez said. "He demands blood. What'll it be?"

"Thanks, but we'll walk all the same," Aidan said. He reached for the locker holding the Winchester 70 and undid the combination.

Mr. Olivarez slammed the locker shut as Aidan opened it.

"It isn't like that."

"But you said we were free to go if we wanted."

"It's never that easy. You are free to go once one of you has paid the price in blood."

"What?" Peter yelled. "That isn't fair. You said…"

"Malifax demands blood, and Malifax will receive blood!" Mr. Olivarez yelled. The people in the crowd cheered Mr. Olivarez.

"Fine. I'll do it," Jax said. "Sacrifice me."

"You don't even know what we propose," Mr. Olivarez said. There was something black and inky about the way his words came out of his mouth. Aidan had never noticed it until then.

"I'm your man, either way," Jax said.

Mr. Olivarez signaled the man with the tattoo sleeves. That man opened the adjacent locker. It was full of garden supplies.

"These came from one of the first crates we opened, and right away, I knew it would be special. The container was headed to some hardware outlets until Black Friday when all the dockworkers were killed. I had the locker brought here, and I inspected it."

He walked over to one of the garden tillers and lifted it up into the air. It was the hand-held kind. The crowd cheered. It had long spikes.

"Throughout history, societies have made sacrifices to their gods. These use special instruments that they consider as sacred as the ritual. I keep my instruments very clean so that there is no chance of infections or sharing any blood borne pathogens. I want you all to know that I take no delight in this."

Jax took his polo off.

"Not you, kung fu kid," Mr. Olivarez said. "You."

"Me?" Aidan said. He had been fine with Jax wanting to prove his love and devotion.

"You're the one in charge, are you not? Then you own the numbers. You can't punt and pass that responsibility."

Aidan set his eyes. "Where do you want me?"

Two men grabbed him and shoved him to the ground, kneeling on his shoulders. Two more men pinned his ankles to the ground.

As he struggled, his friends tried to reach him, but the armed guard stopped them. Val held Alyssa. Aidan could see none of this.

First, he felt pressure against his back. Then he heard Alyssa scream, and he felt more pressure on his back. He tried to glance at it, but he couldn't see what was going on. He couldn't see much of anything. His vision was going blurry.

When he awoke, he saw his blood on Mr. Olivarez's hands and wrists. The garden tiller at his side was also covered in blood. Fresh blood. In his other hand, Mr. Olivarez held Aidan's baby blue polo shirt up for everyone to see. He then tossed it over the side of the bridge. Aidan felt like his body was falling over the bridge, too. Falling, falling, falling.

But two men were holding him up. He wondered, *when did I get up?*

"Are we done?" he managed to gasp to Mr. Olivarez in what he hoped sounded defiant. He didn't think he had the strength for a single word more.

Mr. Olivarez said, "I am sorry, but Malifax spoke to us last night. He will not be satisfied with blood alone. He demands bone and flesh as well. I don't know what you did, but he has a real lust for you, son. He never demands so much."

Aidan didn't hear anything after the words, "bone and flesh." His mind was whirling like his vision. From in front, Mr. Olivarez approach him with a pair of bolt cutters. Out of the corner of his eye, Peter sheltered Colt. Alyssa screamed into Val's arms, and Riley and Jax clung to each other. Only Jax was watching him. Aidan felt a knuckle pop. He didn't know he was so tense. It felt better for a moment until he realized that the knuckle didn't pop – his little finger was gone. Thrown to the sea as the toll for crossing the bridge. Three billy goats gruff. Then he passed out.

When he awoke, his back and hand were on fire. Not flaming fire, but white-hot poker fire. He could not move and started to cry, assuming he was paralyzed. As he cried, though, he felt his foot scrape against the floor. He had never been so happy to feel such pain.

Val was there with Alyssa. When she saw Aidan awake, she ran over to him. She began petting his shaved head. He didn't hear much of what she said, only "recover" and "three days." Then he was out again.

By the third day, he was getting better, but still wasn't ready to walk. Unfortunately, he had no choice. It was time to go.

He placed his journal into his back pocket. He winced with every step, which launched a rocket ship of pain through his central nervous system. On either side of Aidan stood Riley and Alyssa, but his brothers and the rest of the lost boys walked huddled close-by with all their gear and their weapons. He wasn't sure, but he thought they had picked up one or two more kids.

Maybe the kids Peter had mentioned. Definitely Kirk's new guitar buddy. They both had guitars strapped to their backs.

"Is it just me or are there more people in our group now than before we arrived?"

"So much for reducing our numbers. Are you okay?" Alyssa asked. "It's okay if you're not. But you look beyond pained. You look pissed."

"No, I'm not. Just feeling claustrophobic."

"Too bad. We're not letting you go."

"Good. I don't think I could stand."

Before they could begin the walk down the bridge, Mr. Olivarez, Val, and a group of the militia stopped them.

"Aren't you going to let us go, you shithole?" Jax asked.

Mr. Olivarez was watching Aidan with pained eyes. He shook his head.

"You bastard," Jax continued his torrent. "You said we could leave."

Mr. Olivarez rubbed his forehead as he said, "I'm sorry. This has never happened before. The Malifax. It demands more."

"Hell no," Jax said, and he pulled out his parang.

"Your creature changing the game on you?" Aidan mumbled.

"The tribute must be paid."

"Does anyone even talk like that anymore?" Peter grumbled.

"You've got plenty of people here," Jax said. "Have one of them serve up some human sushi to that monster."

"Malifax wants one of you. That much is clear."

"You expect us to roll over and let you chop us up?"

"No. But one of you must die. We have no choice."

"Stop!" Val shouted. Mr. Olivarez turned to his son.

"I know this must be hard, Val, but this is the only way to survive."

"Let them go, Dad."

"We let them go and Malifax will destroy everything. I'm doing this for you," he said.

"Then don't. You can't protect me forever, Dad."

"I will protect you with my last breath if I have to."

"I know. That's why you have to stop."

Mr. Olivarez put his hand on Val's shoulder, then ordered everyone to the top of the bridge. Aidan had to be carried.

"I won't ask you to decide which one of you we will sacrifice," Mr. Olivarez said when everyone reached the top. He pulled out a black bag and handed it to the group, saying, "Inside are black stones and one white. Whoever takes the white stone will be sacrificed."

Kirk reached out for the bag. Peter could tell Kirk was going to throw it back into Mr. Olivarez's face. But then, as Kirk grabbed the bag, Mr. Olivarez shot him in the stomach.

Kirk fell to the asphalt, his new guitar friend next to him. He looked up into her soft blue eyes and said, "I guess it makes sense that the anarchist is killed so randomly." He couldn't hear the words coming out of his mouth. It was like he was watching everything through a tunnel that ended with light and her blue eyes. A third, red eye ripped between the other two, and she fell forward. She was dead before she hit his chest.

"Teach you to leave us," one of the guards growled.

Kirk gave the guard no more recognition than he deserved. To the lost boys he said with his last breath, "Tentacles."

Aidan, who was overly tired and slightly tunnel-visioned himself, thought this was a weird thing to say. Jax was quicker-minded, though, and pulled the lost boys away. "Run!" he yelled as the first tentacle reached over the bridge and grabbed one of the guards.

Somebody pulled Aidan in one direction, and everything was getting cloudy. He didn't know if he was running or flying, but he was definitely moving. Something large knocked him down, and the world turned upside down. He saw a hundred mouths and a thousand eyes, and then he was back on the asphalt and something was flailing on him. He looked up and saw gunfire and tentacles. People were running everywhere. Jax roundhouse kicked one of the guards. In the corner, Val pulled Alyssa to safety and shot at a tentacle. The tentacles were like rain, like a thousand tentacles raining from the sky to grab people and pull them off the bridge.

Alyssa drew close to Val. He was talking to her urgently. Passionately. He started to take off his shirt and they kissed. Was that for real? Did he dream it? No.

"Alyssa!" Aidan yelled. "Come on!"

Alyssa's eyes were full of sorrow and terror. She shook her head to Aidan. Aidan turned away.

Aidan pulled himself back onto his feet, fueled by anger. He stumbled down the bridge. Jax had to stop him.

"We can't go that way!" Jax shouted. He pointed to the bottom of the bridge where wargs were breaking down the barriers. "Where's Alyssa?"

"She's made her choice."

"What does that mean?"

"How do we get off this damn thing, then?" Aidan snapped back.

Jax pointed to the large crane standing out in the middle of the air.

Just then, they heard a large crumbling sound and a crash. A section of the lower portion of the bridge gave way.

"Malifax is bringing the whole place down," Peter yelled. "We have to get off here quick!"

Jax helped Riley to the side. She leaped for the crane and missed. She started to flail her arms and caught a lower trestle. As she climbed up on the crane, Peter was already leaping across. The gymnast had no problem launching at bars through mid-air. He even did a bit of a twirl as he pulled himself up. He reached out his hand to Colt and smiled, saying, "Don't worry. I'll catch you."

Colt looked to Aidan, who nodded. "We will get you out as far as we can. It's not a far jump at all."

As Colt jumped, though, the bridge shook. He faltered and fell. Jax grabbed him by the ankle and hauled him back up. Colt looked at them wide-eyed.

"Second times the charm," Jax said.

Colt shook his head violently. They knew he would never do it again, not after nearly plummeting to his death.

"I've got an idea!" Peter said. He tried to manipulate the crane's cord and push it to them. It was too heavy, though.

Jax ran off.

A tentacle appeared in the sky and watched them with its many eyes. The tentacle struck forward, and a multitude of tiny mouths filled with rows of needle-like teeth jutted out from the black tentacle. Aidan pushed it out of the way with renewed strength.

He saw Mr. Olivarez coming towards them, his gun raised. A tentacle jumped at Mr. Olivarez. The little mouths clamped onto him like a pit bull. First one mouth, then the others latched onto him. The tentacle closed around him. He could not move. When the other mouths began to tunnel into his insides, though, he began to scream. Mr. Olivarez looked into the many eyes of Malifax and vomited. Malifax dropped him, and his head rolled away from the pulp that was his body.

Jax jumped over a tentacle and slashed it with his parang. He had the rifle strapped to his back and rappelling rope wrapped around his waist. Aidan thought to ask him where he got the rope, but honestly, he didn't care. Was just glad he had it.

Jax tossed the rope to Peter, who tied it to the crane. Then Jax tied the other end to a container hold.

"Go, Colt!" Jax yelled. Colt shook his head again.

"You have to do this, Colt. I can't do it for you," Aidan said.

Colt nodded. He took hold of the rope and crawled hand-over-hand, the rope laying under his body and one leg out for balance.

Colt knew better than to look down. He tried to ignore the wind and the way it made the rope sway. With every inch, his mind told him this was too scary and he should turn around. Tears streamed down his eyes as he crawled across the rope, concentrating on the faces of his brother and his open hands.

Peter and Riley grabbed Colt when he was within reach and pulled him the rest of the way to the crane.

"Your turn," Jax said.

"When I say no, I want you to understand it isn't because I'm afraid of heights, but because I physically cannot do this." Jax started doing something with his hands, but Aidan's tunnel vision kept him from seeing what Jax was doing, so he kept talking. "I don't have half the strength needed to cross a rope, nor the functionality in my body to do it. Tell my brothers to be good to each other. Take care of my brothers for me."

"When are you going to understand? Your brothers take pretty damn good care of themselves. If you trust them, they will even take care of you." Jax pushed Aidan, and he fell backwards over the bridge. Suddenly, he was in the air, and there was nothing between him and a hundred-foot death drop. Then the twang of the rope caught him, and his limp body began to arch towards the crane.

Peter and Colt grabbed Aidan. Riley, who had already climbed a little lower to give Peter and Colt more room, looked up at the three brothers' silhouettes huddled together on the crane trestles, and for a moment she thought of birds on a wire. She put her hand out to Colt's leg, which felt good and warm.

Peter flung the unattached end of the rope back to Jax.

Jax grabbed the rope at the same time that Malifax snapped the bridge columns. He heard the rumbling of the bridge and felt the line go tight as the bridge began sliding away from the crane.

He cut a tentacle that had been stalking him and swung out into the open air, his legs flying into oblivion, and prayed that someone would catch him. His body collided with the crane, and Riley grabbed him by his shirt, which nearly ripped right off until she grabbed his arm, too.

As the bridge slid into the shipping channel, the remaining lost boys climbed down the crane as fast as they could.

From the side of the river, they waited for the cover of darkness to move. While they waited, they listened to the sounds of trapped bodies pleading for help from the rubble. Some people who had survived the fall were pulled underwater and drowned by Malifax. Any who escaped Malifax were dragged out of the water and ripped slowly apart by wargs.

With nightfall, the wind direction changed. Smoke billowed towards them, and everyone still alive agreed this was the best cover for escape.

Chapter Eight – Cheerful

The fire truck stopped just beyond the overpass, and Jax cut the engine. The trees were smaller and less dense in this part of the state than in the area they came from. Instead of the pines and cypress of Houston, Central Texas gave them twisted juniper and cedar trees. Dark-barked trees with small tousles of leaf. The roadside was owned by neighborhoods of cactus and limestone.

A few seconds later, the first wet, black-and-caramel-colored disc slipped underneath the mangled barbwire fence, skittered across the road, and entered the ranch land on the opposite side. Aidan put down his journal. Colt wiggled his arms and made barfing noises while Jax tried to stop him. None of the five remaining lost boys had ever seen a cockroach that large before. It was as big as an office desk. As soon as the first roach crossed the road, three more came over the asphalt. Then it was five, then ten, then suddenly the road was swarming with giant, shiny roaches crawling all over each other. They left a giant trail of upturned earth, roach feces, and devastation behind them.

"I think I need a bath," Peter said.

"Our world keeps getting grosser and grosser," Colt said.

"Let's go take a look," Jax said.

They stopped to sleep at the top of a tall overpass in the carcass of an airplane. They inspected it carefully for signs of life, and they noticed that the plane had beak and claw marks along its fuselage. Also, the bodies had been completely picked apart, either by giant roaches or some other creatures. It still stunk, though, which was good because it meant their scent could get overwhelmed by the smell coming from the fuselage. A few of the seats only needed a whack or two with the fireman's axe to ply them from the floor of the plane, so they dragged the seats out into the open, pushed them on their backs, and used the pillows for cushions.

Jax thought of how out in the open this setup was. To a small degree, it terrified him. The safer place to sleep would be inside the fuselage where they were at least protected in case they were attacked. But then again, they had never been attacked by owls or other night prowlers. It also would give them some protection from the cold front that had pushed through earlier.

Colt had taken a mostly-clean skull from one of the passengers. Now he was putting the plane's gas mask on, taking it off the skull, and mumbling quietly to himself. He held up the gas mask, and the skull bobbled in the air. He laughed. It didn't bother anyone.

Under the stars that night, Peter said, "Well, at least you can see a lot more stars at night than you ever could before."

"Do you know any of the constellations?" Colt asked. He tossed the skull and gas mask aside.

"Well, there's Orion up there. Then there's uh, well…Aidan, did you print out any constellation information back at the house?"

"Even if I did, I lost all that back at Bridgetown." Aidan turned on his side, pulled his sleeping bag close to him, and closed his eyes, but he did not sleep.

"I think I see one," Jax said. "It's the constellation X-box."

"X-box? Really?" Colt searched the skies.

"Yeah, right up there. That box with the wire hanging out. See it? And over there is the constellation Tyrion, sitting on a crooked chair. I'm sure if you look closely you'll see all the great ones up there: Gandalf, Wolverine, Victoria's Secret models…."

"I bet Mike's up there. And so is Kirk. Probably playing guitar to that girl he liked," Colt said.

"You know what? I bet he is, too."

Jax pulled up his hecho en Mexico wool blanket. They were all huddled as close as they could get in toppled airline seats to help keep each other warm. The weather was turning colder. They didn't know if it was still November or if December had snuck into their lives, but the chill was setting on them like an ugly tattoo that wouldn't let go. Before he turned in, Aidan had built a shallow coal fire that wouldn't attract much attention but still give off warmth.

"Hey, guess what I got," Peter said. He pulled some cellphones out of his sleeping bag and handed them around. "I found them in a store in that town with the upside-down name sign."

"You mean the one with the 20-foot rattlesnake?" Jax said, smiling. Mockingly, he crowed, *"Oh, c'mon, let's go check it out. It'll be fun."*

"Well, at least now we know what an upside down name sign means."

"Yeah, it means everybody who would be there knows it is no longer a place where anyone should be and only a dumbass would enter."

"Point being," Peter said as sternly as he could, "We don't have phone service or texting or Internet, but we got everything else."

"Oooh, I can take selfies again!" Riley cooed. She climbed partially out of her sleeping bag, held the phone away from her, beamed wildly, snapped a photo of herself, and passed it around.

"When cells are up running again, I'll tag you all in it. Then I will post it online as 'my first extended camping trip.'"

"Wait," Jax said, "This is your first?"

"Well, yeah. I wasn't a girl scout. When I was a kid and my family camped, we did overnight stuff. This is my first camping trip that's gone on for like, two or three months now."

Jax pulled her in for a kiss, but she stopped him. "If you want it, you're going to have to chase it, bucko."

"Now I'm a bucko."

"Welcome to the friend zone, dude," Peter said.

Jax pulled an imaginary knife out of his chest and scooted his bag away from hers. She grabbed his leg and said, "Hell, no. As a friend, you're still keeping me warm tonight. It's cold!"

"I wish there were more of us," Colt said. "I miss Kirk and Alyssa." He inhaled sharply.

"Me, too, Bucko," Riley said.

The cold night air seemed closer then, so they all lay down around each other and went to sleep. Aidan stayed up.

Downtown Austin lay over a river and in the hills. A windstorm had come through the night before, so a thin layer of crackling red and yellow leaves covered the roadways.

"Are you sure about this? We should keep going," Jax said.

"I was going to go to school here," Aidan said. "I want to at least go check it out."

Slowly, the fire truck drove off the freeway and entered the town. The roads were clear. All the pick-ups, sedans, and jeeps had been pushed to the side, some under overhanging rust and sand-colored bedrock where the streets had been carved out of the hillside.

Peter took the family rifle and climbed on top of the fire truck.

In the downtown area, the streets were empty of flesh and steel. It was as if God had called every Ford and Ford-loving cowboy up to Heaven right before the rapture.

Peter pulled the bandana down from over his mouth and yelled, "There's some creepy old guy sitting in the middle of the road!"

The creepy old guy was sitting on a plastic chair – the kind found in classrooms – and smoking a cigarette. The cigarette was almost down to the butt.

"I think he's lost his mind."

The fire truck rolled to a stop, and the lost boys got out. Jax said to the others, "Be careful, and remember what happened the last time we came across a person who wouldn't talk."

To the old man, Jax yelled, "Speak up, grandpa, or we'll shoot you!"

"Don't shoot!" the man said. His voice trembled in the air.

Jax walked up to him while the others waited by the truck. "What happened here?" he demanded to the man sitting on the plastic chair. It was crayon-red. "Who cleared all the roads? Are there any others like you?"

The man didn't say anything more. He had a comb-over and large old man's glasses, though he couldn't have been a day over 45, and he was wearing a scoutmaster's shirt. Hence, the creep-factor. Jax played it cool.

"You a scoutmaster, huh? Hey, we've got an Eagle Scout with us. Maybe you can brighten him up a bit? He's been down in the dumps since we left Bridgetown."

As he was talking, Jax noticed something out of the corner of his eye. Somebody was running up towards them from the alleyway. Slowly it occurred to him that the runner was a soldier. Had to be a soldier because otherwise, it was Alyssa dressed in a ghillie suit like a soldier, and why would she be here in Austin wearing a soldier's outfit? And why was she waving her hands and shouting?

"No! Don't say anything!" she yelled.

But it was too late. At the mention of Bridgetown, the man cocked his face towards Jax.

"You came all the way from Bridgetown? Really?" The man asked. His eyes seemed to roll towards Aidan like the eyes on one of those plastic clown toys. The ones that are always coming alive in horror movies.

Jax looked at Alyssa for a second, not sure what she was talking about or why she was wearing camouflage. This all made no sense, so he answered the man. He could hear the words coming out of his mouth as he tried to reach out and grab them. Alyssa's warning was seeping into him. He trusted her. He shouldn't say anything to the creepy old Scoutmaster, and yet the words were coming out all the same.

"Yes. There's not much left of it, though. People are going to need to find a new commuter route to work, you know?"

"You're them," the man said, bewildered. "You're really them. I can't believe it. You're just kids. Not a one of you twenty. You're them. You're them! It's them! They're here!

It's them!" He started shouting louder and louder until his face turned purple and the veins on his neck stood out.

"How do you know us?" Jax asked, but the man didn't answer. He kept yelling, "It's them!" over and over.

Alyssa ran up behind the man and hit him with a steel tray girder. Blood splattered across Jax's shirt. The man fell down convulsing.

"What are you doing?" Jax tried to understand. "Have you lost your freaking mind? *You* just killed a man."

"We've got to go. It isn't safe anymore out here. They've been warned."

"Who's been warned?"

"If you thought the grackles were bad, you have no idea. Now run. We haven't much time."

At that moment, Jax felt a shadow passing over him. He looked up and saw the sky darkening, like a thunderhead approaching from the river. It wasn't a storm he was seeing, though. Something else. He felt he should now this, should know why the sky was turning from day to night, but the explanation was escaping him. As his senses sharpened, his body hit the fight or flight response, with an emphasis on getting the hell out.

Peter looked up at the black cloud. "What the flip do we do now?"

"Run!" Jax shouted. He ran for the fire truck.

"Not that way!" Alyssa grabbed Jax by the hand and jerked him towards the alley.

The others followed Alyssa into the backdoor of a restaurant with tall ceiling-to-floor windows across the front. "Hidalgo's" was painted in white and green letters across the front windows of the restaurant. Val held the door open while everyone rushed inside. He took the steel tray girder and jammed it in the door's handle. They sat down below the restaurant's windows, partially covered by the tables, and studied the outside road.

"Be very quiet," Alyssa mouthed.

At first, Jax thought the dark cloud was grackles or insects because the creatures were chittering. He had seen those before. A tentacle-like tornado funneled down towards the scoutmaster, who was no longer convulsing. They swarmed and surrounded the old man, and then they spread out across the road and between the buildings. That's when Jax got a close enough view to recognize them. Hundreds of thousands of small, leathery wings. They were crying out and chittering to each other, and then one of the bats landed on the brick wall of the restaurant. It was maybe a foot long, most of it tail, and it had ears almost a quarter the size of its body. Its body quivered and pulsated as it pulled itself along the window's edge with its claws. The bat screamed at the window, then crawled a little farther and screamed again.

Eyes froze wide or shut. Nobody moved. It was like they were back in the house on Vicksburg surrounded by bats and grackles that would locate them if they barely moved or made a noise.

The bat crawled right up to where Alyssa's face should be and screamed again. But while everyone had been staring at the bats, she had donned a ghillie suit helmet. The bat flew away. A few minutes later, after the bats had swarmed through every side street and back alley in the downtown area, the bats left, and the sky turned sunny again.

Alyssa stood up. She looked out of place in the downtown restaurant wearing her camouflaged ghillie suit. She found herself wrapped in Colt's arms. She hugged him back.

"I know," she said. "It's okay." Then Peter and Jax and Riley were all suddenly holding her, too.

"We thought we'd lost you," Colt said.

"I missed you guys, too," she said. She smiled and dropped her chin into their embrace. When they let go, she wiped the tears from her eyes.

"Val found more ghillie suits. You will all need to wear one when you're outside. There aren't many wargs here. We think it's cause of the bats. They run the city."

"Bats? Where are they coming from?" Peter asked.

"Get this," Val said. "Before Black Friday, Austin was known for having the largest urban bat population in America. These bats lived under the bridges, but we went exploring once and didn't find any."

"Of course, with the city pretty much dead, they could be roosting in a building somewhere for all we know," Alyssa added.

"We are pretty safe so long as we stay inside. They are still using echolocation to find us."

"What about the people?" Aidan asked. "It sounded almost like that guy was waiting for us."

Alyssa looked to Val.

"He was. Remember how in Bridgetown, we had made a deal with Malifax? And remember how Malifax could talk to our minds? I still hear him. And he is talking to the people who live here, too, except there is no bargain like my father made, just a demand for the kids who escaped Bridgetown."

"Great," Peter glowered. "So it's not just animals after us, it's people, too?"

"Afraid so," Val said. "The good news is the bats are still using echolocation and not their sense of smell. And it's too cold for them to stay much longer. They will have to migrate south if they are going to survive the winter."

"And the insects are leaving, too," Peter said.

"Right," Val agreed. "I can't look up on the Internet how many insects a bat eats, but it's got to take a lot, so again, they can't stay here much longer."

"Well, neither can I," Aidan said, and he started to leave.

"No, wait!" Alyssa shouted. All social mores were ripped out of their foundation. In front of everyone, she ran up to Aidan and slammed the door shut. The other boys dismissed themselves.

Outside, the door slammed shut. The sound bounced off the alley wall and entered the street. A lone bat hanging from the lamppost turned its head towards the sound, then dropped from the lamppost and flew away.

"Why did you leave us?" Alyssa tried not to yell at him, but she couldn't help it.

"I didn't leave you, you left me!"

"Aidan Kerry Fannin, I haven't left you since Black Friday, so why would you think that I would leave you in Bridgetown?"

"Don't try to put this on me. I saw how you were with him."

"Him?"

"Don't try to deny it. Him. Val. You and he have had eyes for each other ever since we got to Bridgetown."

"You need to stop right there," Alyssa warned him. "I've known Val for a long time now. Since middle school. You don't know what you're talking about."

"I think I do. I'm not blind."

"I won't stop my friendship with him for you."

"Fine, cause you don't have to. I will just take myself out of the equation."

"Stop being such an asshole!"

"I'm the asshole? I saw you and him. He had his shirt off and you were running your hands all over his giant pecs and whatever. You're so gross! And you kissed him!"

Alyssa's mouth dropped, completely mortified.

"You think that…? Val! Val!"

Aidan looked back towards the kitchen. Val was buttoning his shirt. The boys were all looking at Val and back to Aidan. Their eyes were wide with something that looked like a world upended, which was saying a lot. They receded farther back into the kitchen while Val finished buttoning his shirt and walked out.

"Val, get your butt over here right now!"

Val half-trotted to Aidan and Alyssa.

"Show him," she said.

He hesitated. "I already showed the others. How many times do I have to take my shirt off today?"

"Please, just one more time. I don't like asking you to do this, and I know it's kinda demeaning, but I really need you to do this for me. I don't think he'll believe me unless he sees."

Val took a deep breath and unbuttoned his shirt. Aidan looked at two beautifully formed breasts with wide, dark aureoles.

Aidan looked at the breasts, to Val, then to Alyssa, then briefly back to the breasts. Val buttoned his shirt back up.

"Say something," Alyssa said.

"What the fuck?" came out of Aidan's mouth.

Val's eyes twisted, Alyssa's rolled. That's when the giant bat flung itself headfirst through the front window.

Glass burst across the room. The giant bat flung itself around the ceiling, knocked out a light, and landed. It was almost five feet tall, had an ugly, serrated mouth, and bright green phosphorescent patterns that waved across its wings and body.

The rifle was fired several times, and Jax stabbed at the giant bat, but it was hard to pinpoint its location with all the dazzling lights flailing around.

It knocked Riley over, and as it flew back towards the vaulted ceiling, its feet cut Peter across the forehead.

Alyssa grabbed a candlestick from one of the tables and ran back towards the kitchen while everyone else fought the giant bat. She could not see well in the dark. The bat's bioluminescence was as dismaying as a flash bomb. Not able to see well, she ran right into a food prep table, nearly knocking the wind out of herself. She doubled over and clutched her stomach.

"Stop firing! Aidan yelled. "You're just wasting bullets!"

Peter dropped the Winchester and wondered how he was going to fight off a giant bat with just his fists. Then he remembered something, and he, too, ran to the kitchen. Like Alyssa, he couldn't see well. He couldn't hear well, either, because the bat was screeching constantly. So he never saw Alyssa trying to stand in one corner. He waved his hands out until he found the hanging butcher's knives.

Alyssa's hands groped around the back of the oven until she felt the gas line in her fingers. She jerked hard, popping the line. The nauseating smell filled her lungs. She wondered for a second whether or not gas was still pumping through the lines or if what she was smelling the small bit that was left in the line. If it was still pumping, how did it do it? Was it machine operated or did a person somewhere have to pull a switch, or was she lucky enough that this gas line went directly to a large propane tank out back? She had no idea, just the hope that this worked. They had used Molotov cocktails on wargs, so animals were still flammable.

She ran back towards the far end of the kitchen with an unused candle in one hand and a lighter in the other, when something cut across the air in front of her. She ducked, then felt the blade cut into her.

Peter grabbed a couple of chef's knives and a cleaver for himself. He was about to run when he heard something approaching hard and fast from the back of the kitchen. He tried squinting his eyes to see the creature better, but he couldn't make out anything. He put the other knives down except for one chef's knife and one cleaver. Then he prepared for whatever this world was going to throw at him next.

A shape appeared out of the darkness, and he swiped at it with the cleaver. It ducked, and he realized it was somebody, but his other arm was already shooting out at one of his friends. Misery stabbed him as he felt the blade connect with flesh.

Alyssa screamed.

Peter dropped the knives.

"I'm sorry! Where did I get you?"

"Shut up and keep moving!" She pushed him forward. He grabbed the knives and ran.

With her good hand, Alyssa placed the candle on the kitchen table, lit it, and followed Peter back out into the chaos.

The radiating lights had moved beyond brightness flashing in their eyes. It was like trying to fight with strobe lights going off inside their heads. They were no longer looking at the bat while they tried to punch, stab, or grab it. The bat was winning. Already Colt was climbing underneath a table to try to escape the bright whirling green lights. In between flashes, he caught glimpses of his friends. They were being cut up like ribbons of cloth, and he didn't know how much longer they could fight. Jax had the worst of it. With the parang, he posed the biggest threat. He had even gotten a cut of good leathery wing. However, the giant bat had paid him back for that cut with a deep cut to his side.

Then Peter showed up with more knives, and suddenly everyone was armed and chasing after the bat. The bat leapt to the high ceiling.

Alyssa yelled to everyone, "We gotta go!"

This time, they listened and followed her out of the restaurant in time for flames to burst out like a red and orange tongue from the kitchen's agape maw.

In the alley, they escaped to cool, dark corners while a volcano of heat and fire gushed out of the restaurant.

"We've got to keep moving," Aidan said. "This building's on fire."

Wearily, they climbed back into the fire truck. Alyssa crawled into Aidan's lap, and he held her tight. Jax was too cut up to drive, so Peter took the wheel.

Colt pointed to Jax's cuts and said sarcastically, "I think that's going to need stitches."

"Everything's going to be alright now," Peter said.

"No, it isn't," said Aidan. "We lost the Winchester 70. It isn't your fault."

"That was granddad's rifle," Colt said.

Peter was a teenager with the strength to hold his body suspended in the air in a perfect cross on the rings. Years of gymnastics conditioning had prepared him for that amazing feat, and others. But for a young man as strong as he was, he did not have the strength to hold himself up against his guilt.

They drove away from the inferno and the dead town and headed north. For a while, they lost track of time and distance. Every place was just one more challenge to survive in a world they clearly did not own anymore.

The ground shook. Small shards of rock bounced on the hard compact sediment. The lost boys clenched their cheeks and crawled tighter underneath the destroyed home. They were trapped like rabbits, like scared little rabbits with nowhere to go. If these monstrous beasts – which looked like giant elephants with tentacles instead of trunks and four horns each – found them out, they were doomed. They were not fast enough or strong enough to repel their attack.

They were at the mercy of God or Buddha or Karma or fate.

The elephants moved on, heading northeast. When the ground stopped shaking and they could no longer see the monstrous beasts, the lost boys crawled out of their temporary hiding place, found a place to drop trou, then continued north.

Nobody saw the mountain lion coming. They had stopped for lunch and were sitting in random cars on the highway, eating out of cans while the withered remains of humanity dried up in the front seats of the cars. That was when they head the large animal's foot padding somewhere out in the field.

Quietly, they all waited for the animal to appear. Minutes passed, and they say and heard nothing. Then a large creature pushed itself through the high grass on the far side of the highway. They still didn't see it. A car was crushed as the mountain lion climbed up on a sedan. Then came the most awful sound from the invisible creature. Aidan remembered hearing that the sounds of a mountain lion yelling had been mistaken for women wailing. This was the most terrible, horrible wail he had ever heard. If this was supposed to be a woman wailing, Aidan hoped to God he never met the woman on the other side of that wail.

Then the hood of the car dipped, then popped back up, its shocks bearing the weight of the mountain lion they still could not see, even though it was right in front of them.

They waited an hour before anyone was brave enough to go back to the fire truck.

In Abilene, they had to stop and take refuge when three giant turkey buzzards suddenly swooped over the fire truck. Fortunately for the lost boys, the buzzards had no interest in them. The giant buzzards, which had wings as long as parasails, glided over them and came to rest in the middle of the road, where they were eating a dead cow.

The buzzards had sick, fat bellies and a beak like a plow. The most villainous eyes turned to the lost boys half-way through its lunch, seemingly daring one of them to step outside. For effect, maybe, the buzzard hopped over to a car, ripped the door off as easily as if it were shredding paper with those thick talons, and grabbed a corpse out of the car. The turkey buzzard gulped the corpse down like an appetizer, all the while staring at the fire truck and the lost boys. Then it returned to the cow.

When they were done, the vultures pulled themselves up into the air. The force generated by the beating of their wings was enough to make the cars and the fire truck rock back and forth. Then they flew into the sky and left the lost boys alone.

In Lubbock, they stopped for gas. They could not find any at the gas stations outside of town, which they took as a positive sign. It must mean that people were flourishing somewhere. And

Lubbock did not have an upside down population sign, so they drove into town. Aidan, who was driving, stopped the fire truck.

"What's the matter?" Riley asked.

"Do you hear that?" Aidan asked her and turned his ear. Riley also listened. Suddenly, it seemed a lot quieter than it had a minute before, but she couldn't tell why.

"Cut the engine," Jax suggested, and Aidan did. They were all listening now. The wide road was empty and quiet.

Nothing.

Aidan opened the door. "I've got an idea. Peter, can you drive?"

While Peter climbed into the driver's seat, Aidan climbed up on top of the cab, and then thumped the roof when he was ready.

The fire truck's engine started, and the truck began moving slowly down the street while Aidan listened.

Alyssa and Colt and Riley and Jax had rolled down the windows and were trying to listen, too, but the engine was so loud, it was hard to hear anything with the sirens going.

"Hello. Any monsters out there?" Peter squawked over the fire truck's call box.

While Peter talked to the monsters, Aidan listened. Then he heard it from a few blocks down: a buzzing sound, like droning. Then as quickly as the sound appeared, it disappeared. Another buzzing sound came from much closer, maybe from the block over. It stopped, and the further one started again.

He pounded the roof and quickly climbed into the cab behind Peter. "Get the hell outta here," he said, "and roll up those windows."

"Why? What is it?"

"Cicadas. That's what I was hearing. Must be thousands of them hiding in the trees. Somehow they seem to be talking to each other. I don't know what they are saying, and I sure as hell don't want to find out. Let's get out of here."

They were out on the plains driving at night and pushing cars off the road when they saw an unnatural, orange glow on the horizon. It was the glow of civilization, of 24-hour gas stations and road lights. They hadn't seen this kind of light after dark since the first nights after Black Friday. Nothing natural generated light in the middle of the night, at least as far as they knew. Only humans did that. They drove to the light.

It was a large supermarket. They came upon it slowly and cautiously.

A few people were milling around on the far side of the empty parking lot.

"What do you think?" Peter asked as they studied the parking lot from the top of a nearby convenience store.

"They have no weapons," Jax said.

Aidan shook his head. "Have you ever seen a parking lot this empty? Ever? Even before the apocalypse, there would always be at least one car in the lot."

"Something doesn't feel right," Riley said. Colt and Alyssa nodded their agreement. They got back in the fire truck and left. Curiosity got the best of them though, and they circled around the supermarket. That's when they saw that the people weren't people, but appendages of some house-sized spiders that were waiting in ambush just out of reach of the parking lot lights. How they got them on and off, they could only conjecture, but the truth was there: lights meant a trap.

They were resting in the derailed intestines of a southbound train. This was a good spot to camp for the night. They were out on the plains, so they could see an enemy coming from miles away, as long as it wasn't a mountain lion. While Aidan scribbled in his journal, Alyssa rubbed her fingers over the open space where his little finger should be.

"I like it. It's so soft. I never knew you had a soft spot," she teased him.

He reached over and kissed her, and she accepted his warm lips. He put his hand on the wrapped arm, then moved his hand lower on her arm.

"Sorry," he said.

"The only thing you should be sorry about is that you stopped kissing me."

Del Monte, Ranch Style, and Bush's were the choices. After the beans were cooked on the grill they had found among a campsite of dead people, Peter took the cans around to the other lost boys so they could select their can. Val thanked him for the beans and began to shovel them in his mouth using nothing more than his fingers. Aidan and Alyssa sat side-by-side on one end of the fire pit, with the fire truck and most of the derailed train in front of them.

"Stop staring," Alyssa told Aidan.

"It still shocks me."

"He."

"Of course. But the more I look at him, he does look like a her."

"Yes, because he was going through hormone replacement therapy before he could have his operation. Once the lights went out all over the world and companies stopped manufacturing drugs, he started becoming more like a her."

"But he doesn't want to be a her."

"No. He wants to be a him."

"But why not a her?"

"Because that's his choice."

"But it isn't his choice now."

"Now he is more of a him and a her, so he should have a choice."

"What do we call him?"

"I call him Val. You should, too."

"So wait. Is he a boy or a girl, you know…down there."

"I'm both, actually," Val said. "I have a regular-sized vaginal canal and a small phallus."

Aidan blushed and looked down. "Sorry, man, I didn't mean to be rude."

Something splatted against Aidan's fuzzy head. It was beans from Val's can.

"Dude, it's the apocalypse," Val said. "Do I need to buy you a bridge so you can get over it?"

"Yeah," Jax said. "I'm going to make you a t-shirt, Aidan, that says 'Thank God For The Apocalypse – It Killed My Homophobia.'"

Aidan chortled. So did the others. Aidan couldn't stop staring though.

Peter came to Aidan and Alyssa last. Aidan slowly put down the journal (his back was rarely not stiff anymore since Bridgetown). He took the can of baked beans; Alyssa, too. "You should stop staring, Aidan," Peter said. "It's been like at least two or three weeks now."

"More like five days, doofus."

Peter shrugged like Aidan's approval was the last thing on his mind, even though everybody knew it wasn't. To Alyssa, he said, "Again, sorry about the arm."

She flicked her index finger at him and said, "You should stop worrying about it. It's been like at least two or three weeks now. It's almost completely healed. Want to look?"

As she lifted the bandage, Peter ducked away. "God, no!" He took his beans and sat down by the fire, making sure not to face Alyssa.

"This from the man who was making a flash mob of dead people…"

"It's different. They're dead. You're still bleeding."

"I'm tired of beans," Colt said, and he tossed his open can of baked beans into the fire. "I want meat. I want bread. I don't want to eat things we're only eating because they haven't expired yet."

"There's corn and spam, man," Val offered.

Colt moaned.

"It's whatever we can find to get us through another day," Alyssa added. "Be thankful you have it."

"I'm tired of living through another day. I'm tired of 'surviving.' I'm tired of running and fighting and foraging."

"Well, what do you want to do?" Peter said as he came around the campfire.

"I want to do something fun."

"What would be fun to you?"

"I don't know."

"Want to play a game?"

"I hate RPGs. It's all you ever want to do for fun. I don't want to pretend I'm fighting monsters. Every day, we're fighting monsters. I want something fun."

Aidan put down his journal. "I think I know something you will like."

"What's that?" Alyssa asked, as she cocked her half-smile at him. Aidan paused. He fell in love with her all over again every time she showed him that smile. Aidan leaned over and whispered into her ear. All Colt could see was the steam coming from his mouth.

"Are you insane?" Alyssa shot back.

"Why not? It's not like there's a law against it."

Five minutes later, Colt was driving the ladder truck down over the state line to New Mexico, swerving from one lane to another while everyone else was either screaming or laughing.

"Wo!" Aidan yelled while shoving his foot on the brake and the engine skidded to a stop, sliding only a little.

"You almost got us killed," Alyssa yelled at Aidan. She was no longer smiling. Aidan ignored her.

"This time, go slower," he cautioned Colt.

Colt took his foot off the brake and gently applied the gas. The giant truck lurched forward and partly into the shoulder as Colt slammed the brakes back down. "Sorry!"

"Don't worry. You're doing great," Val shouted from the back of the cab.

"Yeah, you're doing fine," Aidan agreed.

"Can I turn the siren on?"

"We're on the plains. There's nobody around for probably fifty miles," Alyssa said.

"You're the driver, Colt. It's your decision."

Grinning impishly, Colt turned the siren on and stomped on the gas. This time, the truck went off the shoulder and crashed through the fence. It bounced up and down in the fields as Colt, barely big enough to get his arms around the steering wheel, tried to control. The whole time, he grinned like a 13-year old given the keys to a monster truck.

"Are you having fun now?" Aidan asked. Colt didn't need to say anything. He just kept grinning.

They came over a small rise in the field as they circled back towards the road. Unfortunately, the other side was much steeper, and suddenly they were looking down at a five-foot drop.

Everybody in the cab screamed. Aidan grabbed the wheel. He wanted to make damn sure Colt didn't turn the wheel sideways and roll them. That would be too much fun. As it was, he was certain they would only lose the truck once it slammed into the rocks in front of them.

At the last second, Colt jerked the wheel free of Aidan, who was having to reach from his side. The ladder truck turned to the left, skirting the rocks. At the same time, the same side of the truck lifted off the ground.

"We're gonna die!" Alyssa shrieked.

Then all four wheels touched the ground, and they were safe.

"You bastard!" Alyssa screamed as she punched Aidan on the back of the shoulder, but they weren't finished yet. The fire truck had entered a wide arroyo, and as Colt turned towards the road, the arroyo tapered and came to a rocky end.

Colt wanted to hit the brakes, but Aidan shouted, "Punch it!"

"But we're going to hit the rocks!"

"Just punch it!"

Colt slammed the gas pedal, and the fire truck, sirens blazing, launched over the rocks and caught air. It flew like a ton of bricks, slamming back down on the ground, first one tire, then another. Aidan was pretty sure that if the first crash didn't destroy the axle, the second one did.

As the fire truck landed, a giant stag appeared in front of them. It was almost as tall as the fire truck, and it had blazing white eyes. The stag barely had time to jump before the fire truck collided with it. Fur and glass and horn exploded everywhere, and the fire truck thumped over the stag and onto the highway.

Colt braked the truck, which was being pulled along its momentum, and once the fire truck slowed down enough, all the lost boys jumped out, including Colt.

"Put it in Park!" Peter shouted as he jumped back to the cab to help Colt.

When Peter and Colt walked back around the fire truck, they saw a trail of blood curling onto the road and to the rear bumper of the fire truck. The dead stag was partly wrapped around the rear axle.

"Oh, my God! You hit a deer!" Alyssa accused Aidan. "You take him for his first driving lesson, and you kill a deer!"

"So?"

"So? That is so redneck cliché. I can't believe you!"

Jax put his hand on Alyssa's shoulder. "Alyssa, you don't get it. We hit a deer."

She looked at all the smiles, and she rolled her eyes.

"Sometimes, y'all are such hicks."

"I don't care," Peter said. "That's venison."

Jax used his parang to chop off the leg, which was really the only part that was wrapped around the axle. They used small knives to remove the rest that was attached to the fire truck. Then Riley took a snapshot of everyone with the fire truck and the giant deer, its head almost as big as Colt. Peter and Aidan checked the axle, and amazingly, it was not cracked. The truck was drivable. After the photo, the part of the deer that had not been wrapped around the axle was tied down to the top of the truck using fire hoses.

Aidan drove them back to the camp across the state line and back into the high plains of West Texas. While Val and Riley got the flames going again, Aidan and Jax skinned the stag.

"You know, we should save the head," Jax said.

"Why's that?"

"Well, when we need to hide again, we could use it."

"I think they'd notice a disembodied deer head."

Jax shrugged. "I guess."

They handed off cuts of butchered meat to Alyssa and Peter and Colt, who set the meat on gathered firewood to cook.

"What we should do, though, is smoke this meat so we can carry it," Jax suggested. "Too bad we don't have any salt. This meat won't last two days, even in a cooler. Maybe we can scavenge some salt when we go into New Mexico. Most people hoarded food and bypassed spice. I think there was a town not far from here. Maybe we can get some there."

"Maybe. Sounds good," Aidan said, shrugging.

The meat, once cooked, was special. It wasn't MREs or beans or Raman. It was fresh meat straight from the deer. The taste was almost overwhelming. As afternoon settled into evening, they sat around grinning and gorging themselves until they began to fall into a protein-rich stupor. As person after person began to pass out, Colt walked away from camp to go pee.

"Thanks for helping me watch over him, man," Aidan said to Peter.

"Hey, it's what you'd do. We're family, right? Besides, I've got to stop screwing up eventually."

"Peter, I…" Aidan started to say, but then Colt screamed.

The footprint sat fat and deep in the sandy plains soil.

"Warg footprint, and it's fresh," Jax said.

"How fresh?" Val asked.

"Do I look like a professional tracker to you? I don't know. But it's deep and there's no soil disturbance. That's new."

"Okay, fan out and let's see if there are any more. Maybe it's just a lone wolf."

A few seconds more of flashlights arching back and forth in the cool twilight, and most of the lost boys had found more footprints. How they had missed all the signs while in camp was unbelievable and could only be blamed on their attention to the deer.

"They're all over the place," Riley said. "And this looks like one was stepping on our gear. We've gotta go."

"Looks like it's going to be a long night," Aidan said. "Let's pack it up and move out."

They were geared up in less than three minutes and ready to travel.

Before they climbed back into the truck, Aidan said, "Head back the way we came earlier today. We can head north into Oklahoma and then cross into Colorado."

"Don't pull that bullshit, Aidan," Jax said. "They are looking for us up north. We gotta do the unexpected and go west."

"North takes us to the cold and less chance of encountering animals. You go west, and every monstercized coyote and cougar will be after you."

"And if we go north, it's bears and wolves. Don't be stupid, Aidan."

"Just as I thought we were starting to get along, Jax."

"Guys, c'mon," Peter said. "Let's stop fighting and get moving."

"I'm heading north," Aidan said.

"You don't have the rifle to boss us around anymore, Aidan. Now I have the weapon. We're going west."

"It's not about rifles and swords and who has the biggest dick. This isn't high school anymore, Jax. You're not the handsome rich kid, and I'm not a geeky journalism student. You can walk that gauntlet west if you want to, but I'm going north. And I'm taking the truck."

"Cut it out, boys," Alyssa said, as she moved between them. It was too late, though. Aidan and Jax were already closing in on each other.

"You want the truck, then you go west with me," Jax said.

"It's my truck, Jax. I found it."

"Look at you. If it weren't for me, you'd be dead. I saved your ass. And this is how you repay me?" Jax swung at him.

Aidan dodged his swing clumsily, and then struck back. Aidan was no match for the trained fighter. By the time he threw a punch, Jax had already hit him hard in the kidneys. Pain erupted in his sides. As he fell forward, Jax kicked him in the chin so powerfully that Aidan flew backwards and landed in the dirt. New pain in his bloody mouth and bruised sides met the old pains in his back and collided like to two trains going opposite directions on the same track, and it left him unable to stand.

Jax moved to strike Aidan again, but Peter reached out and grabbed his leg and tossed it back effortlessly. When Jax regained his balance, he found Peter and Alyssa and Colt standing between him and Aidan.

"You're right," Aidan said from the ground as he spit blood in the dirt. "You did save my ass. And I am nowhere near the fighter you are, Jax. But it's going to take more than some fancy foot moves to survive the winter. And you don't have that."

Jax walked forward, and Peter grabbed his shirt. Jax moved through them, then reached down and dug the keys out of Aidan's pocket. Aidan wanted to stop him, but he didn't have the strength.

"Anybody else coming with me?" Jax said. "Now's your chance."

Nobody moved.

"Fine, but I want to remind everyone staying with the invalid here that there are wargs about, and I'm taking the truck."

Still, nobody moved. Jax climbed into the fire truck and fired it up.

"Wait!" Riley said, as she ran after him, her pack in hand. She opened the door and said, "This changes nothing between us," and got in.

Peter walked towards the truck.

"Peter?" Aidan gasped. His younger brother, who was defending him from Jax, was walking away? It made no sense.

Peter started to say one thing, and then blurted out, "You can search north for Mom and Dad, and I can search west. We can cover more ground this way." But the way he said it, Aidan knew Peter didn't believe they were alive anymore.

As the fire truck left, Aidan looked at who was left and sighed.

"I know," Alyssa said. "You got left with nothing but a kid, an intersex, and a chick with palsy. You have less fingers than you had a month ago, a back that won't stop aching, and no food, no water, and no transportation. But trust me. It will get better. You just have to believe in it."

Part Three: The Black Tooth

Chapter Nine – Thrifty

They had to be thrifty with how much space they used in their backpacks so that they would have enough room to store any food they scrounged off the land. Out on the plains of Oklahoma and Kansas, food was scarce, water scarcer. Between Val, Aidan, and Alyssa, they figured out that barrel cactus had some water, and yucca did, too. A couple of times they caught ground squirrels. (Not having vorpal teeth like the squirrels back home helped.) The uneaten squirrels hung from cords roped to the lashing points and tool loops on their packs.

Colt was always tired. Everybody was. The wind was constant and pushed against them no matter which direction they turned, as if the gods of the winds were also mad at them, and wanted to make life miserable for them. The wind pierced through the clothes they salvaged off a dead family that was trying to hike north. Colts' clothes were rolled up because they were two sizes too big for him, and Alyssa was worse than the others because the dead teen daughter was wearing nothing but flimsy boy band t-shirts and tiny denim shorts. She completely discarded the denim shorts after the first hour of hiking and put on a pair of the father's hiking pants, which were way too big and long for her, but at least they kept her a little bit warmer.

In the distance that morning, they saw a car on the road. They spent most of the morning walking to it. Colt was the first one to the car. It was an old Chevy Bellaire that looked more like an archaeological find than a good scavenge. Aidan traced his remaining fingers along the car's sharp lines. Colt opened the door, pushed the mummified carcass aside, and started the engine. The car didn't turn over.

"Anybody know how to fix a car?" Aidan asked. He wasn't looking for a response. None of them were mechanics, and that was the problem. Except for Alyssa, they were middle-class kids. The skills they learned growing up, like making waffles in the waffle maker, upgrading iTunes, conquering video games, or anything relevant to pop culture, were no longer applicable to the world they lived in. They had no clue how to fix a car. You want your phone set up, they were your guys. You want to fix a car, call someone else.

On the other side of the car lay a giant dead cow. Its head had been ripped off.

Cautiously they circled the cow. It was completely brown and large.

"I think it's a Hereford," Aidan said.

Its underbelly had been ripped open and gutted. Whatever had been disemboweling the cow had not been able to finish, because most of the meat had been left. Flies buzzed around the carcass, and the stench was unbearable except to those who had been around death as much as they had.

They looked around, trying to figure out what happened. Val looked off to the side of the road, and his eyes narrowed with understanding.

Aidan was about to ask him when suddenly, a massive spike of pain erupted behind his temple. It was so sudden and painful he could barely open his eyes. He felt like when he used to visit the eye doctor, who would shine a bright white light into his eyes. Aidan's eyes began to water, and he kneeled down.

Val and Alyssa stooped down to check on him. Colt pointed to the sky. "I think a roc is coming."

Val said, "Quick, get inside the cow! We gotta get cover before that roc sees us."

This was the life they had lived for the past six months of fleeing or hiding or both. They fled in cars, they fled in numbers, they fled quietly so as not to be seen, or they hid in abandoned homes, downed planes, derailed trains, forgotten restaurants, and animal carcasses. The rocs could see them, the bats could hear them, and most animals could smell them better than they smelled themselves. They had been more lucky than good for six months, and they were lucky then that the roc was not searching for them. They had yet to find a way to kill one of the monstrous abominations easily. Head-on encounters had always led to one of them injured or dead, either directly or indirectly.

This winged beast was the largest roc they had ever seen. Easily, it was twice as large as most rocs. And this one wasn't an eagle. They weren't sure what it was, or rather what it had been, but now it was a black-as-night monster with a thick black beak and eyes dark as coals. Maybe it had been a raven or a vulture. It had four wings. On its back rode a warg. The beast was straddling the roc and sitting upright. It used small kicks and nips to keep the creature moving how it wanted. The creature brought fear with it, and it dispensed fear like a biplane spreading pesticide across fields of crops. It was heading straight for them. Colt started to tear up as it approached, and then he suddenly ran outside, crying, "Don't let it get me!" Val scooped him up and plopped him back into the meat sack. He looked back up. The roc and its rider had turned west. As the roc flew overhead, it turned in the air currents and curved away from them. As it disappeared, they walked out of the carcass.

"What the hell was that?" Alyssa asked without requiring an answer.

"It's the scariest thing I've seen," Colt said, rubbing his eyes.

Val looked back at Aidan. "They are continuing to evolve," he said.

Aidan looked up. Seeing the others, he stood up as if whatever had overcome him was gone.

"What's that?" he asked, and pointed to a mound in the ditch.

Val had seen the mound right before the roc appeared. "They are the remains of people who attacked and killed monsters."

"The monsters struck back?" Colt asked.

"Any human who attacks one of the monsters is killed and skinned. I thought you knew. That's partly why they're after all the survivors from Bridgetown. We killed creatures. We attacked Malifax."

"Did we kill him?"

"Hard to say. The monsters only give the information they want us to know, and they are usually images rather than concrete thoughts the way you or I would think of them. It is sometimes difficult to infer what they want."

"So what happened here?" Aidan asked. "I haven't seen anything like this before. Some people tried to make hamburgers, and wargs got to them?"

"Probably. They skinned them and dropped the bodies in the ditch." Val stopped and scanned the roads. Then he pointed. "See up ahead there? It looks like someone hung flags from the telephone poles, but it isn't. Those are human skins. They are a reminder of what happens to people who break the natural order. If they ever catch us, they will do the same to us."

"Man, it sucks not being the apex predator anymore," Aidan said.

For three hundred yards, they crawled on their bellies like snakes in the grass. They came around the far side of the herd so as not to be downwind of the cattle. All four had binoculars spying on the cattle.

"What do you think?" Val asked.

"I think they're just cows, but it's hard to tell. I've seen longhorns that went monster. Then there were the bats. The bats seemed like normal bats, but clearly they weren't."

"That's what I was thinking, too."

"Are you picking up anything from them?" Aidan asked.

Val shook his head. "No, but then again, what do cows think about? Your head hurting?"

"No. Why?"

"Testing a theory. I think they're just cows, man."

"If you're wrong, it's not like you're wrong on a test. You're like, really wrong. Kill us all wrong."

"Well, if it helps, I was a GT kid."

Aidan looked to Alyssa for support, but she was still watching what they were after, a Ford Taurus.

"The Taurus looks in good shape," she said. "There's no way to be one hundred percent sure, but I think it will work. The tires haven't been slashed, the engine hood isn't propped open, no major dents in the body. I think this is the one."

"Usually when one car is left behind, it's because that's the car everyone took gas from," Aidan said.

"Gas tank lid closed, Captain," Alyssa said.

"Well, we going to watch from the benches or we going to dance with the ladies?" Val asked.

"I wish there was a way to know for sure about these cows," Aidan said.

"You could see if they stampede," Val offered. "I don't think the changed cows would stampede. They're too smart for that. Or at least they'd react somehow."

"Okay, but how do we do it? We'll need a loud noise or something to make a disturbance."

"I can help with that," Colt said, and he scrunched his face up and groaned.

"A fart joke now? Really?" Alyssa asked, disgusted.

All the boys started to giggle, but then Colt pulled out a smoke bomb from his backpack.

"Look at you, Mr. deux ex machina," Val said. "Where did you get that?"

Colt shrugged. "Back at that convenience store when y'all were looking for food, I was looking for something useful. It seemed like something Peter would take, so I grabbed them."

"Good job," Aidan said.

"All we need now is a way to launch them," Val said.

"Easy," Aidan said, "We stuff it up Colt's butt then let him launch one across the fields."

"Another fart joke? It hasn't been ten seconds," Alyssa groaned. "I swear, you'd think that after the apocalypse you guys would have deeper conversations. I bet if you could find porn, you'd sit around jerking off until the wargs came to get you."

Aidan and Val nodded in agreement.

"Hey, guys," Colt said as he pulled a rubber slingshot out of his backpack. "I got one of these, too. I thought we could launch water balloons like we used to back home, but then I realized we didn't have much water out here."

Aidan rubbed his head. "Now that's a Fannin!"

They decided to shoot it into an open part of the field. At first, they looked for easy targets that Colt could shoot at. That left the watering hole and a tree, which were both likely to either put out the fuse or at least catch up all the smoke. So they found an open space between the cows to aim for.

Aidan took one side and Val the other. Colt placed the smoke bomb into the cup and pulled it back. Like he had learned from their time at the house, he leaned way back spread-eagled until he was almost on the floor. Alyssa lit the fuse and kissed him on the cheek. "Good luck."

"Watch your aim," Aidan advised, "and keep the open grass in view."

"Got it," Colt said. He closed one eye, took careful aim, and released the smoke bomb just as it was starting to release smoke.

The bomb arched through the blue sky and landed in the dead wintry grass exactly where they had wanted it to go.

"That was awesome!" Aidan said.

"You, sir, know how to shoot a slingshot," Val said, and high-fived Colt.

Plumes of orange smoke billowed upward. Then the wind caught it and dragged the smoke towards one side of the herd. A cow looked towards it. Flicked its ears and licked its lips. Then it returned to eating the grass.

"Good enough," Aidan said.

They crawled the rest of the distance towards the Taurus, each of them expecting at any moment for a demonic hoof to stomp on them, but it never did. They climbed into the car. The keys had fallen out. They looked around, still waiting for some monster cow to go berserk on them. Nothing.

They picked up the keys and started the engine. It whirred to life with an almost electric hum in that way characterized by so many modern cars.

Nothing.

"I guess some animals didn't turn into monsters," Aidan said as Val drove them up the road. They stopped a mile down the road to put their packs into the trunk. The Taurus was a good car, but not roomy enough for four people and their packs. Now Colt was checking the stations without success, and Aidan was trying to find a comfortable way to sit. Nothing seemed to fit his back well, not even car seats.

"I have a theory about that," Val said. "Only some animals evolved into these demonic versions of the animals we are used to. And then, only a small percentage of the 'evolved' creatures became megafauna."

"You mean like mammoths and sabre-tooth tigers," Aidan said for clarification.

"Right. Some animals are still just animals. It makes sense to me. You can't heavily populate that many large creatures all at once. There aren't enough resources for them."

"But there were enough resources during the ice ages," Alyssa said.

"But he's on to something. You ever notice how some animals just seem to be more intelligent, like the grackles. Other animals are still nothing more than what they were, like the oversized blackbirds we met or those cows back there. Nothing really different. The ground squirrels have also been nothing new. Other creatures like rabbits and dogs and cats were horribly monstrous, but they were all domesticized creatures."

"What about Malifax? " Alyssa asked. "What about that large bat or the dryder? I've never seen anything like that."

"Well, he's on to something with holes in it, but I still think he's on to something," Aidan said.

They drove north all day, only stopping to change direction when they came to towns with upside down elevation signs. (Only in Texas do they give population signs). They had no desire for a repeat of what happened in Austin.

Ulysses was one such town. Seeing the upside down sign, they didn't need to investigate why smoke was rising from within the city limits. Colt, who was now driving, and driving pretty well, put the Taurus in reverse, turned around, and headed back south to Hugotown. They headed northeast.

They stayed in farmhouses if they could. Mostly these were quintessential two-story clapboard farmhouses with rustic furniture and chicken statuary. They checked for living people, but never found any. They checked the silo only once, to a disastrous end that nearly took Colt's life. After that, they left the silos alone. Sometimes the houses had food that hadn't spoiled. Soup was good, tuna better. Vienna sausages and deviled ham was like finding gold.

They slept together in the same room at night. If they could find one, they carried an extra bed into the master bedroom so that Colt could sleep with them. Since losing Mike, and then later Peter leaving, Colt never wanted to be out of eyesight of his only remaining family anymore. This was becoming less tolerable to Aidan and Alyssa, who wanted some privacy.

Val slept in his own room.

Before Kansas, the Taurus ran out of gas, and they couldn't find more to scavenge. They left it on the side of a ditch and out of the way of other potential traffic. Alyssa wrote "NO GAS" in lipstick on the front and rear windows.

In the plains states, they often passed entire fields full of crops that had been devoured by locusts or rotted in the husk. On one road, they walked past a mile of burning fields. In the cold winter wearing scavenged clothes, the heat from the flames felt good. Eventually, the heat got too intense, though, and they had to turn around.

One evening, they came to a farm with corn that was still edible. The owners also had a small garden with gourds of squash and pumpkin that had somehow survived. Since the oven was missing from the house, for reasons none could fathom, they took a cooking pan and placed it on the linoleum, which they turned into their cook pit.

Colt grimaced when he looked at the cooked squash and pumpkin.

"Do I have to?"

"You do if you want corn," Alyssa chided him.

"Creamed asparagus, canned beats, squash, and pumpkin. It's like all the Moms in the world created the apocalypse just to make me eat my vegetables. I'm not a kid anymore!" he yelled to nobody in particular. "I want to eat what I want!"

Aidan smiled at his younger brother and wondered that the mention of parents did not sting him. It was like this after all tragedies, he supposed. There was a time period when everyone mourned, and then there came a time when people accepted the reality of the world as forever changed. Then true acceptance came when you realized you didn't think about how different life was without them and you didn't think about the empty spaces they should be taking up anymore. They had blurred into the background. Was he "getting over" the loss of his parents? The thought made him feel guilty.

Eventually, Colt went along with Alyssa and Aidan's prodding him to eat the vegetables, although not without throwing a few moans, and pretending like eating cooked squash was worse than being fed to roc chicks.

Val came into the kitchen with thick curtains in his hands. "Somebody must have stolen the blankets from this house. I took the liberty of pulling the curtains. We can use them for blankets tonight."

With full bellies, they fell sound asleep under the curtains.

Early in the night, Val, who had the first watch, knocked quietly on the bedroom door and came inside.

"You gotta see this," he said.

They walked out under the porch. All the lights were out in the world, so the stars shone brightly. Orion was still not up yet. Val pointed to the wide, flat horizon. Small glowing objects were floating across the sky. They were going too slow to scare, and as they approached, it became obvious what they were: jellyfish, so light they were carried by air currents.

Soon the sky was lit up with dozens of soft-glowing effervescent lights with long tentacles that drifted through the air, too high up to reach anyone. Most of the jellyfish bodies were no bigger than a full-backed office chair, though some were as large as cars, and the smallest ones were as small as baseballs. They grabbed their phones and started taking pictures.

"They're beautiful," Alyssa said as she snapped her photo. Most of the creatures she had seen over the past six months were demonic or at least zombie-like. These animals were almost angelic.

"They are so low to the ground, it's like I could grab them," Val said.

"I've never seen anything like it," Aidan said.

"What do you think they're doing?" Colt wanted to know.

"Hell if I know. There is so little we know about this new world. Case in point: jellyfish fly," Aidan said. After a second of thinking about Colt's question, he said, "Migrating? Like birds?"

The jellyfish drifted along like peaceful bubbles swept along by air currents. In that way, they were like a living aurora borealis, and just as mesmerizing.

That night they slept together in the same room. They slept peacefully in awe and wonder at the beautiful miracle they had witnessed.

The early morning sun felt good on Val's face, even if it was a cold winter's blaze. He picked an ear of corn off a broken stalk and ripped off the husk. The corn was good.

"Not everything is bad, I guess," Val said to himself as he dropped the golden ear of corn into his pack. He looked from the middle of the cornfield to the farmhouse and thought of Alyssa, Aidan, and Colt still asleep. He didn't care for Aidan very much. He could lead fine, and he was great for apocalyptic events, but he was too grim. The guy needed to lighten up. But Alyssa was still very much the girl he had always dreamed about, though he was certain she did not share those feelings.

The stalks here were broken up, as if somebody tried to drive a pick-up through the corn. Mashed stalks and husks were flattened in the mud. Val kneeled down to examine some of the stalks. The corn was a waste. That much was obvious.

Then he saw something printed in the mud that made his heart start beating like a piston. He inhaled sharply and jumped into the corn stalks.

Once in the stalks, Val froze and listened intently. Then he heard what was driving his fear. It was the footfall of something heavy. It had stopped, too.

Val dropped his pack and ran for the house, stepping over the fresh warg tracks as he ran.

Aidan had woken up with his head full of white hot light. From the first floor, he heard the door slam open and Val coming running up the stairs.

"Let's go!"

Aidan looked at Val darkly as he picked up his pack.

"Your head's hurting," Val said as he went to the windows.

"Is it that obvious?"

"We have to hurry. We must leave immediately." Val looked out the window to the cornfield.

"What are you doing?" Alyssa said.

"Searching for a confirmation I hoped never to find." Then a few stalks of corn waved.

"They're in the corn," Val said. "They're coming. We must be leaving."

The rest went to the windows, too. Something was definitely moving in the corn, brushing against some stalks and knocking down others. Two separate trails of trampled corn curled through the field.

"They finally found us," Aidan said.

"Who?" Alyssa asked.

"Wargs." The word sent a shiver down Alyssa's spine.

As one of the black beasts left the cornfield and neared the farmhouse, he stood up into bipedal form. His knees and spine seemed to lock into place for the different range of movement required for walking upright. Out from behind him stepped a man who was dressed in camouflage and a vest that at one time had been bright orange but was now faded and covered in blood and shit. For a brief second, the warg stared at the man, then pointed to the house.

"What is it with us and wargs and houses?" Aidan growled. "C'mon, it's time to go."

They grabbed their packs and rushed downstairs. By the time they got to the foyer, they could see the hunter approaching the front porch.

"We could kill him," Val said.

"We kill him, and the warg will know."

"Maybe we could reason with him."

"He's just a beagle chasing foxes. Let's go out the back. Maybe we can avoid him there."

They stepped quietly, yet urgently across the linoleum. Aidan was the last to exit the house, closing the back door just as the hunter entered through the front.

The hunter walked slowly up the stairs and saw the mattress that had been added to the room. He put his hand on it, then went back downstairs, where he could see last night's fire on the kitchen floor.

The hunter walked back out front and pointed the warg to the back. The warg lifted its nose in the wind. It took a step, extended its nose into the air, and took a second sniff. Then it howled balefully. The sound seemed to fill the open Kansas sky.

"Shit!" Aidan cursed. They were running towards the barn.

Please let there be a fast car in the barn, he thought as they crossed the dirt driveway. *And please let it be automatic.* Val reached the barn first. He flung open the door and ran inside. The barn was empty save for a giant John Deere.

"Damnit!" Aidan cursed again. He could hear Peter in his ear telling him there was no need to swear. *Fuck you*, he yelled back to the Peter who only existed in his head.

A long warehouse building extended from behind the barn. They ran inside, but not before the hunter saw Aidan closing the door. As the hunter made for the barn, the warg came up along the side of the house. The warg looked at the hunter and then kept running towards the far side of the building.

Slowly, the hunter entered the warehouse.

The inside of the warehouse showed it to have been a giant pig farming operation. Four rows of pens stretched to the opposite side of the warehouse. The air was fetid with six-month-old pig crap.

"I don't want no trouble," the hunter yelled into the warehouse through a thick drawl. "Come out, and we kin help each other."

He took a few more steps into the warehouse. When nobody answered, he cursed, then started checking methodically through all the pens.

"Here, piggy, piggy, piggy," the hunter cooed. "You cain't run forever," he added. "Eventually, if they want you, they'll get you."

He was searching at a brisk pace now. He could see into the surrounding pens pretty easily.

"You's just kids," he said. "Rightly scared because of all that's happened. Come with us, and we kin end the fear. You no longer gotta hide in abandoned farmhouses and pigshit."

He finished the row and started down the next aisle. "Fucking kids," he mumbled.

A giant boot came swinging down from above and landed in the hunter's face. Then Aidan helped Alyssa down. The other two jumped off the support beams.

They started running towards the back, but then a shadow of a warg appeared against the far wall. They ran out the way they came.

Alyssa was the first outside. A warg grabbed her in its paws.

"No!" Aidan shouted. The warg raised its open jaw to her head, but it did not bite down. It watched to see their reaction.

"Put your pack down," Val translated for the visions in his head. "It wants us to put our packs down."

Aidan dropped his where he stood while the others unbuckled their packs. The second warg came up behind them.

"Now follow me, single-file," Val instructed, and he walked slowly towards the road. Aidan and Colt, who could not see what Val saw, followed him down the driveway and to the road. In the road stood a box that was made of crisscrossed pine nailed together. It was tall on the ends and not big enough to hold more than a few people.

A hand reached out from one of the holes and spread its fingers. Alyssa jumped when she saw the hand. "Aidan, I'm claustrophobic."

"I know. Me, too."

The wargs lifted each of the lost boys and dropped them into the cell. Colt nearly cracked his skull against the boards. The rest were flung on top of him. There was barely enough room to move around in the narrow cell. There was less room once the hunter with his black eye was placed inside the cell with them.

"You try anything," he told them, "and they'll know. They'll kill you. I'm important to them cause I help them find low-lifes like you. They won't hesitate to kill you to save me."

"We get it," Aidan snapped back, stopping the hunter from saying anything more.

There was a small blond man in the back of the cell. His face was ashen and his eyes drawn tight, like he had been in a constant battle with death for weeks or months. He didn't say anything. Only maneuvered himself so that they could get more room.

Aidan watched the warg through the breaks in the wood. It pulled a cart out of the woods and lifted the wooden prison up onto the cart. Then the warg went back into its four-legged position and began pulling the cart.

A minute later, the companion warg emerged from a line of crops with a second cart with an additional box on top of it. Aidan saw one pale hand hanging out of the prison, but it didn't move.

Even in the cold of winter, the cell was poorly ventilated and steaming hot from all the body perspiration. The lost boys stuck their hands out just for the chance to feel flowing air.

The cart bumped and bounced as the wargs took them west, stopping at every farmhouse to look for more people. The hunter helped them find two more people in another abandoned farmhouse. Every time, he walked out to the house, tried to placate the people, try to convince them to come out. If they did, the wargs snatched them. It was easier for the wargs that way.

"I really hate that guy," Aidan said as the hunter yelled to the wargs that he had found more people.

If the cell was crowded before, they were packed as smuggled parrots in the back of a delivery truck once the additional two were dropped into the cell. As they were flung into the cage, they landed on the lost boys. Aidan and Val pushed them up on their feet. The two new people were an older couple in their thirties that looked in pretty bad shape. The way their clothes drooped off their emaciated bodies, the way they were covered in wounds, and the way their jaws kind of hung from their heads – Aidan thought they looked like zombies.

After the zombies were upright, the hunter was placed back inside. Alyssa stood between him and Aidan. Then things got bad.

About two hours later, Aidan somehow started to drowse off despite the cramped quarters and the pain in his head, leaning against the side of the cell. He awoke to Alyssa elbowing him and saying, "Get off me!"

Aidan saw the hunter with his arm around Alyssa. Aidan didn't think. He reached around her and wrapped his fingers around the hunter's throat. Suddenly, the cart stopped.

"Aidan, stop!" Alyssa shouted. She pulled his hands off the man's throat. His face was already starting to turn blue.

The warg opened the top of the crate and looked around. Nobody moved except the hunter, who was gasping for air. The warg growled and snapped at Aidan.

"That's one," Val said as the top of the cell was slammed shut and the door locked. "There won't be a two."

"You punk ass kid," the hunter gasped. Red marks blotted his neck once the blue went away. "You punk ass kid," he said again once the cart started off. "I own this place, and if I want some hot, young, Latin pussy, it's mine. Try to stop me, and they'll kill you."

"I don't mind dying," Aidan said, "but I will kill you first."

Aidan glared at the hunter with such extreme hatred, the hunter had to look away, but not before saying, "You'll learn. Wait till we get back. You'll learn."

Aidan, Val, and Colt maneuvered themselves into a wall between Alyssa and the hunter. The hunter turned away and stretched his hand out into the open air. Aidan didn't stop burning two eyeholes through the hunter's head.

Eventually, they all turned to face forward again. It just seemed natural to look forward. They peeked through the cracks and watched the land pass them as they bounced and jittered across the open plains.

At nightfall, the wargs came together and dropped the carts. They fell asleep on the ground. Aidan and the others had to sleep pretty much leaning against each other. The cell stunk really badly. The new couple had yet to make a sound. Through a seam in the crowded cell, he noticed they were at least holding hands now.

Aidan woke in the middle of the night to the feel of warm wetness running down his leg. When he looked up, the hunter sneered down at him and said, "Fuck. You." Then he zipped his pants back up. Aidan started to kick him, but the glint in the hunter's eye made him think better.

"C'mon, hot head. Try to take me. The dogs'll get you, and then I'll get me that nice Latin pussy you got. I been dreaming 'bout her. I bet she's tight, ain't she?"

Val put his hand on the hunter's shoulder and looked down at him. He said, "There are four of us and one of you. If the first one doesn't get you, the others will. That's not a threat. I'm just telling you how it is. Your days are numbered."

The hunter laughed out loud, but his eyes belied his fear. "You bitch," he said to Val. The lost boys laughed, but of course, the man didn't know why.

The man shut up and went back to sleep. He woke early, though, and started mumbling about all the unspeakable things he wanted to do to Alyssa. He no longer looked at them. He stared out his hole in the cell, but he asked about her birthmarks and her taste and talked about how he wanted her to have hard nipples because he liked hard nipples.

"How is the headache?" Val asked Aidan, trying to change the subject.

"It's more like a dull pain than a sharp one now."

They weren't fed in the morning, and Colt complained that he had to go to the bathroom. The hunter laughed when he heard this. "There's no potty breaks or rest stops on this road trip, kiddo, so you got to go, go!"

By noon the next day, the cell stunk of piss and shit. The stink was so permeating that Val started to wretch, but there was nothing in his gut except a little stomach acid, which he spit onto the floor in front of him.

The hard part was getting used to the dead bodies. At some point in the night, the ashen-faced blond died, and so did the couple. They passed from this world hand-in-hand. Their corpses leaned against Val and Colt and Alyssa. Colt wanted to cry, but he looked at Aidan, who was watching the hunter, and he pushed back his tears.

The hunter kept rambling about Alyssa's body, but he didn't stop there. He talked about someone named Eliza, who may have been his sister, but was now most likely dead. He talked about the woods and the squirrels and deer and all the things he was going to hunt, like that Latin pussy, which was a phrase he was using more and more often. He also talked about the beasts and about how they talked to him. How aliens talked to him. How balloons talked to him.

"I think he's lost his marbles," Val said when the hunter fell asleep.

"You wonder why people like him didn't die off," Aidan said.

Alyssa wanted to roll her eyes at Aidan, but she didn't feel much like defending some nasty little bug who fantasized about raping her.

Suddenly, Colt grabbed Alyssa's arm. "They're alive!" he gasped. "I felt them moving!"

Colt half-crawled on his friends, causing the bodies to fall forward. Aidan, Val, and Alyssa looked behind them. They saw the dead bodies with stretched arms and clenched jaws. Their bodies looked tight.

"Shhhh," Alyssa placated Colt. "They're not alive. It's rigormortis." They tried to position Colt closer to the front but couldn't do much better. He spent the rest of the night trying not to pay attention to the dead limbs pushing up against him. Before they arrived at the camp the next day, though, the muscles in the bodies had relaxed and the appendages returned to their normal dragging state.

"We're here," the hunter announced. "Home sweet home. The deep black heart of hell."

When the cart stopped, they looked out the holes to see where they were. All they could see was mud and debris and pens. This may have been an old base, or a school district's bus coral. There were buses in the background.

The warg opened the top of the cage and pulled the hunter out.

"She comes with me," he said hungrily to the wargs and pointing to Alyssa. "She comes with me. She comes with me." Then he flipped off Aidan.

The warg closed the locked door. Then it opened it again and snatched Alyssa.

"No!" Aidan screamed. He grabbed onto her leg, but she kicked him.

"Don't!" she warned him. "I want you alive."

Aidan screamed as Alyssa disappeared out of the cage. Val and Colt tried to console him, but he shoved the cage until it nearly toppled over.

"You've got to stop it," Val said. "She didn't want it this way."

Aidan sobbed.

The next time the cage was opened, another warg sniffed at the dead bodies, grimaced, then pulled the three out of the cage. It placed them on the ground. In all from the other cages, ten people stood in a line surrounded by wargs and other humans.

"There are more people helping the beasts," Aidan growled. He spit at one of them.

"Calm down or you'll get us all killed," Val hissed. "They are just like the hunter. Like my father."

Aidan wanted to say something reassuring to Val, but being out of the cage, all he wanted to do was fall down and go to sleep. With Alyssa gone, all the anger gave out in him, and his body was left with nothing to support it. It took every ounce of control to force himself to stay upright. He barely had the concentration to look around the prison camp, which was mostly blurry to him now, so in need of food and rest was he.

Even though every muscle in his legs wanted him to lie down and pass out, Aidan forced himself to stay upright. Being out of the cage at least gave him a chance to get a better look around.

They had arrived at a prison camp at the base of the Rocky Mountains. Men like the hunter walked the perimeters. They had guns. Chain-link fences and barbwire surrounded makeshift cages and pens. Aidan looked for a way out, but the only exit seemed to be through the line of wargs relaxing at one side of the camp. A single fire was burning to keep the wargs warm in the cold.

Colt tugged on Aidan's sleeve. Aidan followed Colt's eyes to a large warg with a scarred, hairless face. The large warg was inspecting all the new prisoners. When the large warg looked at the people in line, he bared his rows of long, toothy black fangs.

A pit sunk in Aidan's stomach.

"We're dead," he said. He looked down at his feet before Black Fang could see him. Colt followed suit.

"What's wrong?" Val wanted to know.

"Old acquaintance. That warg with the scarred face knew us back when we were living in Lakewood."

"You're the one he wants?" Val almost exclaimed too loudly. "Ever since we got close to camp, that warg has been painting my mind with some really ugly pictures of what he wants to do to the people he's been tracking. He's been searching for you for a long time."

"But he doesn't remember what we look like?"

"The images aren't clear, but then again, they're emotional. Images are rarely clear when they are colored with so much hate. Hey, I have something to tell you."

Aidan turned around and Val decked him hard, with all the weight of his body thrown into it. He hit him so hard it hurt his hand. The guards started to react, but Val said, "Finally got that one out of me." So they stopped and went back to their posts.

Aidan got up, his hand to his face.

"Let's see it," Val said, and he pulled back Aidan's hand. Val grimaced. Already the eye was turning discolored and starting to swell. "That's a good shiner."

"What the hell, Val?"

"You can thank me after my disguise works."

Aidan reached down and dug his hands into the snow. His nine fingers pushed into cold black earth. Not for the first time, he wished he had his missing digit. Always with an eye to the wargs, he tightened his grip and pulled up two fistfuls of mud.

Suddenly a warg snapped at him, knocking him over. He dropped the mud he was carrying. When he stood back up, he smeared Colt's face with what little mud he still had between his fingers.

The line pushed forward. A person from the front screamed. The line pushed forward again, and another person screamed. Some people in line were beginning to cry.

Aidan got a glimpse of what was going on.

"Don't worry, Colt," Aidan said. "They're just branding us."

"What?"

"Think of it as a tattoo. You've always wanted a tattoo, right?"

"No."

"No? Okay. Just stay calm, then. The more you struggle, the worse you will make it. It'll be over quickly."

They got to the front of the line. Val was first. He groaned as the mark was placed on his forehead. Then it was Colt's turn, and all Aidan could think about was how much he wished he could save Colt. He didn't deserve this. He should be living a life full of games and running and homework.

"Lord," Aidan said, then stopped. He had long ago given up bartering with God. He cussed under his breath, and then one of the human captors pushed him forward.

He came face-to-face with the monster that had killed his friends, the monster who had been tracking them for months.

Black Fang stared right at him. Aidan's headache spiked in his head. He winced at the pain.

Black Fang reached for him. Placed his awful, stinking hand around Aidan's head, and brushed away the smudges and the grease with his thumb. Aidan knew this was the end. Black Fang stared closely at the boy's black eye and scarred face. Even gave him a second pass. Then his other hand came up, and Aidan felt the warg's claw cut him first up from the base of his right temple. The cut arched across Aidan's forehead. Then he made another cut at the bottom of the first cut, swiping across his cheek. Aidan gritted his teeth. The feeling in his face was hot like lava and knives. Something in the warg's cut continued to burn even after he had been branded.

Black Fang tossed him aside.

In the pens, everyone had similar crosses on their faces. Colt ran up and hugged him. Val pulled them aside. They found a

174

piece of open dirt among the other prisoners and huddled up together. Tired and hungry, they fell asleep.

Aidan awoke to the feeling of something cold being pressed against his black eye and the right side of his face. He had no strength to stop whatever was happening. It made him dreadful of what must be happening to Alyssa. If he had no strength to stop someone from putting something against his face, how would she deal with an insane man?

The entire right side of his face was swollen. He couldn't see out of his eye. He turned his face. His dad was pressing snow against his face. What was his dad doing here? He was saying something in a language Aidan didn't understand. Then he passed out again.

Somewhere in the bowels of the night, Aidan woke up. A tarp had been placed over him and the others. Gently, he stood up. His entire body was stiff, and his back was killing him. He had never fully recovered from the tiller running up and down his back, though it had seemed so long ago. He wasn't sure it ever would. He couldn't go get physical therapy for it or take pills to stop the pain. Val and Colt were already awake. They were playing rock-paper-scissors but stopped when Aidan woke.

"What's up?" Val asked.

"Hallucinating."

"'Bout what?"

He looked at Colt and said, "The past, I guess."

Together, they walked around the pen in the moonlight while everyone else slept. Aidan looked up at the starry sky and wondered briefly about his brother, Peter, and Jax and Riley. He hoped they fared better than he did.

"I could gnaw a warg I'm so damn hungry," Aidan said. "This is a miserable place."

"Glad to see you cheerful again, Aidan. I was worried you might be depressed."

"Where's the food?"

"There is none."

"Well, then."

"Look, I'm not going to babysit your dark side like Peter. If you want food, go find it. Otherwise, I thought we'd talk about more pressing matters."

"Like Alyssa?"

"Alyssa is in another pen, and I wish there was something we could do for her, but I don't even know where she is, so no, that isn't what I was going to suggest talking about."

"Black Fang."

"Yes. The beasts have a different name for him. I don't know how to say it, but it basically translates to 'Keeper of the Kingdom' or 'Warden of the West.' Still, most people refer to him as Black Fang. There is something else we must talk about."

"What?"

"Lower your voice."

Val pulled Aidan away from the nearest people, which was a group that was huddled up so close to each other for warmth that they were like layers of clothes dropped on top of each other.

"Black Fang doesn't know you are the one he's looking for," Val whispered. "And nobody can know it, either. They would surely betray us."

"How would anyone know? To them, I'm just another kid with no parents."

Val shook his head. "You and Colt cannot receive their psychic projections. That makes you different, and different around here is a dangerous thing."

"So what do we do?"

"I will talk for you. If I talk enough, people may think I'm crazy like that hunter. They will think I talk just to talk."

"That's ludicrous. You can't keep that up forever."

"How long do you think you can go before Black Fang remembers you?"

"Not long. Maybe when he wakes up, maybe a day from now or ten or twenty days from now, but yeah, eventually, he will put the two together. The monsters are smarter than they ever were as animals. He'll figure it out."

"And then what?"

"We need to be gone before then. First, though, I need some food. I don't think I've eaten in three days."

They turned to walk away, and they saw a young black woman no older than them with her bright eyes open and staring at them. She was rail-thin and had long, wild hair. She was lying in the pile with her other friends or family members, wrapped in tarps and trying to stay warm.

Aidan started to approach her. He wasn't sure what to do next. She must have heard their conversation. She must know who he was and that he was valued by the enemy.

"Your secret is safe with me," she whispered.

"How do I know?"

"Because I haven't screamed for them. Believe me; it will take less than a thought to reveal your identity."

Aidan glowered. After a moment, he came to a conclusion and stuck out his hand. "Aidan."

"Dre." They shook hands, and then looked at each other for a minute.

"I'm going back to sleep. Don't kill me in my sleep," she said.

"Ditto."

When next he awoke, it was midday again. He opened his eyes and his stomach growled. Lying across the pen was an object that looked like a broken leg bone.

"I think it's going to be awhile, so you might as well shut up," he told his stomach.

On either shoulder slept Val and Colt. They were curled up like balls next to his wide frame. He was getting hot under the tarp, so he stood up. They both complained to him, so he gave the tarp back and walked around a bit.

An old man who was speaking some kind of Asian language waved to him, and Aidan realized this was the man who helped him the first night, the man he had hallucinated as his father. Aidan bowed and said, "Thank you," before moving on.

Next to a cluster of open pens lay several gallon jugs lined up in a row. Some were empty and some were full of water. Nobody was watching over them, so Aidan went and picked up one of the jugs and lifted it to his mouth.

"Careful," Dre said, coming up beside him. "Some of the Renfields come by and fill the tanks back up every week or so. For kicks, they poison the water every once in a while, so you never want to drink until somebody else has had a drink."

"Thanks. I'll remember that." He drank deeply anyway. If he died, he died. He was thirsty. The water was ice cold.

"Another word of advice: always stay wrapped up." She tossed Aidan a black headscarf. "Last thing we need is a Renfield recognizing you."

"Renfield? Like Dracula, right? That's cool."

"I don't think anything's been *cool* since the world turned upside-down, but if that's the word you want to use, fine. Another thing. Don't talk to anyone. Avoid the people who twitch. They've already eaten, and they will likely eat again."

"They don't feed us?"

"The dire dogs? For fun, they will regurgitate into those metal buckets over there. When you are hungry enough, you will try to keep it down, but it will be hard."

"So what's their play? What do they intend to do with us?"

Dre shrugged. "They just make sure we stay in here and don't escape. At most, sometimes they select people to torture. If that happens, don't look them in the eye. Dire dogs hate it when people look them in the eye. It's a challenge, and one they're too eager to take."

"Where are you from, Dre?"

"OKC. You?"

"Houston."

"You've come a long way to hell, man."

"No. Hell's been following us. It nested with us back home, and it's been tracking us ever since."

"How long you been out there?"

"A couple of months, maybe. We were picked up maybe three days ago, but I could be wrong. I've been told I lose track of time."

"And you've been out on your own all this time? Amazing. We've been here since August. It's been hard, but you learn to get by. Then it just becomes monotony. Is it true there are cities still open? Tell me about Houston."

"Houston, Austin, San Angelo. It's all dead."

"I've heard that Seattle and Denver and Toronto are still human-owned. I was hoping that maybe you'd seen places."

"Sorry, Dre, none that were safe. They were occupied by bats or rocs or wargs – what you call dire dogs."

"Bats and Rocs?"

"That's a long story."

Then he heard her voice, coming from across the pens. He ran to the chain link fence. His eyes teared up as he searched across the walkway to the other set of pens. All he saw were clumps of people. He was beginning to think he had only hallucinated her voice. Then he heard it again. It was preceded by a large slap. Hearing that sound made his heart break, and anger welled up inside him.

"Don't you look at me like that again! Watch me – I will tear you apart if you look at me like that one more time. And when I say food, I don't mean maggots or some damn warg vomit. What the hell's wrong with you? Co-mi-da, entiendes?"

But was that…?

Across the pens people moved, and suddenly the image opened up to him. He saw Alyssa. Other than a mark by her ear, she looked well. Better than well. The rest of the lost boys looked like withering bones, but she had been eating since she arrived. Alyssa was setting her incendiary eyes on the crazy hunter, who was scampering away from her on all knees.

"Yes, Miss. I'm sorry, Miss," he said. "I'll go look for some more food."

"If you can't bring us meat, don't come back!" she shouted after him.

Aidan broke out in laughter. Dre had no idea what was going on. Aidan's laughter rolled from him deeply. It kept coming, and his eyes were tearing up now from it. He had to put his four-fingered hand on the pen to keep himself standing.

Alyssa heard the laughter, and she approached the chain link fence, flashing her crooked smile.

"I should have known," Aidan said as he wiped tears from his eyes.

Dre just stared at the strange woman who stood across from the pens looking like an Aztec goddess full of beauty and death. "Who the hell is that?"

"That's the woman of my dreams," Aidan said.

Alyssa grabbed the fence and shook it.

"I miss you!" she shouted jubilantly. Then, "I love you!"

"I love you, too!" he shouted back.

"I'm okay!"

"I see that."

"You've got to stay hidden, Aidan. They're looking for you."

As if on cue, Aidan's head began to hurt. Instinctively, he pulled the headscarf over his face to protect himself and took a few steps back in time for a roc to land in the muddy space between the pens. A warg climbed off and snapped his whip at Alyssa. A red line arched across her arm, and she backed away.

The warg turned to look for Aidan, but he was gone.

Chapter Ten – Brave

In the prison camp, Colt sat on a stack of pallets overlooking the pens. He touched the scab on his face where Black Fang marked him. He didn't have a mirror to see what he looked like, but he guessed it was as gruesome as everyone else, so at least he fit in.

Colt wondered if there were any other kids his age in the camp. He hadn't seen any yet, but that didn't mean they weren't there. He hadn't seen many children at all since Black Friday. There were a couple at Bridgetown, but he didn't have a chance to meet them before the bridge was torn into pieces.

He hopped off the pallet and decided to go search for more teens his age.

"Where you going?" Val asked.

"Nowhere," he said lightly as he walked out into the mud and the snow.

"If you find any food, let me know," Val said.

Colt walked around the camp for hours. The camp wasn't very long or wide. It was mostly a bunch of fences chained together with guards watching them from the outside. Inside, people were huddled together to keep warm. Sometimes he found a stray tarp – he guessed that was how they got covered the night they came in – a generous hand placed the tarp on them while they lay sleeping.

Then Colt heard a playful noise, the kind of noise that tugs at the heartstrings of all people, especially the younger generations. He followed that noise like it was the sound of an ice cream truck on a hot July day. He was walking, then jogging, then running to find it, a big jack o' lantern grin on his face. Colt pressed his face and his fingers against the chain link face and watched, his heart full of love and desire.

The warg pups were not more than a few weeks old. They were like giant balls of fuzz with wet noses and happy eyes. The puppies were no more than 30 pounds, fur and all. They tussled and tramped on each other and pulled on each other's ears.

Colt wanted one. He didn't care if they were the harbingers of doom or murderers of civilization. He wanted one. He just did. And despite everything he had been through – the maiming by Cthulhu, the running, the hiding, the constant fear of death from all animals, especially wargs – he still longed for a puppy companion.

In Colt's mind, he had a black dog, just like the warg puppies he was watching, and together they would take on all the monsters this new world threw at them. They would be best friends and great warriors and they would never leave each other's side, ever. He would do anything to keep the puppy fed and watered and cared for. He would brush its fur and its teeth and feed him all his scraps.

A shadow came up behind him.

"Hey," Aidan said.

"Hey," Colt sighed.

Aidan waited for Colt, but he didn't want to stop watching the giant puppies.

"Sorry, bro, but we don't live in a world where you can get that puppy in the window anymore."

"I know," he grumbled more than he intended.

"C'mon. I think we found some food. Val has it."

Colt watched the puppies play-fight for a moment longer, then forced himself to walk away. It was like ripping his heart out.

Back with Val, he handed them some pine needles he scrounged out of the dirt.

"There isn't much to them, but I remember from one of those survival shows that if you boil them in water, they have Vitamin C in them and at least a few calories."

"How are we going to boil them?"

"Our new friend Dre and her family have let us borrow their pot. (I didn't tell them I was going to boil water – I don't want anyone to steal our food.) I got a couple of gallons of jug water. Now all I need to do is get a fire going. Unfortunately, I have nothing to spark. If we still had our packs, I would have matches, but we don't. Maybe we should eat the needles raw."

Nobody liked that idea.

Aidan looked around. To Colt, he said, "Go get a couple of those bricks."

Then Aidan peeled some strips of wood from the pallets. He also broke down one pallet into tinder and small sticks. In the same pallet, he found a single, non-rusted nail. It was galvanized, and still shiny. He bloodied his fingers removing it. Then he balled up the kindling and placed it between the bricks.

He looked up at the sky. The sun was almost directly overhead.

"Perfect."

He wiped off the nail and played with it for a minute or two. When he got the reflection right, he waited for the first puffs of smoke.

Val and Colt smiled when the fire started. Aidan blew on the smoking bits, then placed some larger sticks on the fire. Val dropped the pine needles in the pot and placed it to boil.

"What are you doing?" Dre asked as she came running up to them. She looked at the long trail of smoke as if it was diseased. Others were coming behind her. Dre kicked over the pot and stamped out the fire. The pine needles were ground into the dirt.

"Hey! That was dinner!" Val accused.

"The one thing they don't tolerate is fire," Dre said. "No humans, not even the Renfields, are allowed to use fire. Only the dires get to use it."

"C'mon, cut us a break," Aidan said.

"Do you think in the middle of winter all this wood would be left lying around unused if fire were tolerated?"

Just then, two wargs jumped the fences. Human prisoners scattered. Aidan pulled his scarf up, but a warg snatched it off his face. The warg nosed him hard enough to push him back against the fence. The beast snarled, the hackles on its back raising. Val and Colt were shoved beside Aidan.

Dre thought she was clear and that the wargs had forgotten about her. She walked away hurriedly, but then a warg stopped her and sniffed the ash on her boots. It shoved her with the others.

"Walk towards the gates," Val said. Colt and Aidan followed him and Dre. They were taking him right back to Black Fang. This time, Aidan was sure the 'Warden of the West' would remember him.

Alyssa stood on top of a shack and watched her dearest loved ones being escorted away by wargs.

"What is going to happen to them?" she asked the hunter, whose name she came to understand through his schizophrenic ramblings was Brandon Buckner.

He tried to ignore her. "Cause I don't want to talk to her, Eliza," he mumbled.

Alyssa had no patience for him. "Don't you ignore me, Mr. Buckner," she said with a condescending tone.

"Fine! They's gone to be taken back to the Black Fang. He's gone take care of them for good. Burn they's bellies wide open. The nine-fingered boy's gone get special treatment, though."

"What do you mean, special treatment?"

"I'm not gone tell."

"Chinga to madre, digame o I'm going to put my boot so far up your culo you won't be able to take a shit for a year, Mr. Buckner!"

Mr. Buckner frowned and said darkly, "That boy's gone wish he was dead. They is gone to make him die from the inside out. You be able to hear him screaming for weeks."

She stood high and looked around for a solution. She had to free them. But there was nothing here but pens, palettes, and shacks. There had to be a way.

"C'mon," she said as she got down off the shack.

The hunter followed behind her, cursing to himself.

She marched past the denizens of the pens and searched from one side to the other, looking for any way to escape or help them out. People who knew her moved aside to let her pass. She heard a few of them whisper her nickname here. She wasn't proud of it, but it was an identity she was willing to take on if it kept her alive. "Bitch of the Yard," someone muttered as she shoved through a crowd. Maybe she was supposed to have come in here to be abused by a mentally unstable species traitor, a "Renfield" as they called him. Like she would let that happen. Most people here were afraid to take charge, and she didn't like doing it either, but somebody had to, and if that meant she had to ruffle some tail feathers and piss a few people off, fine. She was willing to do it. Had she not found ways to deliver food to the children and the weak since she arrived a few short days ago? There was soup now and actual blankets because of how she had manipulated the previous man running the joint, Mr. Buckner. So Bitch of the Yard she could live with.

At the back of the pens, she found her answer.

"Do they work?" she asked Mr. Buckner.

"Righteously," he replied.

Alyssa looked at the big yellow school buses and smiled her crooked smile.

Ten of them were taken in front of Black Fang.

"Be brave," Val said. "The plan is to torture us tonight until we die. This is their version of evening entertainment. Don't show any fear, and don't look at them, or you will be the first to be tortured."

A warg snapped at Val to be quiet while they were marched back into the open.

Aidan thought of running, but where? He had nowhere to go and no energy to get him there. And even if he had energy and a plan, there was still his brother to save and Alyssa left in the other pen. He wasn't leaving without them. He wished he could see her one more time, hold her in his arms, and feel her warmth.

Colt's fingers twined with Aidan's. "Don't leave me," Colt said.

"Never."

With great fear, Colt realized that the evening games had already begun. A body lay split in half on the ground. The warg puppies were running back and forth with strings of intestines in their mouths, happy to play in the dismemberment like dogs with chew toys.

Colt gripped Aidan's hand tighter and fought back his gag reflex. Aidan thought of killing Colt right there. He looked for any sort of weapon nearby like a pipe or a glass. He would spare his brother the pain and suffering with a single slice to the throat or blow to the head. To his despair, he saw nothing he could use.

A large fire was lit in the middle of the open area and maintained by a warg, and to the side was a long flatbed that Aidan hadn't seen before. Black Fang and the rest of his pack lay by the warm fire and watched the ten being marched up onto the flatbed. Once they were in position, the wargs began ripping their clothes off them. The winter cold stung their skins. When they were stripped naked, Black Fang stood up.

Val and the others shirked.

"Oh, my God. The images he is showing. Oh my God!"

Colt and Aidan pretended to shirk, too. Like the others, they were looking down.

Aidan could feel something tugging at the back of his head. Like a cord was wrapped to his brain and being pulled. He followed that cord back, and suddenly, he was seeing what the others saw: people murdered in all sorts of atrocities. But this wasn't just for fun. This was how they did it. Black Fang was showing them how they destroyed the world. City by city, he saw the animals turning monstrous and then turning on their masters. He saw armies fall and bombs explode. He saw nations crumble. This wasn't just America. This was worldwide, and though the animals changed, the people did not. Sometimes it was tigers or jackals or elephants or snakes, but mostly it was the same: dogs and cats and domesticated animals. Goats and pigs and cattle and horses.

One face appeared over and over in his mind, that of the warg with the burned face and the rows of blackened fangs. As the images slowed like the stills in an old-fashioned projector, Aidan opened his eyes and looked at Black Fang. There was no denying it. The Warden of the West knew these were the ones he had been after for so long.

Black Fang stood up on four legs from where he was lying. With revulsion, Aidan realized it was a throne of body parts. Hands and legs and faces fell from under him.

His knees popped, and suddenly Black Fang was standing on two legs. He crossed the muddy field to the flat bed. He had grown since they saw him three months ago in their subdivision. He was thicker now, and matted. And there was something else, something so undeniably insane that Aidan didn't want to admit it at first, but as the warg came up to him and he could get a really good look at his face, it was obvious. This was not the animated face of a living, breathing creature. The face was dead. Aidan felt like he was looking into the eyes of a very angry and very undead wolf.

"What do you want from us?" Aidan yelled at the demon-faced dire wolf.

A low guttural sound surfaced from deep inside Black Fang's chest. The sound grew and grew until it spilled out of his mouth, "Die." The word hung in the air like frosted breath.

Black Fang pointed to a pair of car doors that were slammed together. A body was sandwiched between the doors. The face was almost gone, eaten to the bone by bugs. Another warg pulled the car door off, and the head and limbs fell to the side. Aidan realized that the body parts had been held together by the doors. What was inside was just pulp filled with maggots and slithering bugs. The warg dumped the remains off the door and prepared the doors for Aidan.

One warg ripped Aidan from Colt, who was screaming, and placed Aidan inside the car doors, which were then clamped shut around him. The pressure from the clamps was intense. He felt like his arms and legs were going to break if his head didn't explode first. Honey was poured in his mouth and all over his face.

On the other end, wargs commanded everyone else to lie down on their backs.

"Cold?" Black Fang taunted them. He had a voice as ugly as his scars.

Dark coals from the edge of the fire were placed on each prisoner's belly. At first, the torture victims thought it a Godsend that the wargs weren't using the red-hot coals that would burn through them instantly. But the goal here was not to make them pass out or die, at least not yet. The goal was to make them suffer. So only the black coals from the edge of the fire were used. These coals could cook for hours still.

They started with Colt since he had screamed for Aidan. Colt screamed as the black coal was placed on his chest. The pain was unbelievable. It was as if fireworks were going off on his chest.

"Fight it!" Val yelled.

It took every ounce of concentration to keep Colt from reaching over and throwing it off. As part of their "sport," the wargs left the prisoners unfettered. Any prisoners who tried to reach for the coal would be punished.

Val began chanting, "I am an Olivarez. I am an Olivarez," but he and Dre screamed as coals were placed on their chest.

The others received coals on their stomachs, except for two who were simply ripped limb from limb and thrown into the fire while the wargs watched and laughed with glee.

Alyssa was in near-panic mode as she heard Val scream out. She had jumped the fence with Mr. Buckner's help, and now she was sprinting across open ground where any warg could see her. She hoped that the wargs were too interested in what was happening at the flatbed to notice one girl running across the muddy field.

"Hey," a man growled. Alyssa looked over in time to see an unarmed Renfield running towards her. He was a big guy, so Alyssa was sure she could outrun him. Just in case, she gave Mr. Bunkner a sharp glance.

Mr. Bunkner turned and stood his ground. The Renfield tried to pull a swim move around Mr. Bunkner, but the hunter tackled the large guard. They fell to the ground and began fighting with each other. Mr. Bunkner was no match for the Renfield, though. The Renfield landed three punches on Mr. Bunkner's face, the last punch splitting his nose. Mr. Bunkner put his hands over his face and ran screaming.

While they fought, Alyssa leaped into the open door of the bus. Her fingers slipped as she tried to turn the key that was in the ignition. The second time she turned the key, the engine rumbled to life. She pressed down on the gas, and the bus slipped in the mud. Its back wheels spun wildly and dug deeper in the mud.

Two wargs who had been watching the entertainment turned towards the bus.

Aidan thought of that day not so long ago when the wargs were playing with a man hidden in the shrubs in Lakewood. Aidan had recognized then that the wargs had a playful cruelty, a malevolent humor, to them. Fate had a cruel sense of humor to deliver them back to the wargs so that they could play out their violent games.

A man next to Colt could bear it no longer. He reached up to pull the coal off his abdomen. A warg immediately pounced on him. Laughing, it cut his belly open and shoved the coal deep inside his bowels. The man screamed even more wildly while the dogs laughed. Colt watched the light go out in the man's eyes.

Colt and Val were sweating in pain while the coal seared their flesh. A rotten, horrible smell filled the air – the smell of their own flesh burning.

Aidan saw little of this. His face was covered with golden goo, and his neck felt like it was going to snap. If this was a nightmare, he wanted it to end. He wished he had found that pipe or glass. They deserved better than this. To have traveled so far and lived so long on their own only to be killed here so senselessly... Aidan tried to move from out of the car doors, but he was hopelessly trapped. Flies began to land on his face and suck at the honey.

"C'mon!" Alyssa yelled at the bus. "Go! Go! Go!" The wheels continued to spin deeper in the mud. The first warg rammed the side of the bus, nearly knocking it on its side. The warg could have just as easily broken through the front window and bit her head off, but it was playing with her, probably in a mood of amusement because of the night's festivities. It wanted to make her scared because it found pleasure in her fear, so it stood next to the bus, its paws almost underneath the vehicle. But hitting the bus freed it from its muddy grave. The bus slipped back and forth, then shot forward, running over the warg's arm.

She saw Mr. Bunkner running away, his bloody face in his hands. The Renfield stood in her path. She ran him over.

Black Fang looked up to see the bus enter the fire light. The bus was like a battering ram, slamming into wargs and sending them running.

Alyssa hit the brakes, and the yellow dog skidded into the flatbed, knocking half the tortured people off. The others knocked the coals off their bellies and jumped into the bus.

Black Fang barked an alert to the wargs around camp.

Back at the camp, the tired, half-starved prisoners saw the chaos of the night's activities and they ran to the chain link fences and began pounding on them. The fences, which were held up more by fear than good engineering, collapsed under their weight, and the people spilled out like the blood from a ripped limb and flowed into the fields and ran for the mountains. Some of them jumped into the bus with Alyssa. A few ran like martyrs right at the wargs and tried to overrun them. The wargs stomped on them and bit them, ending their lives quickly.

Dre's uncle was the first one to the bus. As he climbed in, he said to Alyssa, "Let's go! I can drive a bus."

"Not yet!"

"But we got to go now!"

Alyssa grabbed the bus key and ran for Aidan.

Aidan's face was covered in flies and other bugs that were trying to eat at the honey. Alyssa wiped them off his face, which had a hundred tiny nicks and scratches. He smiled at her. Then she unclamped the doors and tossed the top one aside. A great stink rose from the belly of those two doors, and she put out of her mind the image of what would have happened if she had not saved him.

Alyssa helped Aidan up and took him back to the yellow dog. There was just one problem, though. Black Fang stood between them and the bus.

"Leave them alone!" Mr. Bunkner yelled through his bloody face. He threw hot coals that bounced off Black Fang's hide. It was enough, though, for Black Fang to turn and lunge for him. Alyssa and Aidan took advantage of the seconds they had gained to run for the bus. They could practically feel Black Fang's fur brushing against them as they ran past him and jumped into the bus.

Dre's uncle was sitting in the driver's chair. She handed him the key, and he slammed on the gas once the bus was turned back on.

Alyssa and Aidan grabbed a seat as the bus charged towards the nearest road. Black Fang was not going to give up the chase immediately, though. After disposing of Mr. Bunkner, Black Fang dashed towards the bus. His long claws ripped at the side of the bus, shattering glass and screeching torn metal as he tried to grip the bus in his claws. Dre's uncle floored the bus away from Black Fang, who howled in fury.

Colt nestled between Alyssa and Aidan, and even Val put his head on Alyssa's shoulder. Someone in the crowded bus put a tarp over their naked and burned bodies. Then Aidan was truly surprised by the journal that was placed on his lap. He tried to see who gave it to him, but he was too tired to do much about it.

All night, they drove up into the red-granite mountains of Colorado. Outisde, snow fell quietly on the pines above and below them. Aidan hoped Dre's uncle was a good driver. The roads were covered in snow, so they wouldn't see any obstacles that could blow out a tire, which would be deadly this high up.

The bus came to a stop, and the airbrakes hissed.

"What's the problem?" A voice from the back asked.

"Road's out," Dre's uncle replied as he got out, "and I need a break."

Aidan and the lost boys looked out the bus windows. A vast whiteness obliterated the road.

Like the other torture victims, Aidan wore clothes borrowed from other people. He had on an oversized wool sweater and a pair of sweats. He hobbled out of the bus and approached Dre's uncle.

"Aidan," he said, while shaking the man's hand. "Tony," Dre's uncle said. He had a thin crown of grey around his balding dome and a look of exhaustion that he wore too comfortably.

"What do you think?" Aidan asked him.

"I think it is time for me to find a mountain trail and get the hell out of Dodge before those hellhounds show up. They will be coming with a vengeance for you, and I've seen first-hand how well those bastards can track."

"But we need you to drive the bus."

"Shit. That's your problem," he said.

"You really think they won't track you? As good as they are?"

"I think they'll be too busy feasting on your sorry asses to worry about mine."

"You can't survive in winter at this altitude with those clothes. You are better off staying with us. We will find warmth. Hell, the bus has a heater."

"I'll take my chances."

"We need you, Tony. Your family needs you."

"Don't bring them into it. I've been living with them in that Godforsaken hellhole for almost half a year. Now we escape, and I'm supposed to keep helping them? I've earned my freedom."

"Nobody will argue against that, but how will you feel knowing you left your family to the wolves? Knowing you could have saved them, but knowing you ran and left them to die?"

Tony's left came out of nowhere so fast that Aidan didn't see it before he was on the ground and nursing a black eye. Dre jumped out of the bus.

"What'd you say, Aidan?"

Tony pointed a finger at Aidan. "Not my problem. I've absolved my sins." He started up the mountain pass.

"Uncle! Where you goin'?" Dre yelled up after her uncle. Her uncle was quickly becoming nothing more than a spec in the path of the avalanche.

Aidan climbed back into the bus. "Anybody know how to drive a bus?"

An older man with deep furrows in his brow raised his hand. "I drove an RV. Can't be much different."

"Good. You're our new driver."

"Where we going?"

"North."

The bus turned around and found a new road to continue the long voyage northward. They stopped in the first town with a store and raided it. The freed prisoners swarmed through the aisles, taking every last can on the shelf. They dined like homeless people on other people's leftovers. There were canned beats and old pumpkin pie filling, Spam and cream of corn. Rusted tins of sardines and Vienna sausages that were eaten anyway. They left behind a giant pile of opened cans, then climbed back in the bus and started heading north again.

As the bus rolled over the top of one ridge pass, they were met with the most bizarre thing any of them had seen in months.

A scouting convoy.

The old man hit the brakes, making the bus slide dangerously close to the rail. It came to a stop in front of the bright lights of the Hummers and Strykers.

The doors of the vehicles opened, and soldiers ran out like bees from a knocked hive. The soldiers all wore gas masks and white-camo body suits. They carried assault rifles and flamethrowers. They first shouted for everyone to get out of the bus. Once everyone was out of the bus, they were told to lie flat on the ground and not move. Then the soldiers searched them for arms. When they found none, they ordered everyone back onboard the bus.

"Follow us," a tall soldier in a gas mask ordered the old man who was driving the bus. "If you try to run, we will shoot you down. Do you understand?"

The bus driver nodded.

"Hang on a second," Aidan said. Despite Alyssa telling him to shut up, he asked, "What if I don't want to go? Where are you taking us?"

"Denver. The last known human stronghold in the United States. Because it is the last human stronghold, we have to be cautious about who we let in. So we check the roads for more humans to make sure that we aren't surprised by a busload of people showing up in the middle of downtown Denver and seeking refuge. We caught you on our radar a few hours ago. Follow us."

Aidan got back on the bus with the others. It was morning now, and the sun was soon to be coming up over the mountains. Aidan leaned back in the seat.

"I gotta admit," Val said. "I feel a bit safer knowing there are all those people with guns and Hummers out there. It kind of reminds me of Bridgetown, in a weird sort of way."

"That's what I worry about," Aidan said. His head was hurting.

A minute later, the wargs descended from the mountain ridge.

Chapter Eleven – Clean

Black Fang led the charge down the mountainside. The giant dogs padded swiftly and silently down the side of the mountain. Not even the soldiers saw them until the wargs were almost on top of them. The wargs rammed into the bus and the Hummers, and within seconds, the soldiers lit up the world with machine guns and grenades and incendiaries.

The warg hit the bus with such power that it spun the bus sideways so that the middle of the bus t-boned around the Hummer in front of it. Unlike back at the prison camp, the wargs did not simply hit the side of the bus. This was not for sport. A second warg dived through the front windshield and ripped out the bus driver's larynx. Then the warg began snapping at every human within reach.

Machine gun blasts from the convoy drew its attention, turning the warg from the bus towards the soldiers.

Inside, the bus was complete chaos as the wounded prevented everyone else from escaping out the front of the bus. The bus was turning into a logjam of humanity.

"Quick," Aidan said to Alyssa. "Let's sneak out the back."

"No. We wait our turn."

"Are you crazy? We don't have time to wait."

"There is nothing to gain from adding to the problem. It's this 'every-man-for-himself' attitude that gets everyone killed in these kinds of scenarios."

So Aidan stayed in his seat and waited while people jumped off the bus and the sound of gunfire and howls erupted outside. Aidan kept looking around and trying to see what was going on outside, but it was hard to tell. There was a lot of noise and dirt and snow being thrown around. He couldn't figure out where the people who were leaving the bus were running to. In fact, he wasn't sure that people were actually leaving the bus.

"That's it," Aidan announced. He grabbed Alyssa by one hand, found a seam in the humanity, and pushed his way to the back of the bus, with Val and Colt following close behind. He swiveled the Emergency Exit handle to the side, kicked the door open, and jumped out the back just in time to see a young warg (perhaps one of the puppies) jump into the bus cab.

He hoisted Alyssa to the wintry floor, then helped Val and Colt down, too. Neither Val nor Colt could move very quickly. They had been barely coherent during the trip through the mountains because of their severe burns.

They ducked behind a brick wall as one of the wargs came around it. When the warg didn't see them, it put its snout in their footfalls in the snow. They were close enough to hear its excited breathing on the other side of the concrete wall. It was the rapid inhalations of a predator on the hunt who knows the kill is close. The lost boys moved through the snow quickly, always certain that at any point the warg would figure out that they were on the other side and jump over the wall.

As they came around the other side, the warg trailed them to the far side of the wall. Aidan, Alyssa, Val, and Colt sprinted as fast as their tortured, weary bodies would allow back towards the Hummers. There was another explosion, and more howling.

"We've got them on the run," he heard somebody say.

But when Aidan looked out at the pass, he didn't see wolves on the run. The black beasts had stopped at the mountainside, far enough to not be shot. Black Fang was watching Aidan.

"C'mon! Let's go!" the soldiers were shouting as they loaded everyone into separate Strykers. Aidan looked for Dre, but could not find her.

"Wait! We have a friend!"

"Let's go, sir," the soldier said, and forced Aidan into the Stryker. Aidan hoped Dre was okay and with his family.

The small convoy descended out of the mountains and down into the plains of Colorado. They entered a wasteland of suburban ruin. Cars had been moved off the major thoroughfares, creating the appearance of a labyrinth with walls made of automobiles. Aidan wondered if wandering somewhere inside was a giant minotaur with Chrysler horns and a Jeep muzzle. He thought it would probably breathe fire and smell of gasoline, and had a voice like a monster truck rally deejay.

With the Rockies at their backs, Denver rose above them like a second stretch of mountains, though made of steel and glass. The sun was rising behind the towers and casting long shadows across the ruin-scape. Aidan was again reminded of visions he had seen before, of decapitated buildings and a downtown that looked like a massacre of giants.

One-by-one the Humvees and Stryker crossed the North Platte River.

The convoy stopped at a large column-shaped building, a red and tan-painted sports arena.

The soldiers ordered everyone out of the Stryker and they were placed in a line. Aidan thought they all looked like zombies by way of the Holocaust from the looks of the refugees. Most of them were tight skin-sacks with markings on their faces to designate which warg owned them. Others were disfigured and broken and missing body parts. He looked down at Alyssa's hand, which she had placed in his, her finger laying where his used to be.

Aidan saw Dre, who was with his family, and they waved at each other from different sides of the huddle.

A gray-haired soldier announced to everyone, "You are to stay here for quarantine for thirty days. You will be provided food and water. You will be safe from the monsters so long as you stay inside and remain quiet. After thirty days, you will be evaluated by our medical team and either approved for entry to the tower, or you will be required to remain here longer."

He did not ask for any questions, comments, or go-backs. He motioned to the other soldiers, who led the refugees into the arena.

"Great," Dre said, "from one internment camp to another."

They were led through the front entrance with all its many-sectioned, broken windows. They opened double-doors to the inside of the arena. A burst of foul air blew at them. Inside, they could see nothing but black. It was like the darkest, foulest cave.

"You can't be serious," Aidan said to the closest soldier as he covered his mouth. He could taste the nastiness.

"I'm sorry, but it's the rules," the soldier said. It was the same soldier who had talked to him on the bus. He was pretty sure she was a redhead. "We have to make sure you are quarantined from disease before we let you into our settlements."

"This place will be a breeding ground for disease."

"The wargs will smell us from miles away," Colt said while making a disgusted face.

"Be thankful, kid. That stench will protect you. The monsters won't come near it."

The soldiers left them then.

Aidan and the rest entered the vast darkness. A few people refused to enter. Some others even started dry heaving.

After his eyes adjusted to the dark, Aidan could make out lines of cots. A few people were still asleep in their cots and did not get up. In the center was a cornucopia of packaged foods. He fought an internal battle between the desire to escape the rancid smell and the urge to eat for the first time in days. The need to eat won out. Within minutes, the refugees descended on the mass of packaged food. Aidan and the rest of the lost boys grabbed several random packages (there was not enough light to determine what they were), and walked out of the arena. Outside in the cold and away from the malodorous arena, they read the packages.

"Boxed octopus and squid in ink sauce. Of course." Two seconds later, he dumped the boxes into his starving mouth. It was magnificent. They also feasted on canned artichoke hearts, uncooked chicken bouillon cubes, and hardened stovetop dressing. They didn't care if it was settlement leftovers or if there was no water to hydrate the noodles. It was the best meal any of them could remember since the campfire venison in West Texas.

"Remember – don't eat too much," Val said. "It'll mess up your stomach."

"I don't care if it turns my stomach into goo – I'm starving," Alyssa said, and slurped hers out of the box.

"Remember when we had barbecue in Bridgetown and you said it was the best thing ever," Aidan said to Alyssa, "And you two thought the venison was the best eating we'd had. Now look at us, devouring octopus in ink sauce. Have our taste buds changed or what?"

While they enjoyed their meal, Aidan's head started to sting. "I think my warg-sense is going off," he told the others. "Let's get back inside." As they were going in, one of the encampment survivors – a woman with thick bushy hair and the mark of Black Fang – spotted wargs approaching from the East. Nobody wanted to risk staying outside. They had no weapons with which to defend themselves, and they had no local knowledge of the terrain to help with hiding. As everyone went back inside and closed the arena doors, they hoped the soldiers were right and that the wargs would pass by. They stayed quiet as bugs in a cupboard and waited, but the wargs never approached.

"I need some sleep," Val said. The others agreed. The calories were making them instantly sleepy. Val asked a nearby person lying in a cot if he would mind Aidan taking a cot. He didn't realize until he touched the man's iron shoulder that the body was dead. It should have affected them more, but they were too tired. How was finding a body in a cot any different than finding a body lying face-down in the encampments, or finding bodies in farms or small towns, or finding the two dead girls in their subdivision like Jax and Peter did? At least this body was at rest and not viciously torn to pieces.

The lost boys circled the cots together and fell asleep.

Inside the arena, time got kind of funny, so they weren't sure how many days they had been there when the soldiers finally returned, bringing medical personnel with them. They were all wearing masks, which Val joked could have been for disease or stench. One time in the dark, maybe a few days or a few weeks or a few months – nobody was sure of time in there – Alyssa told him, "You'd think you'd get used to the smell. God, it's still horrible. It permeates."

The day the medical staff entered the arena, they brought in privacy dividers. Everybody got in lines and waited. They filled out forms. Aidan was the first of the group to be checked over.

The medical staff started by checking for temperature and then checking the eyes, ears, throat and pulse. He halfway expected his medical person to tell him to turn and cough. He was checked for rashes, too. He peed into a cup. This all felt weirdly normal and comforting, like he was going for his annual physical.

During the check, all Aidan's scars were documented. "I could have used some stitches for that," Aidan said when the medical person examined his missing finger.

"You're lucky you didn't die from infection."

Aidan shrugged. "Wait till you see my back."

"Your back? Can you remove your shirt?"

Aidan did, and the man did not say anything for a while. Aidan thought maybe the man had left the room, or fainted. He glanced over his shoulder, and the man was staring with terror at Aidan's back.

"Mincemeat, right?"

"You have endured as much, if not more, than anyone else I have met," the man behind the surgeon's mask said.

Aidan thought of Mike and Kirk. Then he thought of the torture of Val and Colt and Dre at the hands of the wargs, and he shrugged off the medical person's comment.

"Many have had worse. Besides, we've come a long way."

The man looked at the clipboard and found Aidan's home address. "Houston? That is a long way. Well, I don't see any reason not to pull you out of quarantine. I hope you can find the peace here that you were not able to find in Houston. Welcome to the Tooth, Mr. Fannin."

After the checkups, most everybody was herded into a mass at the near end of the stadium. None had died in the arena. Only a few were still under further quarantine. Five out of forty.

Salves had been placed on burn wounds, and antibiotics given to everyone with cuts. Everybody was directed into another bus that took them the rest of the way into Denver.

The settlement was buried deeper into Denver than some of the gopher holes that his aunt and uncle had to deal with at their ranch in West Texas. No wonder the monsters didn't come for them. First, they had to pass through two lines of razor wire, which probably wouldn't be too difficult. If a warg can take rifle shots, razor wire is probably like dental floss to them. But then it got tougher. There was a moat of liquid fire that wreathed its way through Denver's downtown area. Once they passed through the flaming moat, they had more razor wires, a ring of mines, and another ring that was completely empty. This was the one ring that confused Aidan the most.

"What's in there?" he asked a nearby soldier, who just laughed but didn't say anything.

The black tower shot up like a giant triangular tooth growing out of the diseased gums of the Earth. Aidan noticed that this triangular shape was a trick of the eye. The upper stories had collapsed upon themselves, giving the tower the angled appearance.

"This is all for defense?" Aidan asked.

"Preservation," the soldier across from Aidan said. She was a redhead, maybe 25 years old. She had a badge sewn to her uniform. It looked like an M and an H intersected. A snake was wrapped around the letters.

"What does that mean?" Aidan asked.

"It means when you sleep at night, I keep the nightmares away."

"My name's Aidan." He extended his hand.

"Don't hate me if I don't take you up on your offer for a handshake. What you see is an extension of your friendship, but I see the finality of war. I see a severed hand that will stick in the back of my mind even after I've finally placed it as yours. So please forgive me for not shaking your hand, but I don't need that on my conscience."

Aidan put his hand in his pocket. Alyssa rubbed his shoulder, and they tried to look outside.

The bus came to a stop in front of the tower. Most of the glass had been blown out and shattered. A large sculpture of Atlas had lost its world, so it seemed the air was burdening the titan. The fountain he sat in was filled with fallen leaves. On each corner of the tower, paneling had been added, perhaps to hide a large weapon.

As people began unloading, a man in a worn suit jacket came running through the broken front doors. He had a small crop of hair haloed around the base of his head and a bookish, professorial look to him.

"No! No! No! No! Send them back. We're not ready!" the man said.

Behind came another soldier, but he wasn't wearing a helmet.

"John, the time is up," the soldier said. "We gotta do this."

"But Quincey, we don't have room for them. We are tight on food, water, clothes, and space. At least in the arena they had all those resources."

"The arena is a deathtrap."

"It is not. It is our salvation. These people weren't even properly quarantined. How long were they in the arena – five days maybe? You shouldn't have let them out. Five days isn't enough time to know for sure they don't have any communicable diseases. Just one of these refugees comes in here with the flu or the measles or something worse, and it will spread throughout the whole Tooth. What do we do then?"

"Standard treatment. Quarantine, wash our hands thoroughly."

"With what water? We're already on tight water rationing as it is. You want us to use our reduced water supply to wash?"

"I'll handle this, John."

"You bet your ass you will, cause it's not my problem." The man with the clipboard, who was apparently "John," looked at the forty refugees and said to them, "You hear that? You're not my problem!"

Alyssa leaned over to Aidan. "Does that sound like anybody?"

"Yeah, yeah," Aidan said. "Consider the boot thoroughly on the other foot."

The military man stepped towards the refugees and said, "My name is Colonel Quincey Weatherford, and I apologize. Everything John said is true. We are on food and water rations, and most of you will end up sleeping in hallways with your arm for a pillow and your clothes for a blanket. But that arena is a disgrace for a quarantine zone and a deathtrap. So welcome to the Black Tooth. It used to belong to a global finance group. Now it is our refuge and our safehaven. We have spent the past 6 months barricading human civilization in this tower to protect it from the monsters out there. Rule Number One: We will do anything to keep our safety. If you compromise that safety, you will be given back to the wilds. Do you understand?"

After a chorus of head nods and yeses, Colonel Weatherford pointed to Aidan and the other lost boys.

"You four – the lost boys. Come with me."

As soon as they were out of earshot, the Colonel turned on them. "You're the Boy Scout," he said to Aidan, then added, "You all are the ones that evil mutt called the Warden of the West wants."

Aidan didn't even try to disagree with him. He knew that this was all told to the Colonel on the great psychic monster grapevine. To tell the truth, he wondered why he hadn't heard anything sooner. Were the other refugees just ignoring that fact, or were they too tired to want to turn him in?

"I don't know what he wants with you, and frankly I don't care. I want peace and separation from those monsters."

"You intend to hand us over, don't you?"

"Is there a reason I shouldn't? Are you anything but a gigantic risk to the stability of this settlement?"

"We're leverage if anything happens," Val suggested.

"No. You're a reason for them to attack. And if they do, I want you forewarned, I will hand you over in a second if I think it benefits the Tooth. Until then, you are free to come and go throughout the settlement as you see fit. Obey our rules, which is the basic stuff – no stealing, not murdering, no raping – and I will let you live here. Disobey those rules, and you will find yourselves sent to Casa de Black Fang. Understood?"

"What about John?" Aidan asked. "He seems ready to get rid of us already."

"John thinks you guys dead in the arena would have been better for everyone. He has different opinions than I do on how to keep the peace around here. Don't worry about him now, though. He's probably moved on to a newer problem du jour."

"So what do we do now?" Val asked.

"Now, you go get a bath. Five days in the arena, and you kids smell every inch of it."

Despite the need to ration water, the four were given all the hot water and cleaning supplies they wanted. Aidan shaved his head down again, and Alyssa shampooed, rinsed, and repeated for about twenty times. Val didn't take long at all. He wasn't comfortable with the way his body looked naked. In the weeks since he had left Bridgetown, his body was changing more obviously. It was almost impossible to ignore the curve of his breasts. This wasn't the body he wanted. He didn't shower any longer than he had to.

After the shower, Val and Alyssa gave each other haircuts. Val asked to have his hair cut short. It made him look "butch," but he preferred that to womanly. Aidan teased him a bit, and Val punched him in the arm playfully. Then he presented Alyssa. Her hair was tapered in the back and about fifteen inches taken off. It had started to clump, and there were no combs or brushes in the arena to take care of her hair. She looked spectacular.

"I like it," Aidan said.

"Stop it. I look dreadful. Half my face won't move, and now I have this giant scar over my ear. I'm ugly!" She started to cry. Aidan hugged her while she sobbed. "I know it's stupid. I'm looking at you with your back and your missing finger and this jagged thing all over your face, and I have no right to complain."

"Shush. Don't talk like that. Of course you do. And you know what? I think it looks beautiful. I like it. And I love you, and I'm still attracted to you."

"Really?"

"Hell, yes."

New clothes were left out for them. "Your old clothes will be burned or ripped up and placed in Molotov cocktails," the woman who watched over the showers told them.

After they dressed, they went out into the building's main atrium. A golden garland hung from the second-floor balcony. Giant wreaths were placed above the elevator shafts and at the old guard's table. Most impressive of all was a two-story tall Christmas tree with a star adorning the top. Red and green and silver balls hung from its metal limbs. Oversized boxes of cardboard wrapped in stock Christmas paper and bows were placed underneath the tree. Everywhere they looked, it was Christmas.

"Awesome!" Colt yelled.

"Did you know?" Alyssa asked.

"I didn't, but I guess I should have known. It was Thanksgiving when we were at Bridgetown. Has it only been a month?" *Had it really?* Aidan wondered. It felt like years of wandering through small towns.

"You know what," Val said. "I don't care. If it's Christmas time, I'll take it. When is Christmas?"

"Tomorrow is Christmas Eve," came a voice from behind them. "You almost missed it."

They turned around and saw Jax, Riley, and Peter. Alyssa screamed and jumped into Jax's body. "I knew we'd see you again!" she said.

"Missed you, too," he said as he hugged her.

Colt put his arms around Peter and held him tight. "Don't do that again," he told his older brother. "Ever."

"Okay. I won't."

Aidan hugged Riley. "Good to see you again." Then she hugged Val.

Aidan went over to Peter. He looked different. "What happened to you? A gopher get your ear?" he asked, pointing to Peter's right ear, which was missing most of its lobe.

"New Mexico, bro." Aidan clapped him on the back. It had been less than a month they were separated, yet his brother seemed taller, more mature.

An hour later, they were sitting in a conference room that was decorated with giant western portraits of cattle being driven north and men riding horses. Amid the western chaos, silver and gold bells had been stapled to the walls. They glittered in the lamp light.

The lost boys sat huddled around a small electric lamplight, hot cocoa in their hands. Jax was talking.

"We made it to Albuquerque before we could go no farther west and had to turn north," Jax said, his voice strong in the night. "Snakes and Gila monsters and something we call 'Morning Star' cause it has arms and tails like one. Freaky thing. Then we went north. Up in Colorado we were picked up by a roaming caravan like y'all. We've been here ever since, which has been about three weeks. We look after kids mostly. I teach taekwondo, Riley cheerleading, and Peter gymnastics. We're like the most kick-ass PE teachers these kids ever had. When we aren't doing that, we help out by gathering food supplies.

"Once a week we go with the soldiers out into the burbs. We raid the stores for anything we can find, and then the Humvees and Strykers bring them back here. Every once in a while a food-gathering trip becomes a person-gathering trip, which John hates to no end. He thinks we are almost out of rations, but I've seen it. We're stockpiled for like, two or three months.

"But what's it like here?" Aidan wanted to know. "What's it really like?"

Jax glanced nervously at Val, then said, "It's no Bridgetown, if that's what you're worried about. No ritual sacrifice. Nothing like that. These people really have no connection to the monsters except the psychic link that everyone but us seems to have."

"Any explanation for that yet?" Val asked, wanting to change the subject.

"None yet. John and the Colonel know about it, but they got no more explanation than the doctors we've seen. I guess it's just one of those things. Personally, I'm happy for it. I don't have to see their awful shit, and I won't get the tumor everyone else develops from this psychic crap."

"Watch the language," Peter said.

"Oh, yeah. Your brother – he's been a real treat, Aidan. Always trying to keep my tongue on the good side of the Lord."

"It's Christmas time," Peter said with a little more sternness than Aidan could remember, "Show some respect."

"Christmas. What a concept," Aidan said. "This whole thing is taking me by complete surprise. It's like walking into a Disney movie or something. It's so weird. I half-expect Santa to come riding out of the sky, giving AKs and IEDs to all the good little boys and girls."

"You know what we need to do?" Aidan asked. Without waiting for answer, he reached into his back pocket. "Not sure how I was able to keep the wargs from catching this when we were at the camps. Guess I was lucky I taped it to my journal the day we were picked up."

He slammed down a bag of some dice. Everybody's face lit up. Even the girls smiled through their upturned eyes and covered mouths.

"You guys are such dweebs!" Riley said.

"Maybe so, but this time, y'all are getting into it, too."

They played as late into the night as they could. They fought demons and dragons and found buried treasure hidden deep inside secret vaults. One by one, each player dropped out to go to bed. Finally, it was just Aidan and Peter still awake. Peter had the dice in his hand.

"I'm sorry I left."

"I was angry with you for a long time, but I understand. You had to do what you had to do."

"I didn't find Mom or Dad."

"I know." Then he pulled out an old wedding photo of his parents. It, too, had been taped to his journal. Now it was dirty and faded. Mom and Dad were standing in front of a tall cake. Dad was dressed in a tux, and Mom was in her wedding dress. Mom had a golden retriever leashed to her hand.

"I haven't seen this photo in ages. Where did you get it?" Peter wanted to know.

"One time, back in the subdivision, I went back to the house, and I grabbed a few photos. Some of Mom and Dad and Mike. When we left, I grabbed this one, though. At first, I wasn't sure why. It's not like I could use it to help someone ID Mom and Dad. But now I think it's cause of how happy they look. I want to be that happy some day. I think I can be."

"You know what makes them look so happy?" Peter asked.

"What?"

"They've got each other. When I see you and Alyssa, I think you two have that. One day, I'm going to have it, too, but she'll be a Sports Illustrated Cover Model."

Aidan seemed to be thinking of something while he smiled at Peter, so Peter said, "You've found the right girl."

"I'm going to marry her."

Peter didn't wait a second to respond, and when he did, he made it sound as natural as the sun rising and setting. "When? Christmas would be perfect."

"That'd be lame. Besides, we haven't settled down yet. I want to wait until we find the right place. I have a feeling we're almost there, if we just keep going a little farther."

"I'm glad for you, bro. I think you both will be as happy as Mom and Dad."

"I hope so." Aidan studied the photo in his hands. "I want to get rid of this photo."

"Why?" Peter's voice was pained. "It's the only thing we have left of them."

"Man, you know that isn't true. I see Mom and Dad every time I look at us. I ever tell you why Kirk and I went into the woods together, back when y'all met the dryder?"

"No."

"I thought I saw Mom and Dad. I led Kirk straight into trouble because I thought I saw our parents going into the woods. I was that desperate for them. The funny thing is that before all this happened, before Black Friday, I couldn't wait to get away from them. To get away from all of y'all. I just wanted to escape. Go to college. See new people and have any kind of experience that wasn't from my hometown. Then after that night when the animals changed, all I could think of was keeping us together. Keeping us safe.."

"It was my fault," Peter said, his voice steeled.

"It was no more your fault than our parents. They couldn't do anything to help Michael, and neither could you or I. It's not your fault Michael died. I'm sorry if I led you to think otherwise."

Peter nodded and turned away. Rubbed a tear before Aidan could see it.

"But it is my fault for keeping with this charade. We need to bury our dead."

"But we don't know for sure," Peter allowed.

"No, we do. You do. I do. Colt knows better than the rest of us. I think tomorrow we need to have a ceremony."

Peter went to bed after that, and Aidan stayed up. He stared at the ceiling and watched his breath turn to clouds in the cold. He had not felt so safe in a long time – not since they left Lakewood. He hadn't liked living out in the open, so exposed. Here in the Tooth he could hide or take a stand as he decided.

Chapter Twelve – Revenant

Aidan stood over the small hole in the ground. The rest of the lost boys formed a circle around the hole, Alyssa to his right and Peter and Colt to his left. He held the photo of his parents in his hands. They looked so happy.

He started to say something, but the words would not come. He had been up the rest of the night trying to think of what to say. He could read a list of the people he knew were dead. There were over two hundred. He had their names written down on a sheet of paper in his pocket. He pulled out the wrinkled paper, but thought against it.

Aidan took a second to study the features of the down-turned faces of his friends. They were older beyond their years, even Colt. They were broken, scarred, and missing ears, but they were still here.

He thought maybe then he should say something uplifting. Maybe talk about the struggle to keep going and keep living, but that didn't feel right either. Everybody here knew that they couldn't give up.

Alyssa held his hand in hers, and it felt warm to his skin.

"I need to let go," he finally said. "I need to move forward. I think that's what counselors would say if I were talking to them right now. But counselors are from the old world, just like this photo in my hand. People were truly happy back then with only small cares and small worries. But the world turned upside down on us, and I think the world that created this picture can never come back. So yeah, I need to let go of my parents. Let go of my brother. I need to bury the dead. But more importantly, I need to stop trying to preserve everything tied to that world."

He kissed the wedding photo of his parents and their dog and placed it in the hole in the ground. He was about to leave when Alyssa came forward with a similar picture – a family photo she kept folded up in her pocket. She kissed, it, too, and placed it in the ground. Peter held up a wallet-sized photo of Michael. He smiled, tears streaming freely down his cheeks, and placed it in the ground. "I'm sorry, Michael," he mumbled. Colt and Aidan and Alyssa held him. Jax had an old picture of him and his parents at the zoo when he was a kid. It went into the hole, too. Riley pulled out her cellphone, then put it back in her pocket. Instead, she took off a locket she wore. She opened the locket and looked at the photos of her parents, kissed it, and placed it gently in the ground. Val took out a photo of him and his dad from when he was younger.

"You know, you're going to find this weird, but being with you all," Val said. "My life is actually less complicated than before. I'm not who I want to be, but people either don't know or don't care. And you guys are probably all weirder than me," he said with a laugh, and then placed the photo in the ground. Alyssa wrapped her other arm around him.

"Almost forgot," Jax said. He had a guitar pick. He held it up for everyone to see. "Love ya, buddy," he said, and placed it, too, in the hole.

Then Jax and Riley walked over and held the others.

"Hey, Boy Scout," one of the soldiers said while they were sitting in the conference room they had come to call home. "The Colonel wants to see you."

Aidan hugged Alyssa, and then stood up from their encampment in the conference room. He followed the soldier up to the fourth story of the Tooth. The soldier escorted him to Colonel Weatherford's quarters, and then waited outside.

"What can I do for you, Colonel?" Aidan asked. "Is it time to hand us over?"

"I have four flamethrower turrets. One on every side of the building. They are manned 24-7. I have four hundred and one soldiers protecting three hundred and eighty civilians. My weapons cache boasts RPGs, automatic rifles, and about a ton of bullets.

"We have nine rings protecting us from the outside world. You saw them when you came in?"

"Yes, sir." He felt awkward saying sir, but he knew he would feel more awkward not using the term of respect. "But two of the rings are completely empty."

The old man's eyes twinkled. "Oh, are they? To you and me, they are empty, but they are loaded with pepper spray. Any of those god-damn things try to get a whiff of us, and they'll be blowing snot out their nose for the next week."

"Why are you telling me all this?"

"Cause I want to know what is so damned important about a bunch of kids. I've developed the best chance of man's survival, but the monsters aren't sneezing at it. They want you. Why?"

"I don't know."

"Don't know, or don't want to tell?"

"We have a theory." Aidan hesitated to say anything more. It would sound ridiculous.

"Go on."

"You guys get visions and things when the monsters talk to you on the international psychic hell hotline, right? Well, I don't. None of us do. We're not sure why. Maybe we missed the mind-meld day of the conference or we didn't breathe in the right air at the right time, but we don't hear from them. We're kind of a black hole to them."

The Colonel did not say anything. He just waited and listened. Aidan held up his hand to show his missing finger.

"But then in Bridgetown, the people there did something. They sacrificed my flesh and blood to a creature there called Malifax. We killed Malifax, I'm pretty sure, and then we ran for it. But ever since then, I've been able to know where the monsters are."

Colonel Weatherford folded his hands behind his back and went to one of the windows. He stood there quiet and alone. All Aidan could do was look around the office. Obviously it was some lower management office with a faux-mahogany desk and lots of old-world stock photos. A young man in a button-up shirt and tie, but no jacket, was smiling broadly to a group of people he was giving a presentation to. A chisel-chinned man with new gray who could afford a full suit was pointing out something on a piece of paper to a young Asian woman. Aidan thought to himself, *are they studying Bene Gesserit writings? They look so damn serious.*

"Do you have any idea what these people did?" Aidan asked aloud. "Were they lawyers, sales people, what? All I can tell is they were photogenic and standardized."

"I think it was a temp agency," Colonel Weatherford said. "Aidan, do you know how powerful a weapon you are? Have you seen some of my soldiers with the M-H badge? I created it. It means Monster Hunters. It sounds pretty pulpy if you ask me, but they get into it, and I think it is appropriate. These things out there are dogs and wolves that have turned human. They are werewolves, Aidan. And my monster hunters fight the weres. Guns are not much use. Explosives will stun them, but fire still works best, just like in the old Universal movies. You ever see the old black and whites? You're probably too young."

"No, I get it," Aidan said. "Fire bad. How do you think Black Fang got that scar on his face? I Molotov-cocktailed him."

"You are a boy after my own heart, Aidan. See, we can use you in the M-H. You could lead my soldiers to the weres, and we could burn them. For once, we'd be going after them. That's why they want you dead. You are a threat to their dominion."

"Maybe, but all I want to do is go north and find a place as far away from these monsters as I can."

"Of course you can, and nobody can say anything about it. Self-preservation is the first instinct. The most base and animalistic of our instincts, some would say. Altruism is a call for something higher and nobler."

"You aren't going to convince me to stay. People I love haven't been able to convince me, and frankly, I don't know you."

"You're not one of my soldiers, so I won't force you to stay. When do you plan to leave?"

"We will leave the day after Christmas."

"Good plan. Get some rest and food, and once the spirits are up, move them out. It's what I'd do. But when you are up north, as free of the wild as one can get except for the occasional polar bear or sea otter, you are going to think of what is was to be an Eagle Scout. Oh, yeah. I heard you were one. The Boy Scout. I was an Eagle, too. I still abide by its laws. To be honest and trustworthy and obedient and cheerful, sure. But I think the one that will bother you the most is loyal. Are you being loyal to humanity by leaving us to die when you had the chance to stop all this? Will your oaths mean anything when you have to say them over the bones of the dead? On my honor, to do my best, for God and my country? To help other people at all times. Have you done your best, Aidan? Or are you tucking tail and running for self-preservation?"

"Anything else?"

Colonel Weatherford approached him, hands still behind his back.

"I spent the better part of the last ten years hunting cowards in the Middle East. They ran and hid behind women and children. They dug holes in the ground. They wore disguises. They put up great barriers to keep us out. But eventually, we got them all. You can run and you can hide, and you may live for a decade behind your great white curtain, but eventually the wolves will come for you, Aidan. And when they come for you, you're going to wish you were dead. They will make you watch everyone you know die. All you will have left are the bodies of the people you loved and the oaths you broke. Leave my office."

He turned his back on Aidan.

"Before I go, can you tell me something, sir?"

Colonel Weatherford arched his eyebrow, reminding himself he was working with a civilian. "What is it?"

"I was hoping you could help us piece together some of the puzzle. I have seen so many things that make no sense to me. I've seen jelly fish that fly and elephants with tentacles instead of trunks. I've seen wargs riding rocs. Back in Texas, we came across a giant wall of cars that to this day we still don't know who built it or why. I've seen cars squashed by some giant – thing – that I've never seen. Does any of this make any sense to you?"

"I was at Buckley Air Force Base on Black Friday. 460th Space Wing. We have eyes and ears all over the globe. When this went supernova, it wasn't just an isolated incident, it was everywhere and all at once. The way I see it, when you invade, you scale up your R&D to develop new weapons, the kind your opponent won't see coming because they lack the knowledge or the intuition. We've done it successfully time and time again when we went to war. I guess it was our turn to get the surprise. Within minutes, we saw bases ripped apart by unimaginable monsters. In fact, we were so busy trying to support everywhere else, we didn't keep as good an eye on our front door as we should have. We have preparations, implementations, but there was no procedure for this. Buckley was overrun by the ugliest bison scumdogs you have ever seen. They rammed our F-16Cs before we could scramble. Then came the fire ants and the werewolves. We didn't have a chance. It was a damn massacre. I barely escaped with my life. You put a hundred horror writers in a room, and in a week, they won't be able to come up with the kind of shit I've fought. Maybe in your lifetime, if we live long enough, we will understand it, but I don't expect to live that long."

The soldier escorted Aidan downstairs to the parking garage where there was a line of Humvees. Fenced in was a wall of gasoline in barrels and cans.

"The Colonel wants you to take three. He thinks that will be enough for the seven of you to make it north."

"This is too much," Aidan said.

"The Colonel wants to ensure that you get where you are going and you have the ability to return, should you change your mind. You will have gas, weapons, maps, radios, and food supplies. You will be treated like a king leaving on a royal expedition," he said, derision laced like arsenic on his words.

Aidan returned to the lost boys.

"What did the Colonel want?" Jax asked.

"Doesn't matter. I'm leaving after Christmas to go north. I'm not going to be an ass again and draw a line in the sand or anything. If you want to go, I would love to have you with me, but if you want to stay or go somewhere else, I understand."

"And if we decide to stay," Peter asked. "If we all decide to stay, what will you do?"

Aidan looked at them all. He thought of the people he had buried and the people he had met and traveled with. "I guess I will stay with my family."

"Good answer! You're finally learning! And I'm coming with you," Peter said.

Aidan breathed a sigh of relief. "I was hoping you wouldn't call me on that."

"Look, we believe you are doing the right thing. We just don't need a dictator forcing us down the right path," Val said.

"I'm going with my family," Riley said. "Lead the way."

Jax stared at the ground.

"It's up to you, brother," Aidan said. "I was wrong for what I said to you out in West Texas. I don't want you to follow me blindly, and I'm not going to tell you how to live your life or what to do with it. If you want to stay, I understand. You have a good thing going here, helping the soldiers and teaching martial arts."

Jax considered what Aidan said for a moment, then said, "I can't leave you guys alone. You need somebody to keep you alive. You might meet another giant bat and then Peter will be waving a damn steak knife at it."

There wasn't much to pack. The soldiers made sure they had wool blankets, extra winter clothes and snow gear, MREs, gasoline, backpacks, high-powered Remington 700s with military scopes, hatchets, and survival gear.

"I think we've got everything we could want," Aidan said.

That night, almost all seven hundred eighty people packed the atrium or watched from floor balconies. Only a small handful of soldiers remained at their posts outside the tower. Colonel Weatherford, Mr. Seward, and a few other people who Aidan did not recognize but assumed to be the leaders of the Tooth sat on folding chairs behind the podium.

A woman stood on the erected stage and opened the ceremony by singing "Silent Night." After the song ended, Mr. Seward walked up to the podium. He held a Bible nervously in his hand. He placed the leathered book on the podium in front of him. He opened the book to the marked page said, "Revelations, Chapter 13," then read aloud:

> And I beheld another beast coming up out of the earth; and he had two horns like a lamb, and he spake as a dragon. And he exerciseth all the power of the first beast before him, and causeth the earth and them which dwell therein to worship the first beast, whose deadly wound was healed. And he doeth great wonders, so that he maketh fire come down from heaven on the earth in the sight of men, and deceiveth them that dwell on the earth by the means of those miracles which he had power to do in the sight of the beast; saying to them that dwell on the earth, that they should make an image to the beast, which had the wound by a sword, and did live. And he had power to give life unto the image of the beast, that the image of the beast should both speak, and cause that as many as would not worship the image of the beast should be killed. And he causeth all, both small and great, rich and poor, free and bond, to receive a mark in their right hand, or in their foreheads:

"I know," Seward said, almost apologetically. "Not good Christmas stuff. I've got one better. Luke, Chapter 2."

He turned to another passage and read again:

> And there were in the same country shepherds abiding in the field, keeping watch over their flock by night. And, lo, the angel of the Lord came upon them, and the glory of the Lord shone round about them; and they were sore afraid. And the angel

said unto them, Fear not: for, behold, I bring you good tidings of great joy, which shall be to all people. For unto you is born this day in the city of David a Savior, which is Christ the Lord. And this shall be a sign unto you; Ye shall find the babe wrapped in swaddling clothes, lying in a manger. And suddenly there was with the angel a multitude of the heavenly host praising God, and saying, Glory to God in the highest, and on earth peace, good will toward men.

He closed the book and looked across the atrium. "I'm no preacher, but tonight I will try to be one. For you. For me. The metaphor, or course, has always been that a preacher is the shepherd keeping watch over his flock. Tonight, we celebrate the birth of the king of kings born meekly in a manger surrounded by cows and chickens and donkeys and sheep. I don't know what we did or if it's something we could have done different. Maybe God is mad at us. Maybe this is retribution or penance. I sometimes think he has taken dominion from man and given it back to the animals. I don't know. What I do know is that we have a duty to our loved ones and our neighbors – our community – to act as shepherds for each other. Cause we sure can't be shepherds like the ones in that book. I think that is what I take away tonight. We should try to be more like the one true shepherd, at least for a day. Let us not forget the power of today. The power of brotherly love. The power of compassion and forgiveness. So if you go back to your rooms and you see someone who needs a blanket and you have some extra…maybe you will be a shepherd. Maybe somebody you see is sad or lonely, and I hope you will share a few kind words to keep them going. It doesn't have to be a grand deed, but do one thing tonight to be better shepherds for each other, and maybe in the morning we can work on being better shepherds to the world."

While Mr. Seward led them in prayer, Aidan let the man's words sink in. He had been a shepherd to this motley group that had become his family. Had he been a good shepherd? He knew the answer and didn't like it. It wasn't that he was beginning to doubt his every move since leaving the house on Vicksburg. It was how he treated people he had called family, and how he had sacrificed their feelings and their inputs for his own damn will. Like some Captain Ahab of the Apocalypse, Aidan had led them north on a perilous course, and they had followed, most of the time. But had he considered their opinions, their desires, or had he forced them to his will? Maybe it was time to, like Alyssa, start looking for the right thing to do rather than choose the path that just gave him the best chance to live. That made him feel better inside, and he hadn't realized how hard he had gotten until then. It was time to live the right way.

Mr. Seward closed the book down and went to sit. The woman stood back up and started the crowd into "Away in the Manger," "Hark! The Herald Angels Sing," and "Joy to the World." The songs lifted into the atrium and filled it with warmth and joy.

It was late when they returned back to the conference room. Somebody had gotten the PE system working and started playing Christmas standards over it. In the darkness, the lost boys gave each other gifts of food and drink: Vienna sausages, deviled ham, and tuna. The taste of the deviled ham was almost overpowering to the senses, but the protein felt good in their bellies. Somebody had found a can of Coke, which was passed around and shared. It tickled their throats and made them giddy.

While the others sang Christmas songs, Aidan pulled Alyssa to the side. With the light behind them, he got down on one knee and asked her to marry him. "I don't have a ring or a promise of a better life, but I will never stop taking care of you. I have never stopped loving you, and I will always love you most of all." Before she could say yes, he stopped her, "I am married to you. I have been for a long time now, I just didn't know it. You can say no, but it won't change who I am. You are my forever."

He didn't realize that the others had stopped singing and were watching Alyssa and Aidan.

"Yes, yes, yes!" she said, her eyes smiling with tears. He kissed her, and the lost boys cheered. They congratulated him, and that night, Aidan took her to bed alone with him. It had been months since they had been alone with each other. Always they were surrounded by lost boys or other strangers. Now, they slept in a small office next to the conference room, on a sleeping bag, and they made love while Christmas surrounded them and relieved them.

When Aidan awoke, his body was stiff, and his head felt groggy. Alyssa was still asleep, so he crawled into his clothes and walked down the hallway. People were huddled together in deep Christmas sleep, even the soldiers.

Nothing happened on Christmas, and that was good. The whole world needed a day off, and if this apocalypse was God's work, then this was the day off they had earned over the past six months.

The smell of cocoa drifted down the hallway. Aidan followed it. Lightly playing Muzak versions of Christmas carols danced in the air. Today, he didn't mind. In the cafeteria in the atrium, he found Dre making cocoa.

"Merry Christmas," Dre said. She looked real good. Her long hair was trimmed and ordered, and she had a genuine smile he couldn't remember seeing before today.

"Merry Christmas," Aidan said as they hugged and he accepted a cup. "I haven't seen you in a while. How you been?"

She smiled with abundant satisfaction. "I think we can get used to a place like this. I wish all of us made it here, but you can't control everyone."

Dre's words rang true to Aidan. He also thought of the uncle running off into the mountains of Colorado. He hoped he found someplace to hole up for the winter.

"Good."

"By the way, congratulations," Dre said.

"Word travels quick."

"Yes, it does. And why shouldn't it? Something that beautiful happens and people want to know about it. I'm surprised Mr. Seward isn't already planning your wedding his self. "

Aidan felt something light and cold touch his bare scalp.

"It's snowing."

Dre followed Aidan's eyes upward. Snow was falling softly through the atrium's broken windows. He looked outside. It was a gray morning. Overnight, two inches had fallen.

Aidan crossed the atrium. In each corner of the atrium were large propane tanks. The tanks were kept behind cones and guarded by soldiers. Aidan wondered what the tanks were for. If he got Colonel Weatherford's ear again, he might ask. In the meantime, there were things inside his circle of influence, and things outside it. The tanks were clearly outside his circle.

Aidan walked outside and rubbed his head. The snow was falling so peacefully and picturesquely. He had been born at the bottom of Texas, but he had always preferred colder weather.

He sipped his hot chocolate and stood in the snow and enjoyed the sleepy quiet.

Then it started to nag him, one of those deep-down thoughts rising up from its grave to torment him. Aidan tried to shake it off, but the feeling that something was wrong wouldn't let go. He took another sip of his hot chocolate and looked out at the snow. Then he realized what was wrong, what was bothering him.

No fires.

The fires were out. Why were the fires out? Maybe it was wargs chewing at the front door. Or maybe it was the snow. The pain in his head told him otherwise.

"Hey!" he shouted at the flamethrower's turret.

The man two stories up shook off his sleep and waved down at him. "Merry Christmas! Go back to bed!"

"The fires are out!" Aidan yelled. He pointed his arm to the fires, exaggerating his movements. The soldier saw the flames out, then started yelling into his walkie while the other shot a few preliminary bursts from the flamethrower.

That was when the pounding hit him. It was like an avalanche in his head. He had never felt anything like this before.

Aidan ran towards the atrium while the flamethrowers lit up on something in the distance he could not see. Gunfire erupted from the turrets as more soldiers reacted to whatever was coming towards them. Suddenly, rocs shot out of the thick clouds and stabbed like daggers at the turrets. Some rocs were staved off by curls of flame, but others evaded the tongues of fire and pulled soldiers out of the turrets. Holding them by the beaks, they tossed the soldiers over the side of the tower. The poor departed shouted until their bodies splattered like pulp on the pavement.

Aidan tried to push himself inside, but soldiers were pouring out of the tower like ants from a smashed anthill.

Aidan felt the pull in his head, like a compass with talons. He shouted at a soldier, "Over there! Fire over there!" The soldier took his advice just in time to stave off a leaping warg.

Suddenly, Aidan realized that he knew where they were, all of them. He had to get to the Colonel.

The lost boys awoke to the sound of gunfire.

"Crap!" Colt said, and Peter didn't correct him. He just agreed with him.

Riley bolted out of her sleeping bag. "We gotta get going!" she said. "That's gotta be wargs."

Jax was the last one up. As the foggy fingers of his dreams lifted, only to be left with the sound of gunfire, he didn't stop until he was dragging Riley through the doorway – Colt, Peter, and Val in tow.

In the hallways, people were running from the battle while soldiers ran towards it. Alyssa met them outside.

"We gotta get to the Humvees," Jax said.

"Aidan's gone."

"We've got to go for my brother," Peter said.

Jax looked around. "Okay, you guys run for the Humvees. I'll get Aidan and meet you there, but if we aren't there in like ten minutes, go without us. I will get him. We'll catch up."

In the distance, IEDs were exploding. Soldiers were cheering with each explosion like it was a touchdown, but Aidan knew what was happening. It was too far away for the soldiers to see, but through warg eyes Aidan saw encampment people being forced to enter the minefield. He also saw the bodies stacked on top of the jets of fuel. That was how they clogged the fuel lines. Bodies upon bodies burning like bonfires. If the wind turned direction, the smell would be too much for everyone in the tower.

"There is a something large coming from the south," Aidan directed some soldiers.

"What is it?" Aidan recognized the soldier as the tall red.

"I'm not sure. Maybe a herd?"

The soldiers didn't argue with him. They knew Aidan was the one the monsters were after.

"Take cover!" he shouted to another group of soldiers just as the rocs dove from the sky. The soldiers saw the rocs just in time to drive them away with their guns.

The other soldiers were waiting to lay gunfire on any monstercized heifer that tried to jump the last highway divider. They couldn't have been more wrong. A large bulk reached over the concrete divider and gripped the openings at the bottom. Massive shoulders flung the barrier aside. Hands grabbed a soldier who was shooting at him wildly, and tossed the soldier light as a toy over its back. Aidan jumped back when he saw what emerged from the barriers. It was tall and bulky, and its thick grey hide was impenetrable. It walked on two feet like a man, but roared with the sound of a thousand doors slamming shut on Aidan's life.

The bear grabbed the red-headed woman, lifted her over its head, and pulled her apart as easily as a child ripping apart a doll. Her blood splashed on the nearest soldiers. Aidan staggered backward. It had been no herd, just a monstrous creature more dangerous than an entire herd.

It was crushing them like an avalanche. Except instead of rocks or snow, the lost boys were being smothered by people who were shoving their way towards the stairwells. This was the evacuation procedure of every building in America. Avoid the elevator and take the stairs. But these people weren't trying to exit the building, they were looking for a safe place to hide, and if the safest place to survive a tornado was the stairwell, it was also the most likely place to survive the apocalypse.

Val had an insane thought as he passed the recessed fire extinguisher case. *In case of apocalypse, break glass,* Val thought.

"What is the problem?" Alyssa asked when she heard him laugh.

"Nothing," he said. "Just wish it was an axe instead of a fire extinguisher."

The five, Val, Alyssa, Riley, Colt, and Peter in that order, flattened against the wall next to the extinguisher to allow the crowd of people to press past them towards the stairs. The people had panic in their eyes. Mothers, fathers, kids and teens terrified of what the day was bringing them and whether they would see another day. They were like a herd ready to stampede at the first crack of lightning. For now, they were gently pushing at each other, hands on friends and loved ones and neighbors. But with the right fuse, they would be shoving each other down to escape. Val hoped that didn't happen.

"Could some of y'all lose a little weight?" Peter yelled out, but nobody except the other lost boys heard him. Everyone else was too busy trying to cram themselves into the stairwells in a not-so-orderly fashion.

Inch by inch, Val led them towards the back of the tower. Only Aidan had visited the parking garage, so Val was going on blind faith that it was in the back and not on an upper or lower level. If they had to go back this way, the assault may be over by the time they found the Humvees.

As they worked along the wall, Val thought of the garage and he hoped that it wasn't guarded. Maybe he could talk his way through it, but if not, it would come to violence, and he had nothing to back himself up with. Speaking loud and carrying a big stick is going to suck, he thought. He could only hope that any guards had left their posts to defend the tower.

Alyssa must have seen the fear in Val's eyes because she put her hand on his shoulder and said, "We've got you." He looked at the grenade-throwing cheerleader, the crane-climbing gymnast, a 13-year old who had lived through more battles than most men, and the bitch of the yard. They were high school kids who had become survivors, and so had he. He pushed into the crowd.

Some of the people began shouting, then somebody shoved, and another person shoved back. Riley got the wind knocked out of her when a middle-aged man with a thick moustache bounced into her ribcage and would not move back. Alyssa had to kick the obese man in the knees before he would give Riley any breathing room.

Aidan shoved a man down into the pavement as a roc buzzed over them, its talons like the stretching blades of a harvester. A rush of wind from the downward push of the roc's wings knocked Aidan flat on his butt. It was as if an invisible man shoved him in the chest. He looked up in time to see death in the cold raptor's eyes. Death and maybe something more. Recognition? Aidan suddenly wondered what was showing on the psychic channel and whether or not his image was being broadcasted to the other beasts.

The roc did a quick whirl in the air, flipped, and reached for Aidan. This time, he was not fast enough to dodge the creature. Its cold, hard pinions grabbed him by the side and tossed him in the air. The gray sky did cartwheels around him, and then he was tight in the roc's grip. The tower was racing beside him. The roc screeched a piercing call, a sound so frightening it was painful. As he heard other rocs responding, the Tooth flew to the side, and then impossibly the world raced back up at him, and he was back on the ground. A pain ripped through his shoulder, and his world went black.

When he woke, only moments had passed. Jax stood over him, prying roc claws off of him. Above him, the Tooth was like a giant black ladder reaching up into the skies. At the top of that ladder, Aidan saw giant rocs and worse creatures circling in the sky.

"C'mon! There are more coming for you!"

Aidan blinked and pushed a claw aside. It was like being held by a brick wall. More pain shot through his side. Jax pulled out his parang and chopped the claw off with three strokes. Then he jerked Aidan out and pulled him to his feet.

"You can still run, right?" Jax said.

Aidan nodded, and he followed him back towards the tower. Unfortunately, that took them right back towards the bear.

Tendrils of smoke curled up from its giant back. It stood on the concrete in a circle of dead bodies. As it breathed deeply, the bear made a throaty sound, not of defeat but of rising resolution.

For the first time, Aidan noticed that the bear had four horrible cloudy blue eyes, like cataracts. Once again, he felt like he wasn't looking into the eyes of a living, breathing thing but into the eyes of the dead.

That gave him a crazy idea. He shouted into a soldier's ear, "Aim for the head! Hit it in its eye!" The soldier nodded and lifted his weapon up. The grizzly sensed the movement and looked up to. Right at them.

A bullet parted the air as it drove towards the monster's eyes, and succinctly bounced off the giant cataract.

"Why won't anything work?!" Aidan cursed.

The grizzly raised its massive jaws in the air, and then something truly hideous happened. The bear's jaw split horizontally down the middle, like some nightmarish petal flower. Inside its terrible orifice, two new set of teeth glistened. The beast made a curse similar to Aidan's, but in its language it came out as a terrible roar, and then it leaped towards Aidan and Jax. Jax dragged him away from the bear-monster and into the plaza towards the atrium. Aidan passed under Atlas' muscular frame as the bear swiped at him. Atlas blocked the blow with his own concrete body, but it was not enough to stop the bear. The bear pushed Atlas down. The titan cracked and splintered in the dead fountain.

Around Aidan, soldiers fired on the bear, but the bullets were as useless as pelting acorns against its thick hide.

"Quick! Here!" Jax said, and darted to the side, away from the entrance. They had to leap over a dead soldier's body, but they crossed to the open door just in time. Dre stood there with the door open. She slammed it shut as they entered. A giant open mouth full of dozens of sharp teeth descended on the door, and it was nearly thrown off its hinges as the bear collided with the door. Inside, Aidan saw a large crowd of people stuffed into the stairwell.

A second later, the door was ripped from the foundation and thrown away. The bear chugged air as its cold dead eyes looked on the meaty buffet inside the stairwell.

Nobody moved. It was as if a spell had been cast on everyone in the stairwell, and they no longer had the power to control their limbs. They stared at the demon bear, and it stared at them.

Behind it, the soldiers were holding their fire. If they missed, they would hit the people inside.

The bear placed a paw gently on the floor in front of Aidan and Dre. It then positioned itself to squeeze into the stairwell entrance, which was much too narrow for its broad shoulders. It pulled itself forward, its serrated head entering the stairwell. The smell of blood and death came with it. With its four dead eyes, it studied all the bodies the way a grizzly might study honeycombs, or baby squirrels trapped in the knothole of a tree. It pushed its hulking mass against the doorframe, knocking dust and straining the concrete.

A second time, it reached forward with one paw. Aidan suddenly felt like rabbits trapped in a warren with all the exits sealed. Somebody screamed, and Aidan glanced up the stairwell. People were trying to move to another floor, but the problem was that nobody was moving fast enough for the people on the bottom. The USE HANDRAILS sign didn't seem to deter them from climbing over each other to get to the next floor.

The scream excited the bear, and it reached farther into the stairwell as people tried to push up and away from the bear.

Then a sliver of metal arched towards the ground and cut through one of the bear's claws. It bellowed painfully as it retracted its paw.

"How does that feel, you son of a bitch!" Jax yelled.

"Where you going?" Dre asked.

"The Colonel," Aidan said. "I can help him fight these things off. I know where they are. Do you want to come with us?"

"Thanks, but these people need all the help they can get. You'd think they've never done a mass evacuation before."

Dre shook what was left of Aidan's hand and then he went up the stairs.

The bear charged the stairwell entrance, and Jax and Aidan ran out into the atrium.

In the atrium, the problem was obvious. With stairwells to either side of the building clogged with tower residents hiding from the monsters, there was only one other way up to the fourth floor, the elevator shaft.

"Hang on," Aidan said as Jax pried open the elevator doors.

"We can make it," Jax said as he entered the elevator car and popped the service entry. He leaped up lithe as a panther, pulled himself on top of the car and looked back at Aidan.

"What are you waiting for?"

"Oh, my back, my side, my arms, my gut. Basically, I'm waiting on my entire body to heal up before I can go elevator spelunking. You don't have a healing potion on hand, do you?"

"Sorry, man." Jax looked at him with concern, as if seeing his damaged body for the first time.

"I got an idea," Aidan said, and he left the elevator car. While he was away, Jax listened to the war outside. It sounded like there was a lot of human casualty going on. He only hoped they were holding the monsters back. In the time he and Peter and Riley had spent here before the others arrived, they learned just how protected the Tooth was. There were many layers of protection, much more than the nine rings. If the monsters could get them here, there would be no stopping them, ever.

Aidan appeared in the car again. He had long coaxial cables.

"Do you think that will hold you?"

"I only need it to hold part of me. My legs can take care of the rest. Think you can pull me up?"

"If you lost as much weight as I think you have, yeah."

Jax flashed a smile that was all Hollywood. He put the cable over his shoulder and started climbing cat-like up the elevator shaft cable.

He remembered from climbing ropes with his sensei that the trick was to use the feet to push you up and not to try to climb with the arms. Still, he probably used his arms too much, and by the time he finally reached the fourth floor, he dropped out of the elevator shaft and sucked in air. Little black and white fireflies popped in front of his eyes.

"Throw it down!"

Jax took three more breaths, then began lowering the cable down the shaft.

The problem was not wrapping the coax cables around his body. It was tying the bowline knot. His little finger shouldn't have affected his knot-tying abilities that much, but the cable just wouldn't stay put. He got frustrated. *C'mon, Aidan. The bowline is an easy knot. Beginner Boy Scouts. Maybe Webelos stuff. You just make a loop with one hand, then push the other end of the cable through the hole (the rabbit goes out of his hole), around the extra length of rope (around the tree) and push it back through the hole (and back into his hole).* But the rabbit wasn't cooperating. *Fuck it.* The hand holding the rabbit wasn't working.

A loud booming roar like gunfire magnified through the atrium. Aidan looked across the tiled floor and saw the angry bear on the other side. It had given up on the stairwell and decided to come in through the front doors.

Aidan closed his eyes and took a deep breath.

The bear was woofing from its split mouth as it barreled for the elevators.

He pulled the knot tight, didn't look at it, and yelled, "Pull!"

His body lifted up through the service door just in time for him to feel the bear's hot breath on him. As he stood on top of the car, the bear pushed up through the top, too. Its multiple jaws snapped at Aidan, who hopped to the side. From on top, Jax saw the grizzly coming through the elevator. He heaved on the coax at the same time that Aidan was trying to run up the side of the wall, his hands splayed out for balance.

Aidan climbed to the fourth floor, and they both leaned against the elevator doors.

"Who knew coax cable could be so useful?"

"Right?" Jax added.

There was a large groaning of metal, and they looked down the elevator shaft. The grizzly was climbing. Four eyes focused on them.

"You gotta be kidding me!" Jax yelled.

The boys ran from the shaft and went looking for the Colonel. The cubicle farms were almost completely empty except for soldiers firing out of windows. Every once in a while, the giant shadow of a roc's wing would pass over them, and then it would disappear.

Jax and Aidan ran back towards the front of the building. A plume of crimson and yellow billowed out from beneath them. It was the flamethrower from a turret, which was down one floor.

"What are you boys doing here?" the familiar gruff voice of Colonel Weatherford barked at them.

He was flanked by two soldiers, and he was carrying an RPG launcher.

"Whoa," Jax said.

"Only thing I know that will stop one of these bastards for sure."

Just then, the bear roared from the elevator.

"Fire in the hole!" Colonel Weatherford shouted. He kneeled down and pulled the trigger. The RPG flew over the cube walls and exploded in the shaft, spewing smoke and debris everywhere. Aidan and the others coughed.

"Now *that* is how you get rid of a bear," he said. "Hooyah!"

While the other soldiers cheered, they also prepped the RPG launcher.

"I can help," Aidan said. "I know where they all are."

Colonel Weatherford smiled. "This time, we end it, son."

More cubes. More and more cubes. Val looked around. This was not the parking garage.

"This isn't the way," Alyssa said.

Riley slapped her head. "Sorry. Brain fart. I should have said something. It's back this way."

An empty pit grew in Riley's stomach when she knew she had screwed up. And with a screw-up like this, their lives were at stake. She could hear her mother taunting her. *What were you thinking? You know better!*

"What's the matter?" Alyssa asked her.

"Is it possible that my mother is still criticizing me from the grave?"

"Yes, and ignore her. Where's the garage?"

"Come on."

Aidan had his eyes closed as he tried to concentrate on the images in his head. Once he gave the monsters his full attention, he found it was like being dropped into a large river. The Mississippi of monsters. He had to select which one to follow.

Aidan pointed to his left. "There will be a roc coming over my shoulder in a few seconds. It is diving from up above."

"That doesn't help us much, son," Colonel Weatherford said. "You're going to have to do better than that. 11 o'clock? 12 o'clock? Where?"

The roc zoomed past the open windows. Aidan felt the cold air on his face. Tried again.

"2 o'clock. Coming in three – two – now."

The RPG lifted into the air and collided with a diving roc, which exploded into a fireball of aviary guts and bones.

"That's getting it done!" Colonel Weatherford shouted. "One roc and one bear. Let's see what else you can do."

"What do you call the turrets?" Aidan asked.

"The one below us is Turret One. The numbers go clockwise from there."

"Turret Three. Warg will appear at 3 o'clock in five – four – three – two – now." In his mind's eye, he saw the warg coming over the concrete divider. As Colonel Weatherford called it in, the soldiers fell back. The warg ran towards the closest soldier and was met with a spout of flame. For an instant, Aidan could feel the flames boiling his skin. He jumped out of the stream. Jax grabbed him.

"Why don't you sit down, man?"

They grabbed him a chair. Mr. Seward walked into the room.

"What is he doing here?"

"He just nailed one of the giant falcons and a werewolf."

Mr. Seward took this information in and processed it. He was a man of education and not beyond learning a lesson where it was warranted. If the young man had powers that could save them, so be it.

"Everyone is in the stairwells, Colonel. The door to one was broken off, so the civilians there have retreated to a higher floor, the third to seventh floors."

"Thank you, John," Colonel Weatherford said. They nodded, the only time allowed for such formalities in a battle, and Mr. Seward left the war room.

With the help of Aidan's monster Wi-Fi, rocs were falling from the sky and wargs were shrieking with their coats blazing. The winds of war were shifting in their direction. Then suddenly five rocs came together in a sudden formation. With amazing agility, they banked against the mirrored glass panes and dived on one of the turrets all at once. The soldiers there lit up the rocs like Christmas trees, but it was not enough to deter them. The monsters were cawing out in pain, flames leaping from their backs and reflecting in their eyes as they stomped out the soldiers and ripped apart the flamethrower. Aidan fell out of the chair in pain.

When he got back up, he felt a tug at the back of his head. Something was wrong. He followed the tug back. Felt its many-footed presence.

"I hope we've got traps," he said.

He turned and saw them, hundreds of them, scurrying out of the elevator shaft. Each one was as big as a beagle, but gruesome and hairless, with a long, wicked tail trailing behind it.

"Oh, joy," Jax said as he pulled out his parang.

"Hold on, son," Colonel Weatherford said. "Follow me."

The soldiers fell back, throwing chairs and cabinets in their path. The rats had no trouble climbing over, under, and through the obstacles and were able to stay close. They finally made a leap to one man and pulled him down. Hordes of slick bodies swarmed over him. He screamed as he felt a rat bite his finger off. Screamed again when a rat ripped his belly button off. Screamed one last time when another rat wrapped its giant incisors around his scrotum and bit hard. He would have screamed the hardest then except for the rat that took the chance to enter his opened orifice and bite off his tongue.

Colonel Weatherford opened a door and everyone entered. They were in a windowed conference room with a large oak table and framed photos of the Garden of the Gods. The Colonel didn't close the door behind him, though. He yelled, "Keep going!"

They ran through the adjacent door on the far side of the conference room as the rats followed them inside. This door, the Colonel closed. One of the soldiers ran to the other door and closed it too, while everyone watched the rats crowding into the room.

"What now?" Jax wanted to know.

Colonel Weatherford put his hand on a circular handle. It rested above a large tank with an MSDS sheet he didn't have time to read. The line led from the tank up into the paneled ceiling.

The table was almost unrecognizable with all the pink and white skinned bodies crawling over it, their tails dragging like snakes from the back of chimeras. Chairs toppled from their weight. They began crawling up to the ceiling. One stopped and stared at the group through the window.

The demonic rat growled at them and looked across at its horde. The rats began to retreat out of the conference room or to crawl towards the ceiling panels.

"Die, you bastards!" Colonel Weatherford shouted. He turned the handle. The fire suppression sprinklers turned on, and clear liquid sprayed all over the room. Immediately, the rats began squeaking with misery and their skins began to smoke, boil, and writhe.

"Acid," the Colonel said triumphantly. "One of the many accoutrements to the Tooth. C'mon. There will be more. We didn't get all of them."

They entered another conference room above Turret 2. Aidan sat in a chair while the soldiers set up the remaining RPGs. The Colonel called in their location and asked for a resupply.

"There's not much left, Colonel. We weren't ready for an extended battle. I'll see what I can do," the voice on the other end of the line said.

Then they heard the rats coming at them again.

While Aidan reset his mind to the monsters, the soldiers and Jax pushed forward against the remaining rats. Some of the soldiers shot at the rats, which was only slightly effective.

"Hold your fire!" Jax yelled. "You haven't dealt with rats before today. Guns only knock off ears and tails, but doesn't kill them. Use your knives and stab these motherfuckers."

Dre wanted the crowd moving upward, away from the gunfire. She figured most of the fighting was below the first four or five floors. If she could get the people to move to the sixth floor and above, they would be on much safer ground. As it was now, they were stuck between the second and fourth floors.

She was having a hard time communicating this.

"My son is out there fighting. No way am I leaving him behind!" an obese woman was yelling at her. She had short curly brown hair and pale folds of skin over her eyes.

"The best thing we can do for him is to keep us safe, and we will be safer on higher ground," Dre reassured her.

"What if the stairwell topples?" a gray-haired old man asked.

"Then we will die no matter where we are."

Some people gasped, but Dre sighed. This was tough.

"Just keep moving up in an orderly fashion," she said. "And use the handrails!"

Some of the people on the fourth floor railings began to climb farther up the stairs.

An old man bundled in thick clothes stumbled next to her. Dre reached out to help him. The man's arms felt excessively cold, almost like ice, and hard as iron. She looked into the dead man's eyes and heard the man hiss "dry-der!" as his belly erupted with death and dismemberment.

Aidan concentrated on the river. He heard laughter from somewhere, but he shrugged it off. There was a whole river of thought out there.

But it was not laughter he heard. The raucous railings of the dead and dying cried out from the river. It was a very different river than the one he first dove into. If it was a river, it had changed from a murderous red color to a bright screaming blue. There were fewer and fewer of the thoughts in the river, too.

Then he felt something approaching, like a giant whale coming down the river. No, not a whale. A kraken.

Malifax?

In answer, he did not receive a name but a sound, a boom like the thunders he remembered from Lakewood. And even though he did not hear the particular vowels and consonants, he knew the name in his head.

Why are you doing this?

His head was flooded with laughter. Then the same question was posed to him. Malifax showed him images of the Tooth caving in, crushing wargs and humans alike. Skulls were squashed like jelly donuts and eyes popped like balloons under the great weight of the tower. The next image showed the Tooth intact, with wargs and rocs waiting outside. Humans tossed down their weapons and marched sadly, yet comfortably to the prison camps. There they were given food – grains and nuts and drink.

Fuck you.

His mind bent backward as if Malifax had struck him with one of his many grip-like tentacles. For a second, he remembered the wall of mouths and teeth that was Malifax's tentacles. But these tentacles weren't real, and this was just a feeling, just a sensation, but it was one hell of a strong feeling.

Before he could completely recover from the mental slap, Malifax sent him a crushing wall of images of soldiers being ripped apart limb from limb by the wargs, people in the stairwell being eaten alive by dryders, and the tower overrun by hell-spawned roaches and rats and other creatures that looked like nothing more than shadows with teeth. Bears and pumas of monstrous size pummeled the tower. Rocs carried children up the height of the tower and then dropped them for fun.

He saw each of his friends burning.

No. We will beat you. We are better than you. We have something you will never have.

Malifax did not respond at first. Then he showed Aidan images of Bridgetown falling. He showed pictures of other towns falling by monstercized versions of whatever stock of animal was available: snakes and coyotes in the southwest; eagles and bears in the North, sharks on the coast, and always the monsters that were blasphemies of cats and dogs.

Again, Aidan heard the laughter and ignored it.

Instead, Aidan thought of their victories. He showed Malifax a shot of himself smashing a Molotov on Black Fang's face. He showed the bat being killed. He showed him rocs and wargs on fire on the battlefield. He showed Jax cutting off one of Malifax's tentacles.

The thoughts were coming at him more red and black then ever before. Malifax showed images a thousand times worse than the ones Aidan showed. He showed him a hundred deaths in an instant, each death more disturbing than the last, and Aidan knew each one of them to be true. He did not know the people who died, but he knew how badly they had suffered. Malifax showed him people from Lakewood being skinned. Then he showed him Aaron dead on the lawn while Black Fang sniffed around him. Then he showed the bullet hole smoking in the back of Aaron's head.

He hadn't thought of Aaron in forever. *You forced us to do that.* He heard laughing, but he wasn't sure if it was Malifax or his own stupid conscience laughing at him. He couldn't bullshit here. Nobody forced him to do that. He took Aaron's life because he thought it was the best thing to do for their survival. "He didn't have any bleach." Isn't that what he said? Poor excuse to kill somebody, if there was ever a good reason to kill somebody.

The next set of images seemed to come from a crow or raven perched at Bridgetown. He recognized it. It was him standing there arguing with Jax over Riley. Riley put her hand on Jax's shoulder and pushed him away so that she was centered on Aidan.

"Do you want me to go?" she asked.

Aidan moaned as he remembered his reactions. "It's not that simple," he said.

"No, I think it is." Then like the worst person on earth, Aidan looked away.

I eventually bled for her! I bled for all of them!

He saw Jax taking off his polo and Mr. Olivarez pointing to him. He saw himself and Alyssa on the bus with him trying to push her away from the crowd.

That's not me.

Malifax's silence said enough to Aidan. The case was closed. There was nothing more to discuss. He was not a good person.

I did it for our survival. I only did what I had to stay alive.

The visions in his head showed wolves fighting off spears and elephants fighting off traps. He saw deer running from hunter's guns and cows being slaughtered. He saw a bloom of euthanasia.

Puppies dropped in a box and the box pumped full of gas. The puppies crying out for mothers that wouldn't come.

What are you saying? That you had to do this? That this is your survival?

He felt that slap against his mind like a tooth scraping across his fissures. The next image showed him and Alyssa in a cabin in the far north with nothing but snow and sky to surround them. She was smiling. They had their arms around each other. They leaned into each other, and their shape formed the tower. He was leaving the tower with his friends. They were leaving in the Humvees and leaving everyone behind.

So that was it, then. The grand plan. Leave everything but the Artic alone, and they would leave him alone.

You're making a deal like I'm Mr. Olivarez.

There was no way to answer this, so Malifax showed him again the visions. Malifax upped the stakes by showing him pictures of his family and his children.

That's what separates us from them, he thought. They have no sense of true altruism. He projected a vision of a mother cradling a child. Malifax countered quickly with a dog nursing pups. Aidan showed people sharing food. Malifax showed wolves sharing a carcass. He showed a doctor. Malifax showed a lion licking another lion's wounds.

From him came an image of a boy helping an old woman across the street. It was cartoonish, kind of 90s Nickelodeon because he'd never really seen anyone helping old women across streets, but he thought it would get the point across.

Malifax projected an image of a gorilla fending off other gorillas from a boy who had fallen into their paddock.

Altruism.

Malifax didn't respond. Despite what he had just seen, Aidan wondered if this was the key difference he saw between animals and humans. Not the kindness of kin or similarity, but true altruism with nothing to gain. Was that what separated humankind? Would animals ever be willing to sacrifice themselves for the lives of others the way that humans would.

Again, the laughter. It was deep now. Malifax was gone, and only the laughter remained. Whatever argument he had engaged with Malifax had ended. He didn't know if that was Malifax conceding a point or no longer wanting to argue. Nothing more could be said. They had different beliefs, and that was the end of it.

The laughter was low-bellied. Aidan's mind was tired from swimming in the river. If he were back in his body, he would say the adrenaline had worn off. Something like that happened here, but he had no explanation to equate to adrenaline wearing off. He was weary and tired, and wanted to go to sleep, but he swam a little ways more. He was searching for the laughter. He saw dead bodies in the eyes of those he passed through. Dead bodies in the stairwell and in the turrets. Dead bodies in the field of battle.

He found a very red stream, and in the stream, he saw something that made his soul scream and his body retch. He could not believe what he was looking at. Val, Alyssa, Riley, Colt, and Peter. They were in the garage, surrounded by terrible, snapping wargs. He saw this all through the eyes of Black Fang. That was who was laughing. This was all a distraction while Black Fang captured the rest of the lost boys. While he had been engaged in philosophical wrestling with Malifax, Black Fang had trapped his friends!

Out of the visions, he fell backward. His arms waved wildly as he tried to catch himself from falling out of his chair. Jax, who had slapped him silly to wake him, reached out to grab him. There was a moment of arms flailing and diving, but Jax was able to keep Aidan from falling on his back.

Aidan looked around. There was blood everywhere.

"Where have you been?" Jax asked.

"How long was I out?"

"Five minutes?"

"We gotta get to the garage. Black Fang is here."

Another rat squirmed in his grip. He lopped off its head. Beside him, a soldier stabbed a knife in the back, severing its spine. The mutated rodent began dragging its back squealing in pain. The soldier stabbed it again in the head.

"I think we got them all," Jax said.

"Incoming!" the Colonel yelled. Jax dove aside as a four-winged roc, black as night, came crashing into the side of the building. It squawked and waved its wings like a thunderbird, sending shards of glass spiraling throughout the floor. A warg sat on its back, a spear in its hand. It raised the spear back over its head and prepared to hurl it into Aidan's body.

This was the same monstrous combination that they had seen out on the plains, the one that could instill fear from miles away. The only person who did not try to hide from it was Aidan. The winged damnation reached its beak for Aidan while the warg's throwing arm slid forward. Jax jumped out from behind a desk and used a turned-over desk as a leaping pad to sidekick the bird in the head. The roc turned on Jax and screeched. He leaped back at it, chopping at its giant orbit with his parang. The first cut dinged off the giant eagle's patina. The beast jumped to the side, but Jax didn't let go. While the rider struggled to stay on his mount, the eagle reeled on its side, trying to leap back out. Jax ripped at its patina with his fingers until it blinked. In the instant that it blinked, he struck with his parang, stabbing its giant iris. The roc shook him off. He went flying across the floor, but he was buffeted when he slammed into a cube wall.

The giant eagle dove away. Its warg rider finally lost his grip on the eagle and fell down into an unused flowerbed. The warg strained to lift itself up after the great fall. As it strained, soldiers attacked it, stabbing its mouth, ears, and eyes with their knives until it was dead. On the horizon, the sky started to grow dark.

"What's that?" Colonel Weatherford asked.

"Bats," Aidan said.

For the next scattered minutes, the beasts flung everything they had at the Tooth. It was a fury of blood, wings, and steel. Flame and concussive blasts.

Then Colonel Weatherford called in "the cannon."

"Take cover," he told everyone present. Soldiers climbed behind cubicle walls and steel desks. A minute later, he yelled, "fire in the hole!" into a receiver. A rumbling noise rose from the ground floor.

A giant fountain of flames erupted out of the Tooth from all sides. The heat was so intense that it reddened Jax's skin.

Afterwards, Jax noted that some of the glass panes had begun to melt because of the flame. Fireballs erupted from the top of the tower like the concoctions of some mad wizard. Fire scorched the sky. People inside ducked behind whatever they could find to escape the heat.

Aidan didn't wonder where all the propellant was coming from. He remembered the giant tanks in the atrium. They had been guarded for good reason. Colonel Weatherford was a clever strategist.

Balls of liquid flame splashed on the concrete below. When finally the flames died, the sky was monsterless, as if the marauding rocs and bats had disappeared into fiery oblivion.

"Colonel, I have to go. I have to take care of my family."

The Colonel nodded and shook Aidan's hand, then gave him a can of pepper spray and shouted to the others to get the RPGs loaded. "Don't know how much more ammo we have, but I want to go out swinging, boys!"

Jax and Aidan jumped down the rubble in the elevator shaft, sidestepping the remains of the bear, and ran for the garage.

They found the way to the garage almost completely unblocked. There were still screams from the stairs and the occasional rattle of gunfire, but for now, the Christmas Day battle had found some peace.

Jax burst through the doors of the first level of the garage, knife drawn while Aidan followed slowly behind. Aidan's arm wasn't working since the roc made him fly, and his back was screaming at him to stop and fall down, but he had to find his betrothed, his brothers, and the rest of his family.

"Can you see them like you did the others?" Jax asked.

Aidan shook his head. Something was different. Something had changed.

They ran up the garage, and they saw their friends bound and gagged. Some Renfields had tied them up. The lost boys were trying to say something or at least point with their eyes.

Then Black Fang dropped on them from above. He gripped Jax and shook him like a toy, then flung him across the garage. Jax flipped in the air and crashed into the concrete, hitting his head. The way he hit, all motor control went out of him. His body did not roll, but went down like a football player knocked out during a particularly bad hit. Aidan hoped he was just knocked out.

"You," the warg growled.

Aidan slowly turned his angle so that he was backing up the garage towards his friends. They were tied to the Humvee grilles.

"No fire," the warg growled again. His voice was like granite.

"No gun."

"Useless."

The great Warden of the West licked his lips while he watched Aidan with his yellow eyes. The look was enough to make Aidan want to piss his pants. If he had, he wouldn't have been embarrassed, and years from then, he would gladly retell the fight and always include this part because he was that scared of the warden/dire dog/hellhound/werewolf/whatever it was.

Suddenly, a gunshot rang out across the garage. Black Fang shirked from the impact, then looked to the lower level. It was Mr. Seward. He was holding an old Magnum pistol and firing patiently and deliberately at Black Fang.

"Save your friends!" Mr. Seward yelled to Aidan. "I've got this black-toothed son of a bitch. Try to destroy my friends, will you?"

The great wolf padded towards the old man, who shot again at him, crying out, "I am: yet what I am none cares or knows. My friends forsake me like a memory lost; I am the self-consumer of my woes - they rise and vanish in oblivious host like shades in love and death's oblivion lost. And yet I am! and live with shadows tossed!"

He fired his Magnum to punctuate his speech, and when the end came, he did not flinch nor look away, but looked Black Fang in the eyes as the monster ripped him into two pieces.

While Black Fang cleaved Mr. Seward, Aidan took those precious few seconds to run up and knock over the closest Renfield to him. Then he began untying his friends, and they helped him fight off the other Renfields, who quickly gave up and ran.

"Hurry! We've got an idea!" Val yelled. He and Alyssa and the others began pushing drums of gasoline down to the edge of the garage ramp. Val punctured the first drums using a knife he forced from one of the slaves. Gasoline stunk in the air and turned the white ramp black.

A low rumble emanated from the lower floor as Black Fang released his anger. Colt and Peter hurried to push their drums to the side and dump them.

Aidan reached into the driver side seat of one of the Humvees and grabbed a beer bottle and a bandana, which he stuffed in the bottle. Then he filled the bottle from a gasoline tank that was strapped to the back of the Humvee. His side begged him to put the tank down. Then he lit the bandana with a lighter and ran to the rail.

"Remember this, dog breath?" he shouted as he flung the Molotov at Black Fang. The glass shattered square on his shoulder, and fire exploded all over his side. Flames flickered down and ignited on the fumes before they reached the ground. In a second, the whole garage ramp brightened to solar yellow, and the great wolf screamed in agony.

Aidan high fived Peter and hugged Alyssa, but then the great flaming beast leaped out of the fire pit, waving its arms wildly. It kicked Val in the gut and bit down on Riley's shoulder, shattering every bone.

"No!" Alyssa screamed.

The garage stunk of smoldering flesh. Almost all of Black Fang's hair had burned off, yet the beast came forward, running on pure adrenaline and God knows what else. It knocked Colt down and stomped on him. Something crunched. It tried to bite Colt, but Peter jumped in the way. The wolf gladly bit down on Peter's arm.

It wasn't just pain that Peter felt, but pressure like his arm was pinned between two boulders, and then he was flung out of the way. Aidan pulled Colt clear of the beast as it sank to the floor.

When Peter came to, he looked down and saw the flaming gasoline rolling down the ramp. At the far end lay Jax, his left foot twitching.

Peter climbed up. His arm felt like it had been rolled over by a bulldozer. He limped to the side of the garage and climbed up on the bar. With his perfect balance, he walked the rails down to where Jax was lying, and he checked his pulse. There was a pool of blood under his head, but he still had a heartbeat.

As the flames rolled towards him, he pulled himself and Jax up on the pipes above the flames, then carried him across to the Humvees.

"Gymnast, much?" Alyssa asked as she helped to pull Jax down.

"All State," Peter said.

Colt was barely moving.

"Stay still," Alyssa told Colt. He tried not to cry, but the pain was too much. He would have doubled over, but the pain was so intense, he couldn't move, so he just cried where he lay.

Val also began to move slowly. Aidan got the thumbs up from him, then went to check on Riley.

Riley was gasping for air. "Oh, no," Aidan said despondently.

"We need a doctor!" Val yelled back to Alyssa. "Something's wrong with Riley!"

Alyssa grabbed the first aid kit and ran over. "There are no doctors. What is it?"

"I don't know. She can't breathe."

"What do we do? Didn't you read something about it?" she asked Aidan.

"Maybe."

"There's no time for maybe, Aidan. Do something."

He ran back to the Humvees. "I need something to cut her open and something for air to go into, like a pen."

"How about a straw?" Val pulled one out from between seat cushions.

"That'll work. I need a knife."

"There's an Exacto in the first aid kit," Alyssa said.

Aidan ran back to Riley and took the Exacto out of the kit.

"I'm sorry, Riley. I don't know if this will work, but it's all I can do."

Riley's eyes were rolling and her lips were turning blue. She grabbed Aidan's arm tightly.

Aidan looked to Alyssa, then stabbed Riley's chest with the tip of the knife. Blood began to pour out.

"Okay, now we need to get the straw in there."

He pushed the straw in, but the wound continued to bleed from in and around the straw.

Riley was grabbing him harder as she gasped for air.

"What's happening?" Val asked. "Something's not right."

"Try again" Alyssa said.

"I don't know what I'm doing. I'm just stabbing her to death."

"Try again!"

He stabbed her one more time, gently, and lower in her chest. He took the straw out of the one side of her lung and put it in the other spot. Blood dribbled out from inside the straw.

"I think it's working!" he shouted.

But when they looked up at Riley, she was dead.

They left Jax next to Riley. He had bled out in the back seat of the Humvee while they tried to help Riley. When they came back, he was dead.

"He saved my life about a million times in the past hour," Aidan said. "I never got to say thank you."

They propped him up next to her. Alyssa teared up when she saw how naturally they fit together side-by-side. She reached into Riley's pants pocket and pulled out Riley's cellphone. The first photo was of her in the cold night outside Austin. The last photo was one she took of everyone at the Christmas Eve celebration, not eighteen hours ago. Alyssa wiped her tear and pocketed the phone.

Colt did not want to move, but he hung from Peter's shoulders while Peter carried him, and he tried to force back the tears while they laid him down in the Humvee. Laying him down was the most painful part. He cried effusively as they laid him down. Once he was down, though, he felt much better. Nowhere near okay, but much better. Alyssa made him drink some ibuprofen from the first aid kit.

They drove quietly out of the garage. The battle was mostly over. A few rocs still hovered over the tower, but for the most part, the beasts had fled. The parking lots were littered with the bodies of the dead.

They stopped outside the atrium. Its steel girders had collapsed, and all the glass was blown out.

"I want to check in before we leave."

Part of Aidan wanted to scream at her to leave, but that was only a small part of him now. He smiled and said, "Okay."

"We'll be just a minute," he told the others.

Inside, the place seemed deserted. The few soldiers who remained were covered in blood and ash. They sat down and stared at the spaces in the floors between their knees.

That's when Alyssa heard something. It was a sound that frightened her and scared her and drove her to anger all at once. Aidan heard it too, and followed.

She opened the doorway to the stairs. They heard the sound again, a high-pitched wail, sharp and painful. They ran up the stairs.

The sound went on and on. It was a piercing sound, the kind of sound that made all people want to cry. Something was very wrong, but maybe there was something they could do to help the baby.

At the second floor, the baby stopped to take a breath, and then called out again with that horrible sound that drives people insane. Alyssa didn't know it, but she was crying.

Third floor and they were almost there. The sound was deafening. They were having to step over bodies now. In another lifetime, maybe Alyssa would have cared, but not with this poor creature needing help.

The baby was on the floor, and it was being dragged along by one of the puppy wargs. Aidan and Alyssa charged the puppy. He stabbed it with the Exacto he used to end Riley's life, and she kicked the oversized dog. It howled in pain and limped away. Alyssa lifted the baby and checked it. She thought it would be okay. The beasts had only grabbed it by the blanket.

Aidan tapped her on the shoulder. Two wargs approached, one from either side. There was no way to run. He tried to lift her and the bay up to the ceiling, hoping that maybe she could push the ceiling tiles to the side and escape up there, but the battle had taken its toll on his strength. All he had was the Exacto. He dropped it and kissed her, really kissed her.

"I love you," she said.

"I love you," he responded, and he kissed her as long as he could before the teeth tore him away from her.

Peter waited in the Humvee.

"Maybe we should go in. Go check on them."

"I don't know," Val said. "They probably need a minute."

Colt screamed in alarm before the mostly hairless bear ripped his door off its hinges. The grey grizzly showed its split mouth to Colt as it reached for him.

Peter was a young man trained with the heightened reflexes of someone who has to handle pommel horses and parallel bars while spinning and leaping. This was the abilities he tapped when he jumped over to Colt's side of the Humvee without thinking. He grabbed a gun and fired directly into the bear's open mouth. The bear rose up out of the ash as big as a small tank. As the bear lifted Peter out of the Humvee, Peter yelled to Colt and Val, "Go!"

While Val hit the gas pedal, he glanced into the side view mirror and cringed.

Val drove the Humvee north. Colt sat twisted and moaning in the backseat.

Epilogue

Colt sat in the cabin wearing fleece and wool clothes. His parka hung from a hook on the far wall. The coals in the large fire pit in the middle of the room guarded him against the vast army of cold that constantly fought a war to invade the cabin.

The cabin had a small table and two chairs. There was a case of food – mostly Raman noodles – in one corner of the room. A stack of books lay on the table where Colt sat. He thumbed over the spines dejectedly. Monster's Manual. Dungeon Master's Manual. Some Reader's Digests that Alyssa always found a way to keep around. The Hunter, which Aidan picked up in Austin. The Best of Alan Moore, which they had scavenged in some small town in Kansas. He had read them all a hundred times, even parts of the Reader's Digest. He had to be REALLY bored to read those.

There was another book there, a dirty notebook with a black spine and a faux-granite cover, not unlike the kind of notebook found in every classroom in America. That was a book Colt had not read. It was a book he dared not read.

The walls were decorated with pencil sketchings of all the lost boys. Aidan and Alyssa with their faces close together. Peter with a broad smile on his face, a smile as big as the earth. Jax standing in a military uniform. Riley with her hair pulled back, smiling at the camera, but only half her face showing. Val looking over his shoulder back at him. They were not great drawings, but it was kind of obvious who they were, if you knew them.

Colt went to the boxes and pulled out one. A small phone was inside. He turned the phone on and looked at the photos. Aidan and Alyssa close together. Jax in military uniform. Riley, with only half her face showing. Colt checked the battery – 46%. He turned off the phone and returned it to the box.

From another box, he pulled out the HAM radio. He turned it on, checked the battery and channel information, then said into the speaker, "This is the top of the world. Anyone there? Please respond." He clicked off the talk button and waited. Then he said again, "This is top of the world. Anyone there? Please respond." He waited a bit more. Then he pulled out the sheet of paper and pencil that were kept with the radio, and he wrote down the number. He wrote a giant X over it, then switched the radio dial to the next channel and turned the radio off.

He exhaled deeply and completely, as if all the world's doldrums could be exorcised with that one breath. Then he picked up the Monster Manual and began flipping through it again.

He heard something approaching. It was coming on foot and it was coming fast. Colt didn't have time to grab a rifle or anything. Suddenly, the door opened. It was Val, and he looked distressed.

"You've got to come see this," he said through icy breaths. Val was wearing dark sunglasses that covered most of the scars on his face. Colt had similar scars etched across his forehead and cheek.

"What is it?" he asked, excited at the prospect of anything that wasn't reading or radioing. He hoped maybe it was a carcass or a downed plane.

"I found tracks. Come on. I'll show them to you."

Colt got up, placed his crooked arm into the parka, and then followed Val in his sideways gait out the door.

Val led Colt across the icy tundra, far from their warm shack, past the Humvee, past the rise, and into the bleak white where they had to use a compass to find their way. And even the compass was problematic.

The long evening hung at the horizon. Supposedly, summer was coming, and bringing with it lots of sunshine. Until then, it was just dimness teasing them from a distant shore. It wasn't all bad, though. The northern lights danced above them.

Colt followed Val into the dark, his rifle slung over his back. He pulled his scarf down.

"Is it wargs?" he called out.

"No!" Val shouted back.

"Bears?" They had seen polar bears out on the ice. Always from a distance, bears were some of the only creatures they had seen since arriving here over three months ago.

"No," he said with a hint of laughter in his voice. "This is much better."

"Then what is it?"

"You'll see!"

Colt grunted with frustration. Val was as stubborn as Aidan.

The night wind was cold and full of teeth. No matter how many layers Colt wore, there was never enough, especially when he was out this long. For instance, there was the part around his face that was hooded and warm. There was also a thin area of flesh just inside the hood – maybe half a centimeter wide – and it tingled from the biting wind. The rest of his exposed face, though, felt raw and abused, like somebody had been trying to cut his face open with paper cuts, but it wasn't quite at the proper angle to make him bleed. It was just angled enough to really hurt.

The adrenaline rush was leaving, and so was the fun factor.

"How much further?"

Val turned and looked down at him with his warm smile. "If you start asking me 'are we there yet,' I'm going to leave you for the bears."

"You could try, but I'd find my way home."

"I'll bet you would. It's not that much farther. And the word is farther, not further."

Colt rolled his eyes, and Val laughed.

"What?"

"Nothing, but I see them in you, all of them. C'mon on now. Don't make me have to drag you. You know I will."

Colt's leg began to throb, but mostly it was his hip that hurt. It didn't hurt all the time. Val had said he was sure it was broken, but they had no materials with which to bind it, and even if they did, how would you splint a broken hip? So instead, they found a place to hole up for six to eight weeks while Colt lay in bed. He was never allowed to leave the bed, and after everything that had happened…that bed was the worst place on earth for him. Nothing to do but feel pain, not move, and reminisce about everything that went so horribly, horribly wrong.

Eventually, life got better, and once his hip had healed to the point where Val thought he could travel, they left their hiding spot to go to the Arctic. But even after all this time, his legs still did not want to cooperate with his hip, which caused him to sort of amble with his legs as he walked. He had to relearn how to walk. At first, he couldn't move ten paces without getting tired. Weeks of bedrest had reduced his muscles to nothing. To build endurance, he would walk in circles in the cabin until he was too tired to move, and then he slept. He slept a lot in the cabin.

They were not ten more minutes on the ice when Val stopped and kneeled down. They had been following footprints all through the dark, and the footprints had come to an end.

"Look!" Val said, excitedly.

Colt leaned down next to him, which was always a little difficult to do. He looked at the ice, but he really didn't see it until he glanced sideways across the tundra. The tracks were clear as day. And they were human.

Val and Colt followed the single set of footprints out into the ice. They were maybe a day or two old. He wasn't really certain.

"Do you think we will be able to catch up?" Colt asked.

"Sure. They are walking slow. I'm not sure why I know that, but something about the footprints makes me think they are going slow."

Colt trusted Val on this. He had a way of picking up things he had never done before, like when he decided to make origami one day. He didn't have a book to learn it, and nobody had ever taught him how to fold the paper properly. He just folded the paper until he had crafted a duck. Then he built other animals, like tiny bears and wargs, and then they gleefully burned them all in the fire. They had liked that.

Alone, just the two of them in the cold and the dark, they talked a lot about everyone they left behind or lost. It was good to do it, Val said, because in a way it kept them alive even if they weren't. It also filled up the cabin with people, even if they were only memories of people.

Now there was a new person.

"Do you think it's one of them? Somebody from the Tooth?"

"I think it is someone out on the ice, and they will at least add dialogue outside of comic book debates. Not that I don't love comic book debate night."

They found the crude ice cabin the person had made in the ground. There was a lot of disturbance in the natural lines of the world. Mashed ice and snow clumped together. A shallow pit where the person had been in the ground. And fresh tracks in the snow.

"This all new," Val said. "Whoever was here couldn't have left more than an hour or two ago. They must have had to stop for some reason. But why?"

A gunshot cracked in the distance. The bullet zinged in the air above them. Val and Colt dropped to the ground. After a few seconds, they saw a figure approaching from afar.

Val stood up and made clear that he was putting his rifle down.

"Drop your gun, and do it slowly, and let him see you do it," Val urged Colt.

Colt did just as Val said.

The figure stopped about fifty feet in front of them. It was wrapped in multiple scarves and parkas and all sorts of winter clothing. So many, in fact, that it was hard to tell the shape and size or even sex of the wearer.

Out from behind the figure stepped another person, away from the tracks she had been carefully stepping into to hide their numbers. It was clear who this one was. Colt could not mistake the crooked smile or the baby in her arms.

The End

www.ingramcontent.com/pod-product-compliance
Lightning Source LLC
Chambersburg PA
CBHW070743180626

46818CB00007B/2961

9 781925 225143